Kurt Vonnegut, *Slaughterhouse-Five*:

"You, Stephen, did me a tremendous favor with your script of *Slaughterhouse-Five*. When I am wondering what sort of writing I should be doing during the rest of my life, you ... demonstrated that the way to go is sophisticated, intricate brilliance for an emotionally and intellectually elite audience (i.e. people who know when to laugh or cry), by definition not a large one."

Colin Wilson, *The Outsider*:

"Geller's work is shaped and controlled by a remarkable discipline. He represents something new in American writing-a fine balance of feeling and thought; his vision is ultimately affirmation, which distinguishes him from all his contemporaries, British or American."

George Williams, *Garden of Earthly Delights*:

"*Jews on the Moon* is a dazzling novel, part autobiography, part metaphysical and interplanetary road trip, a comic phantasmagoria intermixed with pitch-perfect burlesques of popular culture, and a quest for the answer to a single question: what is the key to the mystery of the Jews? Geller writes with extraordinary brio and with at least three of the qualities Calvino in *Six Memos for the Next Millennium* considered indispensable for fiction: lightness, quickness, and multiplicity. Highly recommended."

Rel Dowdell, award-winning writer-director of *Train Ride* and *Changing the Game*

"The unlimited creativity and intelligence of literal virtuoso Stephen Geller permeates once again his brilliant new publication, *Jews on the Moon*. ...Anyone with a sharp and open mind will not only appreciate this work, but will be tested viscerally by it. Get ready for a ride with Newman Fears that you will never forget."

Kevin Bliss, adjunct professor of screenwriting:

"Such a wonderful read. Clever and funny. Innovative and clear. It really is the best book I've read this year."

Sabina Griffin, reader, from Amazon.com:

"Stephen Geller is a brilliant storyteller who gets a hold of your imagination from the first page and doesn't let go until the last. He generously treats you to an extraordinary adventure and characters who stay with you long after you finished reading. The books are thought provoking and imaginative, incredibly touching and out-of-this-world funny! You will be blown away as you go on a quest through time and space, meet Will Shakespeare, travel to the days of the third Crusade, visit Hollywood of the 40s and 50s, the Underworld and an assortment of planets and planes and events that are neither possible nor fair to summarize in a brief review. Also, Gods, Goddesses, Muses and Fairies will make regular appearances and challenge you throughout your voyage. This book is a rare gem and a must read!"

Jews Beyond Jupiter

(The Second Book of the 'JEWS ON THE MOON' tetralogy)

By Stephen D. Geller

@ Savannah, GA 2012

Table of Contents

For Tutu Lahiri

My oldest friend, who saw it before I did---a foreverly forest of thanks!

"The creation of personality by Shakespeare irritated Wittgenstein, who preferred Tolstoy."

- Harold Bloom,

'The Best Poems of the English Language.'

The first canto

It was William Shakespeare who had made him piss on his own hands.

Dr. Herschel Fisch was standing in a stall of the men's room of the *Globkelle Teater*, during the intermission of the Jewish Artists' Production of "*Merchant of Venice.*" He had just said, aloud: "It's not going very well."

Beside him, at the next stall, an elegantly tailored bearded man was also in the process of pissing. He had thinning hair, searing dark brown eyes, and a gently ironic smile.

"You are referring to the play at hand?" he asked, quietly. "Or the hand at play?"

"*Sir?*" snapped Fisch, coldly, and cocked an eyebrow.

"What *thing* are you referring to?" asked the bearded man.

"'*Thing*'?" snapped Dr. Fisch, with a nasty edge. "What '*Thing*'? If you are attempting to be *Elizabethan*, sir, then I must assume you are referring to my *fundament*," and then he mumbled, "else you're suffering the loss of a more civilized vocabulary. *Which*, sirrah, did you intend?"

The stranger shook his own thing, put it back into his pants, and gave the pants a forceful zip.

He replied, with a shrug:

"What you will."

And that is when Dr. Fisch looked over to the stall, saw the man's face, and pissed all over his own hands.

The second canto

What was William Shakespeare doing among the Moon-jews of *Noye-Erdkelle,* besides witnessing a strange and, as well shall see, eventful production of "*The Merchant of Venice*"; in fact, the first production of that play, and on the Moon?

Even more oddly, why was Doctor Herschel Fisch back in civilization?

As you may recall in *Jews on the Moon,* Doctor Fisch had been kidnapped by a group of angry academics and kidnapped to the planet Mercury, there to do little but watch re-runs of ancient television works kicking about on solar prominences. How had the grim *amateur of literature* managed to escape from his Mercurial captivity?

Good question.

The even better answer appeared in twenty-four clues, each of which had been left, at every Ivy League university's English Department, throughout the universe: at Oxford's and Cambridge's Shakespearean studies programs on Neptune; at several theater departments and professional companies on Venus, Uranus and Pluto, whose directors were noising it about that William Shakespeare may have been all things to all men, but he certainly wasn't William Shakespeare!

The third canto

The twenty-four clues left by Doctor Fisch had been responsible for eighteen suicides, and six murders.

At the sight of each death had been found: one volume of the 1926 edition of the Oxford English Dictionary, and the written clue, signed by Dr. Herschel Fisch, with the odd initials "Ops WTN" following his name.

It was the Director of the Pluto Shakespearean Trust, an acrostics whiz, who decoded the initials, Ops WTN, to mean:

Since all the directors of the various Shakespeare programs knew that Dr. Herschel Fisch was the brightest Shakespearean scholar and commentator who ever had lived, the suicides spread rapidly. After all, a trip to the "unknown country" was better than knowing that Dr. Fisch was not only alive and well but, worst of all, was on the loose and, like all serious academics, plotting keenly.

The fourth canto

What were the twenty-four clues left on a note beside each volume of the OED?

I'll give you ten of them.

You won't need more.

You'll get the idea.

Beside each volume of the Oxford English Dictionary was written one of the following quotations:

1 -"Some are born great; some achieve greatness; some have greatness thrust upon them."

2 -"I do; I will."

3 -"What's the business,/That such a hideous trumpet calls to parley/The sleepers of the house?"

4 - "The mercy that was quick in us but late/By your own counsel is suppressed and killed."

5 - "What impossible matter will he make easy next?"

6 -"You 'mongst men/Being most unfit to live, I have made you mad."

7 – "I know a bank where the wild thyme blows."

8 – "If it were done when 'tis done, then 'twere well/ It were done quickly."

9 – "There's no remedy, sir. He will fight with you for 's oath's sake."

10 – -"The Prince of Darkness is a gentleman. Modo he's called, and Mahu."

A hit. Twenty-four of them. Most palpable.

Most outrageously of all, there was no possible way anyone could *accuse* Dr. Herschel Fisch of sending a volume of the OED, with a quote from Shakespeare, to each person who had seen to it that Dr. Fisch had been spirited, secretly and extravagantly, to Mercury.

But the perps themselves knew a Fisch Maneuver when they saw one. There could be no greater terror.

What made it even worse was that nobody believed them.

The Universal Forces of Order, the universe's major police/espionage/intelligence gathering and disinformation Bureau, told the academics there were no conceivable means to ensure that every night, on a solar prominence, a production of *Henry V, Midsummer Night's Dream, Julius Caesar, Twelfth Night, King Lear, The Merchant of Venice, Macbeth, Hamlet* and *The Tempest* could be shown. And yet, according to the academics, it *had* happened.

Worse, at the exact point at which those very lines supposedly sent by the Doctor to the professors (*perps*) had been recited, the production of each play had become frozen for all the universe to see, then had audially looped, on the specific and offending line, for twenty-four hours, a deadly secret and private propaganda against...*the perps themselves, who knew.*

To the twenty-four co-conspirators, Dr. Herschel Fisch had become worse than any College President. He had metamorphosed into The Jewish God: vengeful, articulate, savagely cruel, and ready to defend His own.

The only way out for the perps was Suicide - solo and/or in pact.

A dying A.G. Dover-Elliot, the Oxfordian pleader (i.e., one who believed Shakespeare was not Shakespeare, but the Earl of Oxford), had confessed to an investigator from the Universal Forces of Order what the conspirators had done to Dr. Fisch; how the twenty-four academics and stage directors could no longer accept what they considered Fisch's Judaizing of the Bard; how, when the Good Doctor had received the Nobel Prize for his study of cross-dressing in Shakespeare and which was entitled "*This Happy Breed of Men,*" - "and with the subtitle, '*an icon of the Hidden Judaic*'!" - both academics and professional purveyors of

Shakespeare's work secretly met to find a way, "once and forevermore!" to do in the Big Fisch.

Kidnap, then exile to Mercury, appeared to be the most logical solution.

A sweating, fearful Dover-Elliott could not imagine how the volumes of the Oxford English Dictionary had come to be left in the offices of each one of the conspirators. All that the sometimes-man could say, before he expired, was:

A sweating, fearful Dover-Elliott could not imagine how the volumes of the Oxford English Dictionary had come to be left in the offices of each one of the conspirators. All that the sometimes-man could say, before he expired, was:

"The quality of mercy, I fear, has truly been bloodily strained," misquoting the playwright, destroying both iambic and pentameter, and turning the sentence into the prose of a freshman.

Still, the UFO investigators took Dover-Elliott at his word, flew to Mercury, and discovered the learned Fisch on the small, dark side of the planet, playing a Jew's harp while gazing fixedly at three solar prominences. He bade them not to interrupt, for he was watching a four-dimensional version of "Northanger Abbey," and was wondering aloud what it would be like "to perform an erotic act upon Jane Austen's body."

Nonetheless, he *was* interrupted from his reverie, and told that twenty-one male academics and three female academics had died in mysterious ways; that what they all had in common was a volume of the Oxford English Dictionary, signed by him, as well as a quotation from one of Shakespeare's plays.

Fisch's response to that news was: "*A Daniel come to judgment, yea, a Daniel!*"

And yet, clearly, according to George Eliot, the head of the United Forces of Order, there was no way Fisch could have been responsible for their demise. As she pointed out, in her final report:

"*Dr. Fisch has been alone on Mercury for that entire period in which the demises had occurred. Moreover, he is out of his mind with Sun-fever. How has this manifest itself? No Professor ever has had the guts -* even alone *- to express an erotic notion regarding Jane Austen. Admiration and slavish devotion, yes. But Eros, never! Sun-fever therefore must be the most viable explanation. Conclusion: the only thing to do with Dr. Fisch is to return him to the Moon, to his place of origin, and to let his own people deal with him. (i.e., Give him back to the Jews).*"

Case closed.

More about Sun-fever later.

The fifth canto

Dr. Herschel Fisch was known to all Moon-Jews by his original name: Zero Mostel.

However, because of the fact that Dr. Fisch is the most important Stratfordian – i.e., one who believes William Shakespeare is actually William Shakespeare – who ever will live, I prefer to call him Dr. Fisch. In fact, I will translate his compatriots' appellation of Zero as Herschel; of Mostel as Fisch; and of Zero Mostel as Dr. Herschel Fisch.

Bear with me. I understand how confusing this can be.

The Moon-Jew Call Directory – (called *DerYid/Mond Weis Zaytl Oyf Der Telefonish Bukh,* or *ZTB*, for short) - is a testament to world literature, popular culture, science and philosophy. Perusing its pages, one is forced to admire the contribution that the Jews and the children of Israel have made to the planet. And yet, if most everyone is a child of Israel, anyway, what's the big deal?

All the reader has to know, if he or she is flipping through the pages of the *ZTB*, is that Adolf Adorno is not a philosopher but a clothes designer; Ralph Lauren is not a clothes designer but a philosopher. He's not even Ralph Lauren, he's Ralph Rueben Lifshitz. Leonard Bernstein is not a composer-conductor but, rather, a lieutenant in the Universal Forces of Order, Moon Division. The real Leonard Bernstein is called Jerome Robbins, and hates it. (The earthling choreographer, Jerome Robbins, is actually Jerome Rabinowitz).

I don't want to question why Americans find it difficult to take more than one second to learn a person's name. I don't even want to conjecture about different cultural chauvinisms, racism or, simply, jaw-dropping stupidity. Suffice it to say, name-changing for professional reasons – which can mean pretty much anything, by pretty much anyone – has been an American past-time for centuries.

Ask Mark Twain.

Or Billy the Kid.

Go ask Moby Dick.

The sixth canto

Such a past-time, of course, is reflected on the moon.

In the colony of *Noye-Erdkelle*, it is *the* reflection, and it's absolutely mind-boggling. For example: you could have dinner with Felix Mendelssohn, Susan Sontag, June Allyson (nee Eleanor Geisman), Marcel Proust and Albert Einstein. None of them would be composers, essayists, actresses, novelists or scientists. All of them, in fact, would be grandmasters of the Moon-Jew Bridge Club - (*Der Yid/Mond Brik Tslonim*, or *MBTzz* - which has traveled throughout the universe, winning tournament after tournament.

On the dark side of the Moon, at the time of which I write, however, William Shakespeare was (and is, and always will be) William Shakespeare.

And Dr. Herschel Fisch knew it, and yet was terrified that he was pissing on his own digitals, with an hallucination beside him, who was also pissing - but more properly.

"You resemble William Shakespeare," said the shaking critic.

"As you like it," said Shakespeare.

"I like it, I like it, very much, indeed," replied Dr. Fisch. "But I still suffer from Sun-fever. And sometimes the devil tempts us by—"

"---Rest assured," said Shakespeare, smiling sweetly. "I am not an hallucination, but thinking makes it so." He moved to the sink and began to wash his hands, then to straighten his beard, lightly, with a finger, while gazing, with the cool eyes of an experienced actor, into the mirror.

"Then you are *most real*, indeed," Herschel continued.

"I think *you* ought to wash your hands, Dr. Fisch," said the playwright. "They're flicking the lights. Interval's over."

The Doctor was surprised, embarrassed, and curious, and all at once.

"However did you know my name?" he asked, moving beside the playwright and rubbing his hands, like Lady Macbeth, under the water, over the sink.

"Because you've been my noisiest defender, Doctor," said Shakespeare, politely. "Even though we all of us hear you, most extravagantly, I appreciate the thought very much." Almost to himself, Shakespeare continued, "As the years pass, I appear to be called everything. You're one of the few who's stood by me and, simply but eloquently, actually called me by my true name. Shall we go now? I'm very interested in Portia. They appear to be portraying her as a villainess. It's *there,* obviously, hidden, in her lines, but, still, it wasn't meant to be made so explicit. The play is, after all, a comedy. The most daring productions have often portrayed the lady with a certain ambiguity, which I admit is often the case with most of my characterizations. But *this* Portia is being played as a cunt of the first order. Grim, admittedly, but still rather fascinating."

"It's the first production of the "Merchant" that the Moon's ever seen," said Dr. Fisch, politely, "or that's even been done here."

"So I've heard," replied the playwright. "And that's why I've come. I've watched Israeli productions before, and have found the plupart tediously anti-semitic."

"May I take you to dinner afterwards?" asked Dr. Fisch.

"If it's a private place, I would enjoy that very much," said Shakespeare. "I'm afraid I'm being recognized too often, here, so I've taken the liberty of calling myself Milton Zeit. May I ask you to follow my lead?"

"With pleasure," replied Dr. Hersch. "Mr. Zeit."

They entered the auditorium, in which sat sixteen million Moon-jews.

Every seat was taken.

"Oh dear," said Mr. Zeit. "We've become groundlings, I'm afraid."

"We shall have to stand in the aisle," replied Dr. Fisch.

"As we have, so often, and against the falsely sworn," smiled Shakespeare. "Shoulder to shoulder."

The curtain rose.

The seventh canto

In another part of the world, and in another time, a Jew, a Moslem, and a Christian were staring in terror at one another: the Christian had a sword, the Moslem a scimitar, and the Jew a cave, in which he sold spices.

The town itself was in flames: men were being put to the sword; women were being raped; babies were being treated as shish kebab; old people went about wailing, until their heads were detached from their bodies, and then the heads rolled away, wailing more softly, until they wailed no more.

It was predictable, in its brutality. All of it.

And yet the Jew, the Moslem and the Christian had been stunned by the violence, overwhelmed by the behavior of their compatriots, and had sought sanctuary in the cave, which was part of the *souq* around which the main battle was being fought.

The three gazed at each other in mortal terror – there is no other expression to describe the white fear each was feeling - until the Jew asked: “Does anyone want some water? If I don’t have a cup, I’m surely going to vomit.”

The Moslem and Christian continued to stare at one another, waiting for the other to make the first move.

The Jew watched the both of them, then went to the rear of the cave, came back with a wooden bowl of water, drank from it, said, “This is wonderful water, believe me. It comes from a magic well in the depths of this store. In case you don’t know, most *souqs* are underground, or in caves, here, in the northernmost part of Africa, to avoid the harshness of the sun or the winds. Tell me: do either of you find this information as fascinating as I?”

Nobody stirred.

"Well," shrugged the Jew, warningly. "Somebody better drink this before I finish it all," he said. "Going, going---"

Slowly, the Moslem and Christian turned an eye towards the Jew.

"Hand me the bowl," each said, and at the same time.

"You had the same thoughts, and at the exact moment," smiled the Jew. "Are you brothers? Here, put down your swords. Pick a number from one to ten. Closest number gets the bowl first."

"Five," they both said.

"Now that's truly strange," the Jew replied. "I was thinking of five as well. My name's Moshe," said the Jew. "What's yours?"

"Moussa," replied the Moslem, who took the bowl and handed it to the Christian.

"Moses," said the Christian, who sipped from the bowl, then returned it to the Moslem, who drank more thirstily, then handed it back to the Christian. "I am Welsh."

"You said this was magic," replied Moussa to Moshe, wiping his lips and staring once again at the Welshman. "In what sense is it so?"

"It comes from the Well of Friendship," Moshe replied. "All who drink from it share the same source, which is the Rock of God."

"The Jewish God?" asked Moses. "The Christian God? The God of the Infidel?"

"I'm as faithful as you are," said Moussa to Moses. "I am not an infidel."

The Jew watched the both of them, then said:

"So far, none of us are dead. That should you an idea of the magic of this liquid. May I suggest we move to the rear of the cave and continue to drink? Leave your swords here, please. There's not enough room, in the rear, for violence."

Once again, the Christian and the Moslem stared at one another.

"There's also a special way out, in the rear," said Moshe, "if you will help me move several barrels."

Immediately, the Jew and the Moslem nodded, but they still did not move.

"You go first," said the Jew to the both of them. "I'll follow."

Moussa pointed to Moses, who shook his head.

"Take each other by the hand and go!" hissed the Jew. "I have no weapon."

Moussa took Moses by the hand, and both moved into the darkness.

Moshe grabbed the weapons, threw them out of the shop, closed the cave entrance, and hurried after the other pair.

He had no time to see the sword and scimitar hit the ground and instantly turn into two adders, who slithered towards the violence, then had a grand time, adder-fashion, before they too were cut into many parts.

The eighth canto

"I can see nothing," said Moussa.

"Nor can I," Moses added.

"Here," Moshe replied. "Help me move these barrels. There's a special passage to the Rock of God. It leads to the Mount, above the battle."

"The mount that overlooks the city?" asked Moses.

"And which is called The Mount of the Faithful?" added Moussa.

"Indeed," Moshe answered, and put their hands at the side of each barrel. "Every town has a Mount of the Faithful. Please don't consider this Mount anything special. Move these to the left, please."

"We conquered the Mount this morning," said the Welshman.

Moshe pretended not to hear.

"I believe *we* re-took it," Moussa replied, "less than an hour ago."

Moshe grunted, hoping that his grunts would prompt the Christian and the Moslem to work even harder.

But both were staring at each other, in the darkness, and were frightened once more, for it was rumored, by all sides, that whoever occupied the Mount of the Faithful, which overlooked the city, would surely slay all others. Success would be proof that God was on their side.

"Let us go to the Rock of God," Moshe replied, "and bathe ourselves, and drink fresh water, and leave our fate in God's hands."

Moussa muttered, "I always leave my fate in God's hands. I never need to be reminded."

"I trusted enough in the Lord to join this Crusade," replied Moses.

"There now," grinned Moshe. "Aren't we fortunate that God is merciful? Here we are, still alive, the three of us, and there go the barrels. Now, if you don't mind, since we're on the other side of the madness, let us put the barrels back in place, in case my shop is ransacked."

"There's nothing left to ransack," smirked Moses.

"The Jew always hides his things," Moussa replied. "I'm sure there's a great deal he's hidden."

"Please," replied Moshe. "I need the barrels in place. Push harder! The only thing of value in this cave is our safety."

Once again, they strained to put the barrels in place. And after they had finished, they followed Moshe down the musty dirt corridor, and then to the left, down a path that separated into two paths, and then to the right, down another path that separated into three paths, and then, finally, down a central path which took them uphill, and into an enormous chamber in the shape of a heart.

At its center was a large, smooth rock.

From two clefts in its center flowed the sacred water: the rivulet on the right moved as a stream; the one on the left collected into an enormous pool. Far above the rock, light filtered down, illuminating the pool, the stream, and the three men.

Moshe smiled, removed his garments, and jumped into the pool.

Moses and Moussa stared.

"How is it that water?" called the Moslem.

"So refreshing I can't stand it," Moshe replied, and dove under water, emerging a moment later, like a porpoise, and blowing the water heavily about him.

"I can't swim," said Moses. "How am I to bathe?"

"Grasp onto the side of the pool, and I'll hold you up."

Moses undressed and, in his nakedness, surprised both the Jew and the Moslem, for he was circumcised.

"Are you a Jew?" asked Moussa.

"Why do you ask?" replied Moses.

"Because your penis looks like his," said Moussa.

"I'm a Christian," Moses answered. "My penis has always looked this way."

"Perhaps," said Moshe.

"Perhaps what? What do you know about my penis?" said the Welshman. "You don't know me. You've never seen me before, and therefore you cannot possibly have seen my penis."

Moussa turned his back to the others, then slipped quietly into the pool:

"True enough. But I am fairly certain your parents were hiding something from you."

"My parents hid nothing from me!" said the Welshman, angrily. "Moses is a common Welsh name. I know many Welshmen and Welsh ladies named Moses, and Abraham, and Sarah and Deborah and Leah and Isaac!"

"And how many of them were circumcised?" asked Moussa, simply.

"I think we should not talk about penises in the Pool of the Rock of God," said Moshe. "I think we should enjoy the --- My goodness, Moses, you're extraordinarily thin. When was the last time you ate?"

"I don't remember," said the Welshman. "Yesterday, perhaps, or the day before. I might have had some lamb this morning, when we entered the *souq*. I was the only one to eat. Everyone else was doing... other things."

"They certainly were," said Moussa, darkly, and swam towards Moses, threateningly.

"Listen to me, both of you," said Moshe, loudly and quickly. "I think we should consider our situation and accept the fact that if we are going to survive we will need each other's help! Last year the Sultan took back this land from the English. This year the English appear to be taking it back from the Sultan. The land belongs to whom? To God alone, and to Nature. When we die, the land will still be here. The Sultan and the English King will be buried, but the land will remain. Let us give to God and to Nature that which is God's and Nature's. And as for the rest, let us work together to remain alive. If not, then I leave you both to yourselves. I'm cold. I'm getting out of the pool."

"What about me?" called Moses. "Will you help me out?"

"Moussa is beside you," said Moshe. "He can help you up."

Moshe turned away, pretending not to look. They could tear each other apart in the pool, or drown each other. Or realize that they needed each other, and climb out together.

Which they did, but grudgingly.

The ninth canto

"Now what?" asked Moses.

"Now what indeed?" answered Mousssa.

"Now we get dressed," said Moshe. "I have some bread here, and some cheese. With the water from the Rock, we can refresh ourselves and tell each other how it is that a Jew, a Moslem, and a Christian from Wales are all called Moses, and find themselves together, sitting peaceably, eating bread and cheese, while people outside are hacking each other to death."

And he thought:

When we emerge from this cave, what will we see? Who will be left standing? Who will be burying the dead? Who will be left to cry?

"This cheese is good," said Moses. "It's rather like *caerphilly*, from home."

"The bread is honest," Moussa replied. "That is always good. I know a story."

"And I a song," added Moses. "But first, your story, sir."

The tenth canto

For a day and a night, the three men – Moshe, Moussa, and Moses – ate bread and cheese, drank water from the Rock of God, and slept.

When they awoke, they swam in the pool, ate more bread and cheese, told more stories, and sang more songs.

By the third day, Moshe, Moussa and Moses had become friends. They laughed at each other's tales, learned each other's songs, were held, spellbound, by stories of each other's travels. They never spoke of each one's God, or of their duty to their different rulers.

Being in the cave, with no companionship but each other, the rock, the water, the food and the light, they became fast friends.

And when they left the cave, much later, they were all of them hairy and shaggy.

And because they were so odd-looking, and impossible to tell, one from another, all the people took them for fools. Which, in a way, they had become.

This is their story then:

The story of three fools, in a world gone mad with gods, papal princedoms, desperate kings, and dumbstruck human beings.

A first riff to Mnemosyne, before we move on to the eleventh canto

My father was born in Toronto, Canada, in 1914.

Of Toronto, my father remembers being raised in a brick house with a large inner door.

When he was seven years old, there was knock on that door and, through the frosted glass, he saw the outline of his uncle, waving at him.

When he went to open it, nobody was there.

Then, immediately, the phone rang. His mother answered it, and learned that the same uncle had died a half an hour earlier.

When Dad told me the story, he shrugged it off.

To him, Toronto was brick houses, the game of conkers, English teas, violin lessons, King George VI, and ghosts.

Dad had been a musical prodigy, had given his first violin concert in Toronto at the age of six.

When his family moved to Los Angeles for his father's health, dad discovered the trumpet, and the big bands, and how easily his own father became irritated when asked if he could sell his violin for a trumpet.

Because his father refused, dad hawked newspapers until he could buy a cornet. He taught himself to play. Then he took lessons in junior high school. He started a combo, in high school, with his pal, Spike Jones, on drums. During his last year in high school, he became a trumpet player at the Biltmore Theater, downtown.

By the time he was twenty-one, in 1935, he was first trumpet with Benny Goodman's band - nudged between Bunny Berrigan, whom he had replaced, and Harry James, who would later replace him.

Then Dad went to work at RKO studios, and was first trumpet, and musical arranger.

And now I'll tell you a story about my father and about that time, which I love:

In Dad's studio there was a photograph of George and Ira Gershwin, Fred Astaire and himself. Dad was in his mid-twenties, Astaire in his mid thirties, as were the Gershwins.

It's an awkward pose: Dad is happy and embarrassed; Astaire is grinning, and looks as if he's ready to leap off the photo; George Gershwin is smiling pleasantly, and Ira appears to be thinking he'd rather be in a bookstore.

During the time dad was at RKO, all the wonderful Astaire/Rogers musicals were being filmed there. RKO wasn't a major player in Hollywood, like MGM, Fox or Paramount. It also wasn't run like a sweatshop, like Warner Bros. It raced behind the big studios, and in its very real way made history, and some of the best musicals - *The Gay Divorcee; Follow the Fleet; Swing Time; Shall We Dance; A Damsel in Distress; Carefree; The Story of Vernon and Irene Castle; Roberta* - with the musical scores and lyrics written mainly by Irving Berlin, Jerome Kern and Dorothy Fields, Cole Porter, and the Gershwins.

And my Dad was there, in the studio orchestra, recording them.

And this is the story:

Development of the first riff to Mnemosyne, before we move on to the eleventh canto

Astaire and Rodgers are scoring "Let's Call the Whole Thing Off," for the Gershwin musical, 'Shall We Dance.'

They're in Central Park, in the late afternoon; they're bored with themselves, with each other, and don't know what to do. So they put on roller skates, and start to move around the open air rink. They become excited, then happy, then goofy on the skates.

The film's producer realizes he needs more bars of music, and which must reflect the couple's up-tempo emotions. So he calls dad up from the orchestra and asks him if he could write and then insert sixty-four bars of music that would sound like Benny Goodman's band, in an otherwise straight arrangement, composed by the talented Nat Shilkret.

Dad says, "Sure, what kind of voicing, and at what tempo?"

The producer, Pandro S. Berman, takes him into an office, and dad finds himself facing the George and Ira Gershwin.

Dad had played in the Biltmore pit downtown, during the first West Coast production of "Porgy and Bess," and was in awe of the work. He had taken dozens of photos of the production from the pit itself; but to be facing both George and Ira simultaneously was like facing a two-headed God.

"This is what we want, kid," George says, and explains the voicing. Then he asks, "Can you do it in half an hour?"

Dad replies, "Fine, no problem, but what's the tempo?"

"Oh, jeez," says George, "I really don't know. Follow me."

They walk across the lot to a sound-stage, where Astaire is filming a scene. During a lighting set-up, he crosses over to the group. George asks

Astaire about the tempo, so the dancer goes through the whole routine as if he were on skates, and Dad says, almost immediately, "Got it."

"Great," repliesd George Gershwin. "Is there anything else you need?"

"Well," says Dad, "actually, there is."

Astaire, George and Ira Gershwin, and the producer, Pandro Berman, look at the young and awkward horn-player-arranger, and wait.

"See, nobody's ever going to believe me when I tell them this story," Dad smiles. "Do you think I could have a photo, of all of us, together?"

Immediately Astaire grabs the set photographer.

They pose.

And that's the photo.

Further development of the first riff to Mnemosyne, before we move on to the eleventhh canto

My dad was not and never had been star-struck. But this was different.

This was the real thing, and not some dream factory cheesecake.

This was what the real life was about:

People making things. Everybody getting together and making music, dances, films, plays.

To him, it was the only thing that mattered.

And it's pretty much the only thing that matters to me too, besides teaching, which is another way of sharing what I've learned, and with others who are also interesting in making things:

Taking a melody or a step or a chord or your own language further than it's ever gone, and losing yourself in the doing, that's what matters and, if done well, transcends matter.

With the knowledge of the real thing – the music of the Gershwins, the dancing of Fred Astaire – the doing of the real thing, with real artists, teaches you that *anything less* is crap.

It makes your soul dance to the music.

With my dad's life as an example, I saw and understood how the commitment to art and technique also made life easier, but more difficult, too, because the marketplace wanted to get into the act and, more often than not, paid for the act. The people in the marketplace wanted as much of a piece of the marketplace as they could get, and for an artist, for someone who had knowledge of the real thing, and who did the real thing, that would not make for a good marriage.

Sometimes it even qualified as a rape.

Dad had a fucked-up and brilliant career because he hated the marketplace, and pretended to pander to it until he could get away with murder, which was art, and when he was caught and convicted, he either escaped or was sent into exile, then the cycle began again, for him, somewhere else.

The Astaire and Gershwin talents were superior to everything and most everyone around them, in Hollywood and New York. In order to get their work to the world, however, they had to deal with lots of people whose talents, if they had any, were minimal, at best. Did this make for a happy union?

The answer is easy. Think of it this way:

Have you ever seen a movie or a play or a musical about the theater or film that deals lovingly or affectionately with the environment and its people?

And don't say: SINGIN' IN THE RAIN.

It's about a liar, a stripper and an ass-kisser.

And those are the good guys.

The eleventh canto

"May I ask you a question?" said Dr. Fisch of his new friend.

They were dining at the *Bistro Lunaire*, a Belgian style café, of twelve tables, that served *pommes frites*, Crab Nebulae *moules*, and, their specialty, *mondtjewaffeltjes*, or Moonie-wafflies. Nobody knew what they were, but they were soft and fluffy, fruity with a slight tang of salt, and they made you want to commandeer another order.

"If you must, you must," Shakespeare replied, to Fisch's question about asking a question. "But do bear in mind that I cannot tell you *which version of my plays is the correct one*, because I don't remember at all. Most of them were published after my time. The scholarship which followed dulled my soul, and to the dreariest degree! Worst of all were the interpretations of my characters. Besides all that, however, I cannot begin to *describe* the years of Elizabeth or James to those who came after ourselves: the shape of the theater, the size of the audiences, the use of boys in women's parts, the very problems we had faced under Elizabeth and Burleigh and, later, James and the Puritans, but which would mean nothing, one hundred years later; all of this demands an explication I am hard put to remember, much less to consider, with anything but tedium."

He paused, took a sip of his Floreffe Trappist beer, wiped his moustache with a cloth, and said, "I'm sorry if I've offended you in any way, but I do believe in - how do you put it? – 'cutting to the chase? '

"Not at all, not at all," said Dr. Fisch. "I wasn't going to ask you anything about your plays," he smiled. "Although we could discuss this production, if you wish. Not at all, sir. My question was altogether different."

"Mmm, and how different?" said Shakespeare, pursing his lips as a spicy *moule* slid down his throat and he breathed a sigh. "Wondrous," he whispered to himself. "I think I might order another round."

"Please," said Dr. Fisch. "It would be my pleasure," and he summoned the waitress, who swiftly returned to their table.

Shakespeare regarded the woman with comic interest.

"What do you call this specialty?" he asked.

"The Crab Nebula *moule*," she said. "It is the only one we have found beyond Saturn. There are three Saturnian moons and two Jovian moons producing *moules*, but nothing with the finesse and delicacy of the Crab Nebula moule."

"You prefer the Crab Nebula, do you?"

"Undoubtedly, sir. Your face is familiar."

"This is my friend, Milton Zeit," said Dr. Fisch "He's a veterinarian."

"And thus my interest in mussels," Shakespeare replied.

The waitress went off to place the order.

"Sure you wouldn't want to try a Jovian mussel as well?" asked Hirsch of the playwright.

"The finesse and delicacy, so I have been told, abounds in the Nebula of the Crab," replied Shakespeare, with near-perfect mimicry of the waitress.

Hirsch smiled.

"You do listen well, sir," he said. "I am not surprised."

"Languages," said Shakespeare "Did you notice how she pronounced Saturn? She turned it into three syllables. Sa-too-rin. It was as if her mouth had refused to let the word expand and vanish. Crab Nebula was the winner –she spit it out so it was near impossible to understand: Crep-nep-yoola! I'd wager she herself is a monstrous consumer of the Saturn *moule*."

Dr. Hirsch nodded.

"I shall ask her," he said, "when she returns. You must have been a fine actor," he added. "Your ear is so acute."

"When you've been raised in a very small town," said Shakespeare, "then London becomes a traffic of sounds. I took to it with great pleasure. Had I been born in London, I never could have written as many different characters as I'd managed, because their sounds would have been so familiar I'd have ceased to hear them. The Eastcheap taverns were my schoolrooms. Mistress Quickly and her friends were my professors, Justice Shallow my tutor. But of course, so was the Earl of Southampton."

"And who was Falstaff, sir?"

Shakespeare smiled, shrugged.

"Perhaps he was my appetite."

The *moules* arrived.

"Thank you," said Shakespeare, as the waitress put the spicy seafood before him. "Tell me: what are the differences between the Saturnian *moules*?"

The waitress smiled warmly.

Dr. Hirsch raised his eyebrows, recognizing at once that Shakespeare's perception was spot-on:

"Titan, of course, has the largest mussels," she said. "If you're starving, they're the best. Three of 'em will make your evening. But I love the Rhean and Dionian mussels. I don't know why. Maybe it's the combination of the atmosphere and the gravity. My friend was there last year, and he said that everybody imports Enceladian mussels because of their shape, which is odd, but they go down well, I can see why, but somehow the Rhean mussels have a good cold rough sea-taste. You know you're dealing with a chilly ocean. It's like a hardy and refreshing swim."

She leaned in, looking conspiratorially towards the kitchen:

"Don't get me wrong," she whispered. "You're eating the most famous mussels, and probably the best. But I could live on Rheans. Whoops. I have to go."

Shakespeare smiled.

"Let us split an order of Rheans, nurse," he called after her.

"No, please," said the waitress. "After Crab Nebula *moules*, the chef will know I've been touting the Saturns."

"Then I promise to return tomorrow night," said the playwright.

The waitress smiled, and blew Shakespeare a kiss. He blushed, which surprised Fisch, who wondered: *is that blush proof that our playwright's interest in humanity is that of a collector rather than that of a saint? Is that why the humanity of his plays is so enormous, yet his compassion so...rare? Is his blush a giveaway of the distance he unconsciously puts between himself and the world? And yet, he observes. Like Cassius. Iago. Edmund. Prospero. And, of course, Hamlet.*

Dr. Fisch continued his meditations:

It's interesting how so many of his major characters all have followers, devoted slaves, audiences in the plays. Even the comic rogues have followers: Andrew Aguecheek follows Sir Toby; Justice Shallow follows Falstaff; they are all promised romances. The protagonists pimp their followers, directly or indirectly. Even though Hamlet is alone, Horatio follows him, but so does the audience. Playwrights, all of them. Like the Master before me. Drama begs the existence of audience.

Dr. Fisch thought to himself: If I am correct, I must be forewarned: *Worship his plays, but do not fall in love with their playwright.*

The twelfth canto

"What I wish to ask of you," said Dr. Herschel Fisch of his dinner guest, "is the meaning of the '*second-best bed.*'"

Shakespeare pursed his lips slightly.

"If I tell you," he said, with mock sobriety, "you will destroy a great many academic careers."

"I already have," said Dr. Fisch, with a slight smile. "The more, the merrier."

"In my will," Shakespeare began, "when I left Anne my 'second-best bed,' I was alluding to a private joke between ourselves."

He paused and looked away.

For a moment, his eyes seemed haunted.

"Our first best bed, as we called it, was a field outside of the town. That was our private joke. Thus we referred to the bed in our home as 'our second-best bed.' In between that midsummer's night in the field and the birth of Susannah, my eldest daughter, we married."

"Was it really midsummer's night?" asked Fisch, surprised by the revelation.

"In truth," said Shakespeare, "I don't remember. But I did write a great deal about young people running away and having it out in the woods, the woods of Navarre, the forest of Arden, a wood outside of Athens...Have you raised a fire in the woods yourself, sir? You provoke many forces, rubbing together, in the woods. I loved the woods. The only dying I loved in the woods was my own."

'These trees shall be my books.' said Dr. Fisch, quietly.

"Quite," Shakespeare replied. "After ten years in London, I couldn't wait to return to Stratford. I sent most of my earnings to Anne, who continued to build up our farm and holdings. When I removed to Stratford, for good, she'd created a piece of heaven for ourselves."

"So there was no tension between the two of you."

"Tension?" said Shakespeare, surprised. "No more than most; rather, less than most. I respected and loved her wholeheartedly. She was the one who presented me to Nature, brought me children, and made me honor much of life."

"Excellent woman - whom the critics..."

"Answer me this, and then answer me no more," said Shakespeare, and nodded to the waitress as she deposited twelve Saturnian mussels before him. Although they were not as delicate-looking as the Crab Nebula mussels, they were finely toddied and burgeon'd. Shakespeare took two and slurped them down, saying: "Doctor Fisch: would you want to believe anyone who told the world *how you lived, and whom you loved, hundreds of years after you'd departed this earth?* If you did believe 'em, you would also have to believe that these mussels are from France - as am I - and that they are called French turds - as are you."

(No anger, thought Herschel Fisch. Just the human distance, once again.)

"I'm so glad you had a wondrous marriage," he said.

"Please be none too glad," replied the playwright, "for, in truth, why should you care at all? Now be a friend, and explain this dessert menu to me."

The thirteenth canto

The destruction was complete. Bodies, furniture, objects and relics within temples and mosques, were broken and strewn over the streets and alleys; the few Jews and Moslems who remained were old or weary or in such a state of shock that they were left alone to grieve, ignored as if already they'd become invisible.

The Crusaders had been given three days by the Knights and priests to loot the town, to destroy whatever and whomever they wished.

And destroy they did.

Drunkenness occurred the first day.

By the second day there was nothing left to drink, except water.

On the third day, the Crusaders took stock of their profits, forgot their experiences, and became human once again.

The effect was chilling.

Moshe and Moussa agreed that, if they were going to remain together, they had three choices: to walk inland towards the mountains, and to hunt for their food; to remain in the city among the Crusaders, and to beg for their lives; to beseech God for forgiveness, then slit their own throats.

None of the choices were very good.

Moses wanted nothing more to do with the Crusaders.

He was such an innocent he'd had no idea that looting meant rape, theft, and dismemberment. At last, he understood that it had nothing to do with God, although the priests themselves had given it their blessing.

Of the three men, Moses was the most upset, and spent the days after the city's fall with a very unhappy heart. Even though he now resembled a beggar, he refused to look any of his former compatriots in the eye.

He wanted to return home, to Wales, but he was sure nobody would take Moshe and Moussa with him. He desperately wanted to visit a woman in his village who had cures to remove the Evil from his soul. There was such Darkness surrounding him now, he had violent need of the woman's tonics. Moses thought:

Nothing was worth this kind of destruction.

What kind of God could countenance such behavior?

And in the name of Christ Jesus?

Moshe knew exactly what Moses was feeling, and respected his silence.

Moussa tried, at first, to tell him how his own people, when they had re-taken the town from the Crusaders the previous year, had behaved in an even worse fashion.

"The Koran insists we defend ourselves when attacked," he said, "but it does not give us the privilege of taking lives and maidenheads. It insists we do not kill women and children. But we behaved as horribly as your people. Even worse, actually."

"That's good to know, isn't it, Moses?" said Moshe, smiling brightly. "That, in spite of our languages and accents and cultures, people are the same everywhere?"

Moses looked at Moshe, surprised:

"What do you mean?"

"They're impossible and shitty," nodded Moshe, smiling at Moses as if he were a child.

But Moses did not return his smile.

"Yes," added Moussa. "And that is proof that Satan is alive and working in this very town. I saw him once, you know. But did I tell you? He looked like a Bedou chieftain. He was handsome and well-spoken. Everyone in the town thought he was a holy man, which of course he was. Satan was born holy. More than any prophet or helper. He is even holier than Mohammed himself. Satan told us what was going to happen, and he was right. It made him twice as popular with the townspeople."

"How did you know he was Satan?" asked Moshe.

"Because his farts smelled of sulphur," replied Moussa. "It's always an obvious sign. I mentioned it to my cousin, who told me to hold my tongue, that such talk was offensive to everybody. So I left town in order to offend nobody, and one day later the Crusaders came to our shores. I owe my life to the fact that I am able to smell the presence of shit quicker than most others."

"You're right, Moussa. Satan must still be here," said Moshe. "It's not even been a week, has it?"

"I am very sorry to say I *am* right," Moussa replied. "Look about you: this kind of evil can only have been directed by Satan."

"*My people did it*," said Moses, sorrowfully, and crying to himself. "Even if Satan had directed them, they had still had had the choice not to kill children – can you imagine! - and old people – not to respect the elderly? - and to do those terrible things they did to the women – that was such an abomination! - and now they're behaving as if nothing ever had happened. And so many of those men believe themselves followers of the ways of King Arthur, chivalrous souls, all of them, full of the ideals of the Christ, yet behaving like pirates!"

Once again, he began to cry.

"Let's take him back to the pool," said Moshe.

But too late, for a guard of Crusaders had come around the corner, and immediately had surrounded them.

"Moses ap Daffyd," said the head of the guard, staring at the Welshman. "Is that you?"

"He doesn't speak English," Moshe replied, without missing a beat. "He is my brother, and an idiot. He cries at the sight of a butterfly or a starving dog, can you imagine?"

The guard continued to stare at Moses, curiously.

"I know Moses ap Daffyd, and I say that is he."

"I'm a Jew," said Moshe. "And so is my idiot brother."

And as he said this, Moshe lifted his own robe and dropped his pants. In Hebrew, he commanded Moses to do the same.

"All right, that's enough," snapped the guard. "I believe you. God in Heaven, why do you people do that to yourselves? Do you really believe that is a sign of the Covenant with God? What kind of a God would demand such a thing?"

Moshe shrugged:

"I never asked," he said, then turned to Moussa this time and said, in Hebrew: "Show him your penis!"

Moussa turned away from the soldiers, as if he were shy, and lifted his robe as well, dropping his pants and exposing his arse.

"All right, we've seen enough!" snapped the guard. "We believe you!"

"Please forgive me," said Moshe, "but I'm the only one of my brothers who speaks your blessed language."

"March!" yelled the head of the guard to the others, and they moved as swiftly away from the trio as they had first appeared.

When they had gone, Moshe said, quietly, to Moses:

"It is such a pleasure to see you smile again, Welshman."

And to Moussa he asked, "So you speak Hebrew?"

"Enough to show them my arse," said Moussa. "I think we must take to the hills as quickly at possible."

"I agree," Moshe replied.

"Perhaps one day we might find a caravel returning to England," whispered Moses. "My father has a farm, we can work for him until I come of age."

"Absolutely," said Moussa, with a conspiratorial glance at Moshe.

"A wonderful idea," Moshe added, returning the look. "In the meantime, let's get out of here and talk about Wales when we're a bit safer, shall we?"

Around the corner, the guard and his escorts stopped at once.

"Moses ap Daffyd had a Jew's penis," he said, suddenly. "I've seen it when he was pissing. The first one I've ever seen, and it was remarkable for its shape. We've been tricked! That man was lying. Let's find those fools and finish God's handiwork!"

They ran back to the street's corner, but the three Moses had already vanished.

The guard looked about him: one road let to the distant mountains; another to the port; a third further into the town.

"Into the town!," he called, and the Crusaders followed.

Never having performed a full-length circumcision before, the Crusaders began to believe the day might possess great potential.

From the top of the hillock, on the path leading deep into the mountains, Moshe, Moussa and Moses saw the Crusader and his men running in and out of dwellings, yelling, and dragging people into the street.

"Say goodbye to the town," whispered Moussa.

"Goodbye, town," said Moses and Moshe.

And they walked slowly towards the mountain, admiring the fleecy white clouds that seemed to float happily above them.

"We call that mountain, straight ahead, The Home of the Green and One-Eyed Djinn," said Moussa.

"Why is that?" asked Moses.

Moussa turned to him and smiled, with a shrug:

"Hopefully, my dear Welshman, you'll never have to know."

A second riff to Mnemosyne,

Before we proceed to the fourteenth canto:

The humor of a jazz musician or hipster articulates itself in weird voices, physical shtick, and a fabulous sense of the grotesque.

More often than not, its theme is exposure of bullshit.

Which explains the comedy of Lenny Bruce, Peter Sellers, Spike Milligan, even Craig Ferguson (who began as a stand-up comic in Scotland by calling himself "Bing Hitler" – how superb is that?)

My father loved Charles Dickens because he loved the grotesque characterizations expressed in their voices. *Pickwick Papers*, especially. I think Sam Weller was his favorite character, the way that W.C. Fields was his favorite performer.

It was all about language, the put-on, the pause, improvisation, timing. Musical stuff.

Dad loved Stravinski the same way he loved Perelman – S.J., as much as Itzhak. And he adored Ravel and Debussy in the same way that he broke up over Lord Buckley and Lenny Bruce: the intelligence, imagination, new ways of using the language, the surprise and drama of their dynamics, the orchestration, or voicing, of characters and themes.

One afternoon, dad and the writer Danny Arnold were driving from NBC, to our house, in two separate cars. At the busy intersection of Ventura and Van Nuys Boulevards, dad bumped into the rear of Danny's car.

Danny stopped, ran out of his car, and began an argument.

Dad emerged from his car, and the two of them began to yell at each other. Then they started wrestling.

By now the traffic had stopped, and people were watching, fascinated and fearful.

Danny and Dad began rolling all over the street, throwing false punches, flailing about the pavement, stumbling into every lane. Needless to say, all traffic had stopped.

However, as soon as they heard the sirens, they both stood up, shook hands, then kissed each other.

Dad got into Danny's car, Danny into Dad's. Both headed off in different directions, with an audience of several hundred witnesses frozen in time and space.

The most bizarre moment with Dad and Danny occurred the summer of my freshman year in college:

Several of my friends had come to California to visit, and we had all gone out to dinner at a restaurant in the Valley. After we had parked our cars, Dad and Danny disappeared.

We were reading the menus, my mom, school chums and I, when Dad finally appeared, with Danny leading him:

Dad was wearing sun-glasses, and walking haltingly.

Danny, holding his arm, was the good Samaritan.

He was leading the blind.

Crossing towards our table, Dad became confused, turned around, and crashed into a table of five people, all involved in their meal, deliberately trying to ignoring his pathetic condition. He leaned atop a woman's salad dish, smearing the vegetables unwittingly over her face, then turned and sat on another person's main course. Danny ran over, making excuses, with Dad stammering, "Where am I? Who are you? What are we eating? I didn't order yet," and all the while creating more chaos with the food, the diners, and the table itself.

My friends were stunned, my mother furious, but all knew they could not laugh, because that would be far more dangerous.

Eventually Danny extricated Dad from the table, led him to us, and called to the waiters to send another round of food to those people whose table had been trashed.

Order was restored.

Ten minutes passed.

New food was brought to the table, when suddenly Dad rose – blind still – and said, loudly, "I believe the time has come to cleanse my bowels of yesterday's detritus."

The people who had been savaged by the blind man looked up, stunned, to see the man, headed in their direction once again. The paterfamilias rose, trying to block the blind man, who stormed straight at him, intoning like W.C. Fields, "It's essential I place the contents of my bladder in a sparkling white bowl, sirs, or I'm a goner!" and then he slammed into the man, who fell over backwards into his mother-in-law's plate, with dad now on top of him. Both rolled over the table, food flying around the restaurant, and people screaming.

"Is there a fire?" my father yelled. "Fire, dammit! Hurry, before the pair of us are baked like lobsters in a Twopenny bus-man's *ragout*!"

Danny picked up my father, then helped up the paterfamilias, handed him fifty dollars, and led dad out of the restaurant.

By now my school-friends were terrified, and turned to my mother, gazing at her, hopefully, for some kind of explanation, or assurance. Ignoring them all, she looked at me, with a faraway smile:

"I think it was in 1935," she began, seemingly *a propos* of nothing. "Your father and I were driving to the Santa Monica Pier, where Goodman was giving a Sunday concert. Suddenly a car pulled up alongside us, challenging us to race. It was a hot day, but all the windows in that car were rolled up. Inside were Gene Krupa and Benny's brother, Harry, the bass player. They were obviously smoking marijuana and didn't want any of the smoke to leave the car. Anyway, your father raced them until he saw a police car, but they didn't. Dad suddenly turned down another street, and Gene kept going, then the police car put on its siren, dad turned around, and followed the chase. Krupa saw the cop and sped up and drove right onto the Santa Monica Pier and sailed past the casino then smashed through the barrier, and he, and Harry Goodman, and their car went careening skywards, then into the Pacific Ocean."

My friends stared.

What was the point of the story?

"Strange as he is, your father never went that far," mom continued, gazing at me ruminatively. "Gene gave him some marijuana, once, when they were in Chicago, and your father smoked it and became so paranoid that in the middle of a solo he put down his trumpet and left the stand and went up to his room and lay down on the bed, convinced he was going to die. He was still in his tux, as I recall."

With a small shrug, she smiled at me.

"He doesn't need to do drugs," she said. "But you already know that, sweetie. Well, what are we going to eat? You boys decide yet?"

"Umm," said one of my friends, shakily. "Does---I mean, did they live?"

"Did who live?" asked mom, frowning at the menu.

"Gene Krupa and Benny Goodman's brother. After they went over the railing?"

Mom cocked her head, frowning and staring, still, at the menu:

"Gene has a house somewhere in L.A.," she began, "and Harry was a bachelor and lived sometimes with his mother. Crazy people never die," she said. "Or the world wouldn't be what it is."

I wish she were right.

In *her* way.

Still, even if she wasn't, it was one of those times in which I very much loved my parents, and couldn't decide who was funnier.

The fourteenth canto

Shakespeare was staying at the Lunar Holiday Inn Express because, as he said, he "very much enjoyed their breakfasts."

At the Lunar Holiday Inn Express, no guest but himself ever ate the grits, which came in tiny packages, or the rashers of bacon, covered with grey sauce and peas. He was thrilled by the continuous beaker of coffee, ready to be drunk, and the different kinds of breads "one put in an especial oven, where no flame was to be seen." Or the machine that made pancakes from a miniature packet!

Every morning, from seven a.m. until the room closed, at ten a.m., Will remained at a table, watching re-runs of CNN News, broadcasts from the 21st Century, evidently a terrible time for Earthlings. People were forgetting how to speak; instead, were sending odd messages on tiny antiquated machines, filled with letters that made no sense: LOL TGFT WTF etc.

And yet, watching CNN, of three hundred years past, was like reading the *London Times,* in 1894, or Addison and Steele's *Spectator,* in 1762.

Oddly, the women who read the news on CNN looked so much alike, and wore such dreadful sweaters and dresses that Shakespeare could not imagine how anyone human could design such shit; the morning after "Merchant of Venice," he sat in the breakfast area of the hotel, wondering "*what kind of tasteless sow existed*" who had made the decision for those ladies to wear such hateful outfits!

The playwright had been up for several hours, and had forgotten that he had agreed to spend the day with Dr. Fisch.

He growled to himself when he saw the heavy-set fellow moving slowly across the lobby of the hotel, examining a small volume held closely to his eyes. Immediately Shakespeare recognized the book as the Oxford edition of his Sonnets and Poems, and thought to himself: *I don't care if he's become my best friend. I will not give him the identity of the Dark Lady!*

Doctor Fisch, reading the finer print, had walked directly into a wall; then he stopped, looking about dizzily; spotted the breakfast room, which was the hotel's daily meeting room, after ten a.m. Shakespeare was seated by the window, six cups of coffee and four plates of bacon, grits, English muffins and ham before him. At least two-thirds of each plate showed signs of a violent struggle.

The playwright, who was chewing grits and bacon and grey sauce, took a napkin, wiped his mouth, and rose, pointing to the chair opposite him. Dr. Herschel Fisch smiled, then slipped the volume into the pocket of his greatcoat.

"Good morning," he said, and patted his pocket. "I've been so enjoying your sonnets. Ravishing, as always."

"Mmm----mmmm," Shakespeare replied.

"And don't bother yourself thinking I'm about to ask you the identity of the Dark Lady," smiled Dr. Fisch, cannily. "I could care less. All that matters to me, and to the world, is that you wrote these poems, sir. The rest is irrelevant."

Shakespeare nodded, and yet felt slightly perturbed. He disliked being one-upped. Especially by someone who resembled Dr. Johnson, but wasn't. Dr. Fisch may have been very bright, but he was also a *fan*. Dr. Johnson was *nobody's* fan.

Shakespeare enjoyed that.

Eccentricity was far more interesting than applause.

He'd adored Tolstoi's anger against *King Lear*, and thought Shaw's essay, *Shaw vs. Shakes*, a comic attempt to use himself as a whipping-post, as a means for Shaw to test his own considerable verbal gifts. Shaw lost, of course, but the effort, in the main, was sparkling.

"I met G.B.S. once," he said, and Dr. Fisch looked up from his own concentration upon the bacon. "An Irishman, you know," he added.

"Excuse me?" said Herschel Fisch, staring hard, once again, and in spite of himself, at the plate of bacon.

"Please. That's my third plate of rashers. Take as many as you wish," said Shakespeare.

"Thank you," replied Dr. Fisch, and lifted two pieces of bacon very daintily, between thumb and forefinger. "Of *course* Shaw was Irish - as Voltaire was Swiss."

"French," said Shakespeare. "Voltaire's French. Arouet is his name. Born near Paris. He's a friend, though he secretly hates me. Or friendly, though he secretly loves me. One never really *knows* what he means, though his clarity is, as always, superb."

"Really?" smiled Fisch. "How odd. Perhaps I was getting him confused with Rousseau."

"J-J wasn't French," said Shakespeare.

"Swiss, of course," nodded Fisch. "Born in Geneva. Buried in the Pantheon, however. In Paris."

"And the Swiss let him go, just like that," said Shakespeare, with a straight face. "We never knew very much about the Swiss. Still don't. There's Calvin, of course, but then there's also Duerrenmatt. Good writers, although neither of them handled comedy very well."

"They've always been strange, the Swiss," said Fisch, nodding.

"Indeed. They either celebrate you as one of their own by loudly ignoring you, or they instantly deport you to Germany," Shakespeare nodded as well.

"But tell me," asked Fisch, reaching for another piece of bacon. "What did you think of last night's production?"

Shakespeare shrugged:

"Well, the director and cast seemed to understand that I thought everybody in the play absurd, and that's rarely the case in most productions of *Merchant of Venice*. People take Antonio so seriously – he's played as a weak or tragic figure, generally attracted to Bassanio; and they turn Rosalind---"

"Portia," corrected Fisch, unthinkingly.

"Sorry, yes. Portia," smiled Shakespeare, frowning. "-- into a saint. I'm delighted to see that she was portrayed every bit as wickedly as the rest of the Venetians, but I think they went slightly over the top. She is never a *victim* in the play, but also she's *not* Lady Macbeth. Have you tried these grits, incidentally? They come in little packages. Very interesting. You add water, and suddenly you've this pleasant concoction. I tried them with butter, then with fruit, next with that fascinating grey sauce whose contents nobody seems to be able to recognize, but small matter, for it works, and if it works, then logic be damned!"

"Bravo," grinned Herschel Fisch. "I myself pointed out the severe illogicality of what I consider to be the greatest play ever written - your *Hamlet*, of course - and I said precisely the same thing: Who cares if the action occurs in six weeks, and begins with Hamlet at the age of nineteen and ends six weeks later, with Hamlet at the age of thirty-one? It works, and, as you say, that's all that matters."

"Yes, of course, an obvious point," said Shakespeare, with a wave of his hand. "But I'm glad you caught it. Few do. *My* favorite moment of absurdity in the play is with Hamlet and the pirates," nodded the playwright, smiling to himself. "I had to get him back to Denmark quickly, so I thought of the pirates. Outrageously propitious! Or the illogicality of Claudius sending Hamlet to England for no real reason at all, and then later deciding to send along the young man's death-sentence, with Rosencrantz and Guildenstern, *after* he'd already decided to send Hamlet off anyway. I wince, every time I see it."

"Are you saying you were 'winging' the drama as you wrote it?" asked Herschel, surprised.

"Obviously," said Shakespeare. "Doesn't everyone? I'd already written one draft, many years earlier, and it was so foolish, we never performed it. But I did remember the general thrust of the play. I had no more than a few weeks to write it, doctor, before the play was to be performed. Little time to consider anything but the moment, which is never a bad thing, actually, for a dramatist."

Shakespeare stroked his beard, and then chuckled to himself.

"Even Rosencrantz and Guildenstern are absurd creations," he said.

"Weren't they *meant* to be?" frowned the critic.

"I've been speaking of the *craft of drama*," said Shakespeare, somewhat snippily. "Horatio's *already* present, so why bother creating *them*? Why didn't the King and Queen express their concerns about Hamlet's melancholy to sweet Horatio? Because I hadn't thought very much about Horatio, that's why, and when I realized that I wasn't allowing anybody but Horatio to be speaking honestly to Hamlet, I decided to continue in that vein, and make use of that, for great fun. So Rosencrantz and Guildenstern became perfect foils: I turned them into old friends, but liars, and insufficient courtiers."

"That's rather interesting," said Dr. Fisch. "If you'd given Horatio the same role as you'd given Rosencrantz and Guildenstern..."

(*How good it is,* thought Dr. Fisch, *to be discussing the possibilities of theatrical choice with Shakespeare!*)

"If I'd done the same thing with Horatio, Herschel," said the playwright, as if to a fool, "then Hamlet wouldn't have had any friend at all! He'd have ended up talking to himself even more than he does already. I'd certainly have lost the audience. Still, you can't say that

Hamlet cared that much about Horatio, can you? The poor fellow wanted to commit suicide because he loved Hamlet, but Hamlet told him not to – not because he gave a fig for his friend's life, but because he himself needed decent publicity, somebody to stay alive to tell the story. That's how smart and self-serving Hamlet really is: if he'd died and nobody but Horatio knew why, then the slaughter at the end of the play would have remained ambiguous - to Fortinbras and the Danes. In fact, the whole story would have been much ado about nothing."

"Somehow, Maestro," said Dr. Fisch, "your remarks are beginning to sadden me."

"Are they?" said Shakespeare, with small concern. "The point is: you can do anything in a play, no matter how absurd, as long as you have one of the more trustworthy characters question its absurdity. The audience will accept anything, as long as the play retains its momentum. And, of course, everybody knows that a vengeance play is the easiest to write. One keeps increasing the violence until everybody's dead. I wrote that kind of shit, decades earlier, with *Titus Andronicus.* I didn't care about the logic at all. I didn't even care about the audience. I knew the play would work. Audiences loved it. You begin with ritual sacrifice, and end up baking characters in a pie and eating them. Piece of cake, that kind of writing. The only character I liked in *Titus* was my precursor to Hamlet: Aaron the Moor."

"But, sir: didn't you *care at all* about Hamlet?" asked Dr. Fisch, feeling, in spite of himself, betrayed: *Aaron the Moor as Prince Hamlet? How could he even dream such a thought?*

"Of course I cared about Hamlet," said Shakespeare, coolly, and poured himself a twentieth cup of coffee. "He's the only one in the play I *did* care about. I let the audience think I was writing another vengeance play when, in fact, I was writing a blackly comic poem about mortality."

Dr. Herschel Fisch gulped. Stared at the playwright. Then sighed:

"In my book on your theater, I was going to call *Hamlet* 'the poem unlimited,' but a colleague of mine beat me to it," he said, now dreadfully unhappy.

"I'm afraid *I* beat both you and your colleague to it - or, rather, Polonius did," replied Shakespeare. "Odd quoting Polonius for the title to an essay about Hamlet. Especially in the context of that speech of the old man's. I'd written "*poem unlimited*,' as Polonius says it, to mean: a work filled with endless pretension. I never thought of the play itself as pretentious. I've been accused of many things, but never pretension. Marlowe was pretentious, adorably so, and Jonson *tried* to be. As men of the theater, the both of us - Marlowe and I - left poor young Ben in the dust."

Fisch was surprised.

Then confused.

Shakespeare appeared not to notice, or maybe he did, and went on:

"The good thing about a vengeance play, of course, is that you can have great fun with all the characters. You've all the time in the world to play games with them while you bake your pies, and stew your narrative. That's what Marlowe showed me, before he was murdered. He taught me this wonderful fact about writing dramas: as long as the old bomb of Time appears to be ticking away, the audience will be so terrified they won't see what you're really doing, and thus you can do whatever you wish and say whatever you need while the ticks tock, and Polonius gives his addle-headed speeches, and Ophelia goes mad, and Claudius rages about his stepson, and Osric behaves like a stereotypical fop, and the gravedigger has his moment, for the groundlings, and everyone can be absurdly comic, or comically absurd. And thus, in the midst of all this tickory-talkory, there's myself sermonizing about how flat and stale and unprofitable is this world, how Denmark's a prison; how a cloud is shaped like a camel, and of all married couples, all but one shall live; and

– most importantly to me – there is a special providence in the fall of a sparrow, and the readiness is all. I keep harping about mortality, don't I, as I did in *Lear*, and of course in Jaques' speech, and in *Macbeth.* Maybe that was the only thing I really thought worth saying, in all my work: '*Life's shit, we're all going to die, so get ready for it* - and while you're getting ready for it, doctor, have some more bacon."

Shakespeare sighed, and looked about him vaguely, almost whispering to himself:

"Banal piece of philosophizing, I admit, but what else is to be expected from a rustic who possesses none of Jonson's schooling, or Marlowe's? Still, I ask myself: how many productions of Jonson's work tread the boards each year? Or Marlowe's? Meanwhile, beneath the surface of this our waxing moon, Portia holds forth in gay bitchery---You seem to be enjoying the bacon, doctor. Please, I insist you have some more."

My God, thought Dr. Hirsch: The man's not Hamlet at all. He's a gentleman *not* to be trusted! A Falstaff, and no other!

"So you believe that the Portia we heard last night was over the top?" asked Dr. Fisch, clearing his throat, and moving away from *Hamlet* because he was now so thoroughly depressed, and had had so many questions to ask Shakespeare about that miraculous play, and Shakespeare was ruining everything for him - although in the poet's own mind he wasn't ruining anything at all: he was simply explaining the craft of playwriting to a critic, and the critic, because it came with the territory, had understood nothing the playwright was saying.

"*The Merchant of Venice* is a comedy," said Shakespeare, simply. "The closest other play of mine it resembles is *Troilus and Cressida.* In *Merchant,* all the Christians are feeble-minded and greedy, and the principal Jew is the Christians' own shadow. Jessica seeks revenge upon her father. Portia will do anything to get married to the man she desires. And once she does, she castrates him with the ring trick. If I'd been Bassanio, I would have run out of the court, jumped into the Adriatic and drowned myself. Nobody is worth a penny in that play. Take Portia's speech, which every actress I've ever seen, except for the one last night, delivers miserably: Portia doesn't believe a word she's saying. Do you think these are lovely words? "The quality of mercy is not strained. It droppeth from the heavens as gentle rain." I laughed myself into a stupor after I wrote that. It's such an obvious cliché, and even the most witless groundling understood it as such. Portia's playing the Virgin Mary, but then what does she do? She ensures that the Jew is legally robbed, by the court of Venice, and all his property given to her friends! Then he's made to convert to the kind of Christianity those greedy bastards practice! What 'mercy unstrained'? How does Portia one-up Shylock's pound of flesh? By showing how merciless a Christian can be. But last night's Portia was a bit too much the schemer."

"If you would have directed her---"

"I would have cast her as Shylock," yawned Shakespeare.

Dr. Fisch laughed, in spite of himself.

"You are droll, sir," he said.

"The play is a comedy," Shakespeare yawned once again, and stretched. "I would have hoped drollery the least of it."

"Are you Catholic?" Fisch asked, suddenly.

Shakespeare looked up.

"Have some more bacon, *Jew...*" he said.

The fifteenth canto

"Thank you for saving my life," said Moses to Moshe.

They were seated at the top of the hill, several leagues from the center of the smoking town. Beyond the fires, spreading outwards from the boundaries of Moussa's former world, the sea itself stretched to a white-capped, whipped-up infinitude of adventures.

"When I lie, it's for a good reason," shrugged Moshe. "Saving a man's life is always a good reason to lie."

Moussa smiled:

"I wouldn't call it lying," he said. "Telling a tale, that's a brighter way to look at it than calling it a lie," he said. "We live on tales. Our lives are tales. Some tales are more urgent, perhaps, more profound. Our lies, of course, may be urgent, but they can be profound."

"Still," frowned Moses, and staring at his two friends. "If you always tell tales, how can you know the difference between a truth and a lie?"

"That depends upon the teller," said Moussa, politely. "What does he intend by telling the tale? You see, to tell a tale properly, you must have a reason. A good listener appreciates the care put into the tale, while trying to understand the reason for its existence. Perhaps you think we are liars, Moses, but we are not. We invent so many different ways of seeing the world, and of enjoying it. Besides, as soon as we have thought of a tale, the law of God asserts that such a tale might indeed be happening somewhere, and so indeed it has become or perhaps will become very real."

"You mentioned a green-skinned one-eyed *djinn*," said Moshe.

"What is a *djinn*?" asked Moses.

"A spirit who lives in a certain place, and who has certain rules which must be obeyed," replied Moussa.

"Or else?" continued Moses.

"Or else he will cause great harm, and in a thousand different ways."

"And is there a *djinn* who lives in the mountain before us?" asked Moshe.

"Most assuredly," Moussa replied. "I myself have seen him twice. Perhaps three times, although I was not prepared to see him thoroughly, because there was a storm, and it was only during the lightning's flash that I spotted him grinning at me, behind an enormous rock. And when the lightning went off again, he was gone. Then I heard him laughing behind me, but when I turned, he had vanished. My poor donkey died of fright."

For a moment nobody spoke. Then Moses nodded.

"There are strange beings and even stranger beasts in Wales," he said. "There are mountains and caves, and magical quarries where special minerals are sought, gems known only to the dragons themselves, and which give them their ability to breathe flame and fly."

"I have heard of them," said Moussa, nodding and frowning. "The dragons of Wales are known, indeed, to the world." He turned to Moshe. "Do Jews have special beings?"

"You have a home, Moussa, which is here, and in the desert," said Moshe. "Moses has a home in Wales. We Jews are wanderers. What remains with us is God and His Angels. And they are everywhere, for God is everywhere. That's enough awe for us. When we have forgotten it, God makes himself known with all sorts of unpleasantness."

"If you had a home," said Moussa, "and were no longer a wanderer, then you would come to know the spirits of place as well as any of us. Perhaps one day you will have a home."

Moshe shrugged.

"I am at home anywhere and nowhere," he said, simply. "I am a guest on this earth, and then I am dead, and then hopefully my spirit returns to God."

"You have no Heaven," said Moussa. "For this I am truly sorry."

"I thought Jews had a Heaven," Moses answered. "How could you have angels and no heaven?"

"That's a very good question," said Moshe. "And one that I will be able to answer after I am dead."

"Aren't you afraid?" replied Moses.

"Afraid of what?" Moshe answered.

"That there is no Heaven for Jews?" said Moses.

"If I am dead, why should I be afraid?"

"You frighten me," Moses replied. "You are saying we have no future."

"Ahh, life," smiled Moshe, and pointed at the town. "Ahh, mankind. Look what has been done, today, in God's name. How many of your people have been guaranteed a place in Heaven for what you've done? Stolen land, destroyed people's lives, burned their futures? You can't look your own countrymen in the eyes while you are alive, and yet you ask: what will it be like for us poor Jews in Heaven? Let me ask you this, my friend: will God welcome your comrades for skewering babies, raping women, destroying temples and mosques, and dismembering the elderly? Is that your idea of Heaven? I have learned to expect nothing from anyone, and even less from God. Thus, every day to me is a surprise, and sometimes even a delight. "

"I find that very depressing," said Moses.

"Rather unsettling," nodded Moussa.

"Really?" Moses replied. "Who would have thought the three of us would meet in this despicable battle and turn our backs on everything but each other? Who would have thought we would even have the same names?"

Suddenly, in a cloudless sky, there came head a clap of thunder.

And before them, glaring through a large yellow eye set in the center of his forehead, stood the most astonishing figure they had ever seen: he was naked, green, with six long claws on each foot, and hands like those of a crab.

He lifted his right hand in the air, and another clap of thunder exploded around him.

Stars appeared.

They spelled out: *DJINN.*

A third riff to Mnemosyne,
Before we learn what happens in the sixteenth canto

My mother was born in Lublin, Poland, in 1913, and came to the United States in 1923. Her grandmother was a kabbalist, a card reader, and an herbalist.

Every year, before Rosh Hashanah, she swung a chicken over the head of each family member. The *qlipot*, or negativities clinging or surrounding each person, were said to transfer to the chicken, which was then sacrificed.

At the Temple, the sounding of the shofar removed any further nastiness, and connected the congregants with the higher aspect of spirit.

The soul of the chicken, if I remember correctly, was also said to be elevated.

To my mother, the whole thing was "*bubbe meitzes*," or an old grandmother's tale.

Many years later, when her own father was dying in an old folk's home, mother sent me to visit him. It was eleven at night. She knew he was dead. I knew he was dead. But she was too frightened to see for herself.

I went to the home.
Grandfather was indeed dead.
The smell of death was particularly pungent: sweet and acrid.

Several days later, we were preparing to sit *shiva* for grandfather, in my mom's apartment.

I was packing my bags to go back to Rome, where I lived, when I smelled the same odor I had sensed in my grandfather's room.

"So you've come to visit?" I said to my grandfather. "Shouldn't you be with your friends, and moving on?"

The smell went away.

"I'm sorry if I'm chasing you away from *shiva*," I said. "I didn't mean to be rude. Please, grandpa. Stay as long as you want."

But he did not return.

I went downstairs. Mom was in the kitchen, turned to me and said, "Is he upstairs?"

I nodded.

She replied, "Thought so. Heard you talking," and continued to prepare for *shiva*.

Mom wasn't religious. She despised the local Rabbi, whom she believed was money-grubbing for the Temple.

"Why, Harriet," he had said, when he saw her at our neighbor's son's Bar Mitzvah. "Whatever brought *you* here?"

"You know me, Rabbi," she answered, breezily. "I always go where the food is free," and turned away.

Ethically, the Polish chicken continued to work for her all her life.

Socially, mom lived in a smorgasbord of a world inhabited by Dostoievski, the big bands, dramatic literature, and human stupidity. She wanted to improve life around her through art, education, and a compassion born of anger. But she was too idiosyncratic to be a Communist; too much the Polish Jew to trust assimilation within the Norman Rockwell model; too restless to pursue her already burgeoning career as a stage actress and, later, pre-school teacher and child psychologist.

As I'd written elsewhere, she and my father were married to each other four times. Although she had several loves afterwards, she never remarried. Instead, she taught in the Los Angeles Head Start system, got her degree in early childhood education, and worked in the UCLA Pre-School Program, both as a teacher and, simultaneously, as a trainer of other pre-school teachers.

"How could you call your grandmother's practice of Kabbalah *bubbe meitzes*?" I asked. "If you admitted the possibility of grandpa's presence upstairs?"

"Because my grandmother always read cards for the *shabbas goys* and always said what they wanted to hear."

"But was she right?"

"What do you mean, was she right? To lie to those poor Polish girls?"

"No," I said. "Was she right in her predictions?"

"Always," she said. "But I never believed her."

Mothers can be fun.

"How could you not believe her if she was always right?" I asked.

"Because the stuff she did was too scary, that's why."

Now mom was becoming irritable, and triying to evade the issue of her grandmother's efficacy as a practicing herbalist, witch, kabbalist.

"It's superstition," she said. "All of it. Don't tell me *you* believe that shit."

"I believe my senses and my head and my heart," I replied. "I don't care what others think. I trust my own senses and my response to things."

"Listen, kiddo," said mom. "When you're dead, you're dead. And all that card-reading nonsense and wearing red string, it was just--"

"Red string?"

"I had red strings in my ears from the moment I was born," she said. "We all did. It was supposed to keep away evil."

"And did it?"

"*Bubbe meitzes,*" she said.

"So tell me how you knew grandpa was upstairs just now?" I asked.

She looked at me, and in her eyes I saw her grandmother, and generations of practicing magicians and artists and craftsmen, and story-tellers and liars, and all of them making the most of the misery that is life's companion, and turning that misery into magic and art and story.

"If it gets you through the day, who am I to put you down?" she said. "Believe whatever in hell you want, kiddo."

I realized then that, for most of her life, although she'd lived a great part of it in Hollywood, the other had still remained in Lublin, watching her grandmother read the cards to Polish girls who helped the family on the Sabbath.

"Did I tell you how sad Judy Garland used to be," she cut into my thoughts. "Even *before* she became a star? She lived a couple of blocks away, and used to come over here all the time, when Harry was with Artie Shaw's band, hoping that Artie himself would show up. She knew that Artie liked me and always wanted me to travel with the band, so she became my best friend. I felt sorry for her. She was such a *meeskeit*, a homely little kid, but an amazing talent."

"What makes you think she wasn't coming over here to see dad?"

She stopped for a moment, then shook her head.

"No way. I would have known."

"How?"

But she didn't answer.

I watched mom bringing out the plates and cups for *shivas*, and realized that I'd never really known my parents, this town, these different cultures; that everything changed so quickly; that in order to know anything, we not only had to live with such focus in the present but, at the same time, had to transcend time and space and find eternal values within the human response to the present.

We had to live in at least four worlds: the world of nature, and the world of forms, of patterns; the world of ideas, and then of pure spirit. We had to navigate them simultaneously, if they were to make sense. There never was a single answer.To anything.

"I wish I'd known your grandmother," I said.

"She was quite a character," mom replied, and moved the plates into the dining-room, closing a door to her own magic room and, for the moment, locking it, and hiding the key.

The sixteenth canto

Moses stared, shocked.

Moshe smiled, oddly, shaking his head and whispering rapidly to himself, in Hebrew.

Moussa nodded, politely, and sat down.

The Djinn sat as well.

Both Moussa and the Djinn leaned towards each other and spoke in a dialect Moshe had never heard. Moussa appeared to be treating the Djinn as if he were an old friend!

Moshe thought: Perhaps Moussa is a magician, and this is a dramatic illustration of what he had said about ideas and thoughts becoming reality. In which case, is the Djinn his thought, or does it exist independently of himself? And why am I not the least bit frightened? Poor Moses is moaning and praying and staring in terror at the creature, and why do I find it funny? Something, thought Moshe, must be wrong with me.

"The djinn asks us to give him a goat at once, or we must leave the mountain," said Moussa.

"I have something better than a goat," Moshe replied, instantly.

The Djinn turned to Moshe, and spoke in a harsh, coughing language only Moussa could understand.

"What is it that you possess?" asked Moussa. "He wants to know what you have that is better than a goat."

"A spell," Moshe replied. "To capture Djinns with a snap of my finger. Like this."

He snapped his fingers, and there was another thunderclap, and at once the Djinn disappeared.

"And now I suggest we run as far away, and as fast as we can," said Moshe, and helped up a stunned Moussa, while lifting Moses by the arm.

The three of them ran and slipped and fell and struggled up and stumbled forward until they had left the road far behind.

Finally, when none of them could move further, they stopped, and looked back, but could see nothing, for a fog had moved down from the mountain.

"We'd better seek shelter," said Moussa. "This fog smells of rain."

Panting, nodding, they turned, and found themselves facing six *djinni.*

All had green skin, yellow eyes, and claws for hands and feet.

And all were very angry.

"Wonderful," said Moussa, sullenly. "Now we'll have to find *six* goats."

The seventeenth canto

"I thought you might like to see the *Froyschule Kulturmuzei* – sorry, the Free School Cultural Museum," said Dr. Fisch. "Unless you'd prefer to see the *Noye-Erdkelle* Sociohistorical Library, which has an excellent collection of holo-vids."

"Actually," said Shakespeare, "I wouldn't mind going back to that *boite,* where we ate the mussels."

"But it's breakfast time still," Fisch replied. "They won't open until noon."

"Do you have a Starbucks?" asked Shakespeare, with some annoyance.

"You mean a City Hall? Of course. Would you like to meet the janitor?"

Shakespeare frowned, then smiled to himself: "I forgot," he said. "The mayor is the Janitor here. Still, if it's the only way to get a decent coffee, I'm your man. I'm afraid the Hilton gave me heartburn."

"It's a few blocks, if you don't mind the walk."

"Not at all," said Shakespeare.

They began to stroll the holo-street.

At this time of day, *Noy-Erdkelle's* main thoroughfare resembled Vienna at the height of the *Belle Epoque*. In thirty-three minutes, the grand allee would morph into downtown Santa Fe, during the opera season.

"Do you speak Yiddish, doctor?" asked the playwright.

"I'm an expert in many languages," replied Dr. Fisch.

"Yiddish is more of a dialect, though, isn't it?"

"Originally, yes," nodded Fisch. "It was a patois of Hebrew, German, Russian and Polish. But eventually it became its own world. Why do you ask?"

"I've been studying it at the hotel," said Shakespeare. "Its sounds are immensely comic. I would imagine there must be many writers in Yiddish. It appears to lend itself to drama and to poetry."

"You get two free Starbucks lattes for that answer," smiled Herschel Fisch. "It had a great literature, which we are still translating, nearly seven hundred years later."

"I'd be interested in meeting with the translators," said William Shakespeare. "I've had some experience with my own work in different tongues. Perhaps I might be of some service. I've noted you've a *King Lear* in Yiddish."

"Your most Jewish play," said Dr. Fisch, and Shakespeare smiled, warmly.

"I take that as a compliment," he replied.

"To you, perhaps," said Herschel Fisch, "but not to me or mine."

As they walked towards the Janitor's closet, many stared at Shakespeare, and were amazed – too amazed to say anything. However, a well-dressed and elderly woman came right up to the man from Stratford, stood aggressively before him, and began poking him in the chest.

"Shakespeare, listen to me," she said, and poked him yet again. "I like your plays, some of them. We had to read them in high school, and believe me, we were just too young. But your *Merchant of Venice*? You should be ashamed."

"And why is that, madame?" he asked, eyebrows raised like an owl's, and his lips keeping from forming a grin.

"What you put Shylock through shouldn't happen to a dog!"

"Dogs have been through much worse," he replied. "In fact, I had a mastiff, many centuries ago, whose thing got stuck in a bitch's cunt, and even the three of us, tugging at the flanks of both creatures, could do nothing to relieve either beast of its suffering. We threw water at them, made harsh noises, finally tossed them into a pond, but to no avail."

"Whoosh!" said the woman. "So what happened?"

Shakespeare shrugged.

"They drowned, that pair, albeit happily."

Then he bowed, rather stiffly, and said, "Good morning, madam."

The eighteenth canto

Herschel Fisch knocked on the closet door. Immediately it was opened by Ahasuerus, the Janitor (Mayor) of *Noye-Erdkelle*.

"Well, well, well," he said. "William Shakespeare. We meet again."

Shakespeare was surprised, and blushed. "Has the Wandering Jew finally ceased his wandering?" he asked, in a quiet, choked voice.

Ahasuerus shrugged.

"Wandering, shmandering," he said. "Here I have *enough* to do. My wandering days are over."

"So you know each other?" asked Dr. Fisch, surprised.

"He came through Stratford twice," Shakespeare replied. "My father, I'm afraid, treated him miserably. I was so furious with Mister John that I followed this gentleman out of town, and brought him food and drink."

"And yet you asked me questions about forsaking Jesus," added Ahasuerus, raising a finger pedantically.

"Wouldn't *you*?" asked Shakespeare, "were you a young and naïve boy?" He turned to Fisch, as if the latter were a more responsive member of the jury. "Here was the man, we were told, doomed to travel throughout eternity, because he had refused to give succor to our Lord. Some legends even narrate that Jesus himself had cursed him."

Ahasuerus shrugged:

"You believe that? It's not his style. Come in. Do you have a moment?"

Dr. Fisch glanced at Shakespeare, who was staring at Ahasuerus with interest and a certain concern.

"Of course I do," said William Shakespeare. "We've all the time in the world, don't we, doctor?"

"My time is your time," replied Dr. Fisch.

"There's someone I'd like you to meet," said Ahasuerus. "Come into my closet."

Said the spider to the fly, thought Dr. Fisch to himself, and then, with a shudder:

This does not augur well.

The nineteenth canto

The closet was dark, so Ahasuerus lit a candle, then placed it upon the sixth rung of a ladder leaning against the wall.

"Many centuries ago, William, my boy," began the Wandering Jew, "you asked me what I thought of the Christian community. And I replied, 'There are many Christians, and many different communities.' Do you remember your answer?"

"Whatever it was," Shakespeare replied, "I'm certain it was foolish, so now I ask your forgiveness."

"In fact," said Ahasuerus, "it was not foolish at all. You told me, 'What you did was human, and much of humanity is frail. You behaved as would most of humanity. I believe – you told me – that you, Ahasuerus, were given the task of taking humanity's lack of compassion and frailty upon yourself. In a certain respect – you said - you are doomed to live for our thoughtlessness, and our lack of compassion for others. People treat you miserably because they see themselves in you, and do not wish to be reminded of their heart's own conceit. To my eyes, therefore, you have become the eternal martyr. You are a saint.' Then – do you remember this? - you asked me: 'if you found yourself in the same situation once again, in which you are asked to carry the cross of Christ, would you do it?'"

"And you answered: "I *am* carrying the cross of Christ," Shakespeare replied.

Dr. Herschel Fisch watched the pair, silent and stunned.

Ahasuerus nodded:

"But you also said, Mister Shakespeare: '*Then it must have been meant to be. A greater poet than God does not exist.*' Do you remember that as well?"

Shakespeare nodded, eyes closed in memory of the event:

"I thought," he began, "I believed that people turned away from *you* because, by your presence, you made them imagine they themselves would have chosen to carry Christ's cross. Your presence gave them hope and self-affirmation. You were as vital a figure as John the Baptist. And, of course, like John and Jesus, you too were – are - a Jew.'"

"Then you *are* a Catholic," said Dr. Fisch, staring at Shakespeare, and whispering to himself.

But the playwright did not answer, for he was still staring at Ahasuerus with a combination of fascination and fear:

"I wanted to write about you," said Shakespeare, simply, and almost as an excuse to himself. "Every thought I had always led back to you. Your rags became the rags of Edgar; your rage against your own condition and that of the world became that of Lear, and Gloucester; I could not obliterate the sight of you on that rain-drenched track, when I followed you, and the dogs were howling, and the whizzing exhalations of thunder and of lightning rent the welkin, and I led you to a sheepcote and gave you food and drink, and your eyes were terrible, and I said: 'You are Ahasuerus. You are the Wandering Jew.' And you began to rage and then to cry."

It was Ahasuerus who stared, this time, and said nothing. Shakespeare was moving beyond his memory, and was confessing.

Even Dr. Hirsch sensed that.

"I myself could have been you," Shakespeare continued, after a moment. "The way my father was you, and all the others who taunted and tormented you. Although you existed to remind them of Jesus' passion, they themselves had become Pharisees, and were re-enacting the Passion without realizing what they were doing - *and that was the point, wasn't it.*"

Ahasuerus began to shed tears, but said nothing.

"I thought, even then," Shakespeare continued: *why is God giving man the choice to crucify Jesus every day? And I realized that every choice a character makes, in every scene, is a function of story, be it comedy or tragedy; that the choices the character makes reveals the deepest part of himself. The dramatic moment is always the moment of choice. The consequence of those choices creates the full arc of the drama. The tone the character takes regarding those choices distinguishes comedy from tragedy. But whether it's comedy, drama or romance,there's really no difference. It's all the same: it's about choice, and choice which alters character. And the choice is always the same: Do I pick up the Cross, or do I turn my back?"*

Dr. Hirsch shook his head, tightly.

Shakespeare had ceased to be a man of God, and had become, once again, *the* man of theater. Was *that* the lesson he had learned from Ahasuerus? That God was not God, but a Playwright, and that we were His characters, and had become, ourselves, minor playwrights ?

"The only one who understands this fully, of course, is Hamlet," Shakespeare continued, as much to himself as to the others. *"How to make the correct choice? How will History view us? And God? Hamlet was the only character I ever wrote who addressed that problem. Everyone else was too busy to realize the consequences of choice. The few people who knew this but who refused to examine it I turned into villains. All of them became manipulators of their worlds. In other words, playwrights who love to write revenge tragedies: Richard III, Iago, Edmund, Aaron, Cassius, even Prince Hal, all of them deliberately making choices that promote only themselves, and not the common good. By the time Richard II understands this, it is too late, and he is martyred. Prospero, of course, is myself. The magus. The author. God, with a small "g. The only dramatic question I raise of any real meaning in The Tempest is what Prospero intends to do with the villains whom he has brought to the island. And the answer, of*

course, is the solace of forgiveness. Redemption. He had been carrying the Cross all of his life, and has understood Christ's message."

He paused, for a moment, and Herschel Fisch jumped in and asked: "And what does Carrying the Cross mean to you, personally?"

"As a metaphor," said Shakespeare, with a tiny sigh, "obviously it means accepting and alleviating mankind's woes. As a personal device, it means imitating Christ - a role in which I am thoroughly uninterested, and incapable of performing."

"But if we're God's children, aren't we already doing that?" replied Hirsch.

Shakespeare frowned:

"As God's children---which I am inclined to question, given our dreary histories--- we have the choice to pick up the Cross or not. To imitate Christ means to live his life: to be charitable, to be honest, to be *good*. To recognize the truth in nature as God's truth, which means, the truth of ourselves. To treat others as we would wish to be treated. That alone is the most difficult act of mankind. How we hate each other and ourselves to the degree that we do is one of the great comedies, tragedies and, of course, mysteries of living."

Dr. Fisch did not like the playwright's tone, which seemed to imply that the Hebrew Bible was nothing but a preparation for the coming of Christ.

"Jesus was a righteous man," said Dr. Herschel Fisch. "You probably are not aware of this, sir, but he imitated all *tzaddikim*, all righteous men. And as a result, he performed what every righteous man performed, and he performed it as a child of Israel, of the house of David."

Shakespeare was surprised by Hirsch's heat, and nodded for the critic to continue.

"And what did every righteous man do?" he asked.

"The *tzaddik* preached God's words," said Fisch, "which is the Torah; he healed the sick; he cast out madness; he raised the dead; he created wine out of water; he altered the weather; he took on what *you* call the Cross of mankind, but which we call *Geburah* and *Chesed*, or Mercy and Loving-kindness."

Shakespeare listened, frowning with thought, but said nothing.

Being in a dark closet, with two smart Jews, was not a liberating experience.

"I honor you, sir," continued Dr. Fisch, staring in the half-light at Shakespeare. "You were responding to Ahasuerus as Jesus responded to a *tzaddik*, a righteous man. You understood the role he had to play, which is not as dreadful as Judas' role, but without which Jesus himself could never have played the role required of him."

Still, Shakespeare did not speak.

After a moment, Ahasuerus said, "You're very quiet."

"You said you there was someone you wanted me to meet," asked the playwright.

"Ahh," replied Ahasuerus. "Did I indeed? I don't remember."

The twentieth canto

"Stealing goats is not my idea of living a good life," said Moshe. "Especially if the goats belong to a Bedou chieftain."

"We have no choice," said Moussa.

"I agree," Moses replied.

"We *do* have a choice," said Moshe. "Either we steal six goats from the Bedou and run the risk of having our heads cut off, or we try to escape the *djinni,* and run the risk of losing our souls."

"Suppose we lose our souls but not our heads," began Moses. "We'd still survive, yes?"

"As eternal slaves to the *djinni,*" Moussa replied.

"Actually," said Moshe, after a moment. "There *is* a third choice."

"What is that?" asked Moses.

"We ask – no---Let *me* speak---Let me speak to the *djinn.* All you have to do is agree with everything I say."

"I can't do that," replied Moussa.

"Then let us decide whether to run away from the *djinni,* or to steal goats from the Bedou," said Moshe, calmly, turning away from the others.

They were seated at the mouth of a cave, high above the town, and nearly a quarter of the way up the mountain itself.

The *djinni* had given them one hour to decide what to do, and with the warning that if they didn't do it, they would take their souls and turn them into *death-slaves:* bodies without souls, who wandered the lands without any sort of feeling, and who would only behave through the use of commands by the *djinni.* They would be turned into the living-dead.

For a moment, Moshe thought he could escape, with a snap of his fingers. The first *djinn* he had met was so stupid he had believed Moshe would render him invisible. It had run away as soon as Moshe had made the sound.

So many possibilities, thought Moshe....I wonder how many more spirits of place are living on the mountain. If so, we'll never be able to cross it. We need to get through without encountering other *djinni.*

Inside the cave, Moussa and Moses sat solemnly and fearfully, awaiting the return of the six demons.

"Still, I don't see how it is possible to steal six goats from the Bedou," Moussa was saying. "They post guards about them. The goats will bleat and awaken the entire tribe. We won't even have time to have our heads cut off. Heaven only knows how many arrows they'll have shot at us, or how quickly their scimitars will have severed our heads from our bodies..."

"Perhaps we should have listened to Moshe," said Moses.

Moussa shook his head:

"At this point the *djinn* knows Moshe is a trickster. He'll be on the lookout for surprises. It's no use."

For another minute both were silent.

Then they smelled the *djinni* approach, and heard their barking coughs that approximated language.

"Where's Moshe?" whispered the Welshman, querulously. 'Do you think he ran away?"

Before Moussa could answer, the six *djinni* entered the cave. Behind them stood a three-eyed giant, carrying a scimitar of gold. He had a long red beard, and was covered with red hair as well. He wore a long blue cloak, the color of early evening, which was fastened by a silver dagger the size of a man.

"Where is the magus?" asked the first *djinn.*

Neither Moussa nor Moses could answer.

"Behind you and before you," said a voice at the mouth of the cave.

All turned.

"The man whose voice you hear stands before you, but he is not speaking. My invisible troops, standing behind you, are waiting for you to enslave him and his friends. When you do, be aware of what is going to happen to you all: First, your giant will lose his beard. Then his silver dagger will disappear. His red hairs will become engulfed in flames. I dare not say what will happen to the six of *you*, except that you will be taken to the land of ice and slowly frozen to the point of death. Then the Python of Eternal Misery will appear, to swallow each one of you, once a week, eternally, into his terrible days and nights. Within his stomach you will lose your ice, and slowly be poisoned and burned by the foul-smelling brews bubbling in the Python's stomach. Can you see this, as I speak? Because as soon as I have spoken, the thought in the ether has materialized into genuine and true fact. Even now, the Python of Misery is coming this way."

The *djinni* began to step forward, but the Giant held up a hand, staring at Moshe:

"I see what you say, and it is indeed terrible. Tell your troops to be patient with us, and stop the Python from its wrath. What do you require of me, magus?"

"We wish to cross the mountain with safety," said Moshe."We do not wish to see any more *djinni,* or to be asked to perform impossible tasks."

"Dismiss your invisible troops, and I will guarantee your safety," said the Giant.

Moshe shook his head.

"They will not be dismissed until we are safely down the other side of the mountain."

The Giant turned to the *djinni.*

Its leader shook his head, angrily, but the others nodded, agreeing with the Giant.

"You must all accept my offer, or the troops----no!" screamed Moshe, suddenly, turning behind him and holding up his hand. "Do not raise your weapons! Stop, I say!"

The *Djinni* began to scream as well, and the Giant to quake. They all turned, starting to rush to the mouth of the cave.

"Don't go outside!" yelled Moshe, holding up a hand. "The Python is around the corner. Do you promise our safety until we are down the other side?"

"We promise!" yelled the Giant.

"*Ob salabaq salaq din qos*!" intoned Moshe. "*Ob tanabaq sen selaz*!"

Then he moved to the Giant and cried, "Run, quickly! Take the *djinni* with you and flee! I've stopped the Python, for sixty falling sands! Hurry!"

Gathering the *djinni* in his hands as if they were pomegranate seeds, the Giant lowered his head and tore through the mouth of the cave, disappearing down the dirt-path until he had become as dark as the night, and as powerless as newborn calves.

The twenty-first canto

In the cave, Moshe turned to his friends:

"The third way embraces intelligence and imagination," he said, "turning life into a tale in which no one is harmed."

"Some tales, however, have very bad endings," said Moussa, begrudgingly.

"And some have impossible ones," added Moses, angry with himself for not having listened to Moshe when he had spoken of the third way. There were, after all, three of them. Whatever that meant. (It had to mean something!)

"Perhaps," Moshe replied. "In the meantime, the *djinn* dropped six pieces of gold, and ten pieces of silver, and the Giant left his pouch, which the three of us might be able to carry."

"Leave it," said Moussa. "When he discovers its absence, he'll search for it."

"Very well," Moshe replied, staring, still, with curiousity at its clasp.

"Please, let's not be curious," said Moses. "Let us go at once."

Without curiousity, but with six pieces of gold, ten pieces of silver and, most importantly, with their ability to continue breathing, Moshe, Moussa and Moses left the cave, and continued their climb, in the darkness.

The twenty-second canto

Eventually, their path was lit by what Moussa called "Al Zuhra," Moses "Gwener," and Moshe "HaNogah."

In English, we call it Venus.

And then, at the edge of the mountain's top appeared, to Moussa, "Al Quamar"; to Moses, "Lleuad." To Moshe, "HaYareah."

But we call it "The Moon."

Soon they were conjunct, locked in love, the Moon and Venus.
Al Zhura and *Al Quamar.*
Gwnener and *Lleuad.*
Nogah and *Yareah.*

Moshe smiled to himself, when he saw Moussa and Moses also smiling.

"None of us are married," he said, "though all of us have sisters."

"What are you thinking?" asked Moussa politely.

Moses pointed at the Moon and Venus.

And all three sighed, as one.

"Perhaps, one day..."

"Perhaps."

"I would hope."

You do not need to know who said what, for now all were thinking as one.

The mountain, still, loomed darkly, before them. But the sun would appear, and it would bring with it a new day, and with more possibilities for the three fools to exercise the surprising third way - telling a tale woven of intelligence and imagination.

Without realizing it, Moshe had turned his friends into professional story-tellers, and they could never turn back.

If they did, surely, as they now understood, they would perish.

Their lives were committed, now, to the telling of the tale.

On the other side of the mountain, the sun was rising in a stately but friendly manner.

"*Al Shams*," whispered Moussa.

"*Haul*," whispered Moses.

"*HaShemesh*," whispered Moshe.

"The sun," said all three, and began to laugh, with the fullness of the coming day.

A fourth riff to Mnemosyne, Before we arrive at the twenty-third canto

Why did Robert Graves write: "There is one story and one story only worth the telling."

What kind of story is that?

Of course, it is the love story.

And why is it the one story worth the telling?

Because love poses the greatest joy, and the greatest threat, to every human experience.

The great story, the love story, has value because it engages our imagination and intelligence and our passion; it makes our blood run hot or cold, makes us dream, enfolds our ambitions, worldly thrusts, our sense of elegance and beauty and honesty and truths, and gives us greater knowledge of ourselves and others, with understanding of hidden meanings, and the full wisdom of time and experience.

The love story, more than any other, has the capacity to engage all of these elements, and makes of the story-teller: an otherworldly creature; in some cultures, a holy man; an artist who contains and shares the history of the tribe or race through its art; an entertainer, in some societies, who finds the earth's holiness and man's wisdom and history something to be learned only in school, or practiced on Sundays in church; a "shmuck with a typewriter," in places who believe stories are things you sell in the market-place, and in which the practice of "dumbing-down" exists to pull the whole place – through its media – down to the level of the seller, which means to forget that love, wisdom, holiness, history, intelligence and art exist at all; in other words, to believe and thus to turn humanity into curs who not only chase their own tails, but who happily chomp away on their own shit.

"Shmucks with typewriters," entertainers, artists, holy men: all go up the Loving Tree of Life and, in their art, tell us what they see.

Some shmucks, entertainers and artists, choose instead to climb the other Tree, which leads to judgment and useless competition and ultimately the very marketplace that is helping the other bastards destroy our culture and of course our planet.

But why am I telling you this?

Because Shakespeare is locked in a closet with a critic and a religious figure, and is fighting to justify his art.

And because Moses, Moshe and Moussa have just discovered that life is so dangerous that only a good story could save their arses.

Once I add love to the mix, however, they're all going to be lucky to get out of this polyphony alive.

But I might not do that. So disregard this last riff.

But then, again, I might.

Perhaps it's best to disregard nothing.

The twenty-third canto

"Not that I would object," began Shakespeare, as he and Dr. Fisch headed to the *Bistro Lunaire*, "but am I correct to assume you are going to rummage through my work, in your well-known and magisterial *modus operandi*, to prove to the world that I am a Catholic?"

"And to what end?" asked Dr. Fisch, blushing, for that was precisely what he had in mind. "Whatever for?"

Shakespeare shrugged, and took a deep breath. It was good to be relieved of the darkness of the closet.

"I haven't the vaguest idea, sir," replied the playwright. "Perhaps the object is 'to explain certain passages previously considered difficult, which might well relegate the more normative if not catholic interpretations of the Master's more popular monologues to a less revered status, rendering them, in fact, trite, and therefore dramatically useless.'"

"*Master*," said Dr. Fisch, frowning intensely. "*How am I to prove anything?* Quote: 'In a recent conversation with William Shakespeare, on the dark side of the moon, while among certain wise and ancient Jews, I learned that the greatest playwright in the English language, if not in all languages, was a secret Catholic.' Who would believe me? Reading that, I certainly wouldn't. It smacks of conspiracy theory!"

"Worse things have been written," said Shakespeare.

"Such as?"

"An embarrassment of riches," he grimaced. "Have you gone to Barnes and Noble recently? It makes the Barnes and Noble of several hundred years ago – those feverish and glittering years of Stephen King, Michael Crichton, John Grisham, Erica Jong, James Patterson, Dawn Steel and Norman Mailer's last novel (Whatever was he thinking?), as well as the poetry of Jewel and that poor man's Villon, Charles Bukowski, not to mention the odd, flat narrative works of John Updike and the endless *oeuvre* of the endlessly fertile Joyce Carol Oates and the...'ironists,' as you call them: Bret Easton Ellis, Raymond Carver, Donald Barthelme, Cormac MacCarthy, (whose vengeance dramas have no antagonists but a solemnized and purposeless history), and all the youthful wordsmiths who have learned to appreciate their words so much more, in writing programs, (among themselves), than in the world, (among others) – a 'virtual plastic' renaissance of the literary spirit."

"You mis-intend me, sir. I exist, distinctly and alone, to raise the bar to its height," pronounced Dr. Herschel Fisch. "Not to celebrate *Sentina Mundi*, the Cesspool of the World."

"Still," said Shakespeare, not listening to Herschel Fisch's rationalization of his own existence, "If I were you, I would cast your revelatory essay about my supposed Catholicism in a more fictive mode: a science-fiction-mystery drama, say. In which a body is discovered in a distant cathedral on a distant planet, and the murderer eventually pursued and cornered on an asteroid, his knife still hot, and smoking, from the carnage. Cornered, the murderer claims he is Shakespeare. His victim? Obviously, Thomas Stearns, or T.S., Eliot."

Fisch smiled to himself:

"I rather like the idea of Eliot bleeding on a cathedral floor," he said. "In fact, had I lived at the time of Eliot, I would have committed his murder in a cathedral myself. But truly, Will, I relish if not worship the fictive imagination, though I do not possess it."

Shakespeare smiled:

"I see your point, Hersch, and I appreciate your candor. It's simply that yet another book about me is by now so far beyond good taste that it will arrive still-born. There are at least two thousand books written about me, my work, my times, each year. Naturally, the further these writers live from my life and times, the odder their pronouncements."

"You are for all times, Master," said Herschel Fisch, with a faint inclination of his head.

"No," smiled Shakespeare, and spotted the restaurant across the street, set beside the holographic image of a canal, whose location was in fourteenth century Bruges. "My work appears to be long-lasting but, let me assure you, sir, you are not even seeing a *shade* of my former self."

"Still, I'd like to ask you about one particular shade," said Dr. Fisch, quietly but firmly.

"After a few *moules Saturniennes,*" replied the playwright. "Only then might I be persuaded to talk."

The twenty-fourth canto

The afternoon waitress was tall, with thick russet hair, dark and most brown eyes, coy dimples, and a saucy manner. She appeared to be in her late twenties or early thirties. When she handed Shakespeare a menu, she remained at the table, feeling the cloth of his greatcoat.

"You're not from here," she said. "Or this dirty fine woolen is especially imported. I've never seen such tailoring. We've thousands of tailors here, but I'm sure you must have been asked to sell your costume a hundred times over."

"It's a *suit*, not a costume," said Shakespeare, and beckoned her with a finger, whispering something into her ear, which Dr. Fisch could not hear.

She smiled, returned the whisper.

"411," he replied, quietly. "But I won't be there until after 10:30. Is that too late?"

She shook her head.

"Then let's have a half-dozen Enceladians," said Shakespeare, loudly, and pointed at the menu: "Also, let me try these Neptunes: half a dozen Naiads, three Thalassas, and...three Galateas."

"You can eat all that?" the waitress replied.

"If I cannot consume a Naiad and take on three Galateas, I am not worthy of dining in this *boite*. What kind of ale do you have?"

"Well," she said, frowning, and putting a finger to her lips: "With the Neptunes, I'd go for Triton High Albedo. It's the coldest and far and away the smokiest, which you're going to need. Yes, you are *definitely* a stranger here. I love your accent. It's so ancient and odd."

Dr. Fisch was about to speak, but Shakespeare shot him a warning look.

"Your hair is delicious," he said, "Miss Yentl."

The woman smiled. Dr. Fisch noted that she possessed a slightly vampiric pair of eye-teeth, which gave her face a look of danger.

"I'll see you shortly, with your order," she said, quietly, huskily.

Shakespeare nodded, put the menu on the table, then leaned back, arms behind his head, feet outstretched. With unconventional mussels on their way, a new kind of ale, and a tryst, he was the picture of a very contented playwright.

"Where do you live?" asked Dr. Herschel Fisch. "When you're not on the Moon or elsewhere?"

"In the hearts of men," Shakespeare replied, and yawned.

"No, seriously. When you're not coming down to see the odd production of your work, where do you go?"

"To a place you would adore, doctor, but to which you will never be allowed to enter."

"And that is where?" asked Fisch.

"It is a plane of Muses," he smiled, and yawned. "Critics decidedly unwelcome."

"Really?" said Dr. Fisch, not even stung by the remark. "I assume that Proust and Dickens, Jane Austen and George Eliot and Balzac and Hugo—"

"All there. The great and the near-great. All who could never be recycled."

"What about Ezra Pound?" asked Herschel.

"The lunatic?" smiled the playwright. "He tried to keep me from coming here. Said that I knew nothing of Venice, and however did I expect a company of Jews to do a decent job of the play?"

"Still at it, is he?" asked Fisch.

"Anti-semitism's his only constant theme," said Shakespeare, ironically. "But even that infection can't keep a good man down."

"I assume you meant that ironically," said Dr. Fisch. "What about Tolstoi and Dostoievsky?"

"'The sloe-eyed Christers,' S.J. calls them," sighed the playwright, and pursed his lips to keep from grinning.

"S.J. *Perelman*?" asked Dr. Fisch.

"Who else?" smiled Shakespeare. "The only American I continue to read with a pleasure amounting to envy. In fact, the only American who seems to love language, other than Irving Berlin and Ira Gershwin, Cole Porter and Johnny Mercer. Men of the theater, all of them. My kind of club. Fine friends. Especially Mercer. Some of his lyrics are as good as anything I've ever written. Better, several of them."

"Such as?"

"Oh, let me see: *Skylark; Out of this World; Blues in the Night*, that's a veritable play. *Something's Gotta Give* is adorable. 'Old Implacable heart, immovable object,' great fun, and unlike Cole's work, clever without calling attention to itself."

"Yes, I can understand that. But, still, Cole Porter---"

"You're going to say 'Like the moon growing dim/ on the rim of the hill/, in the chill, still of the night,' very clever, and if the music weren't so lovely, too clever for words. My favorite Porter is 'Night and Day,' of course, the pulse of it, I think he's got something wonderful there.'

"And you'd put Irving Berlin up as well, along with Porter and Gershwin?" said Fisch, with a frown, as if he were comparing the chiaroscuro of a Caravaggio with Georges de la Tour, or the British one penny black stamp with the Post Office Mauritius.

"You're *surprised*, doctor?" asked Shakespeare, and took the ale from Miss Yentl without looking at the woman, drinking heartily for a half-moment."He's certainly all there, and has every right to be," he said, smacking his lips, and waving two fingers at the waitress.

"Two more?" she asked.

"Two tankards," he said, staring at Fisch. "I'm surprised, doctor: as a Jew and a literary gentleman, I should have thought you would have recognized how the Divine Irving was the first to distinguish American from Continental English. He created modern American speech, single-handedly. Putting aside all those jingoistic pieces - we all do that, occasionally, his 'God bless America' is no different from my own 'Into the breach!" or Gaunt's speech "this earth of majesty, this seat of Mars." Embarrassing, I admit, but part of our story-telling, our capacity to turn ourselves and our world to myth. Putting aside all that, doctor, every line he wrote had...*charm.* 'But if you've got something that must be done, and it can only be done by one, there is nothing more to say, except it's a lovely day for saying: it's a lovely day.' Astonishing in its' simplicity. As if everyone listening to it personally had thought of it, although only Berlin had. That's a sign of genius."

Dr. Fisch thought: Here I am, listening to William Shakespeare singing Irving Berlin. However can I write that William Shakespeare thinks Irving Berlin and S.J. Perelman are the only real American writers? Whatever happened to Henry James, Herman Melville, Walt Whitman? Is this a form of snobbism? Of cultural superiority?

As if he had read his mind, which he had, Shakespeare finished the ale, put down the glass and continued:

"Tolstoi has some moments of fine ironic observation," he said, as if he'd had this conversation dozens of times before. "And Dostoievsky creates some monstrously good monologues. Still, I could have written forty plays in the amount of time it took me to finish reading "*The Brothers Karamazov.*" I much prefer "*The Idiot*," for Freddy's ability to take the situation in hand and control it. "*Brothers Karamazov*" means a great deal to most Russians, and I do understand that. Which is why I'm learning Yiddish. But here comes the first of our *moules*, served by the tangy Molly the Mollusc herself."

Fisch started to laugh, then felt guilty, thinking: how can the man make an assignation with a Mollusc?

"Your name is not really Yentl, is it?" asked Shakespeare of the waitress.

"It's Moluskiewicz," said the woman. "Hermione. But my mom called me Molly."

"I stand corrected," said Dr. Herschel Fisch, aloud.

Then he felt a cold chill, and turned to Shakespeare:

"*How did you know what I was thinking, or this young woman's nickname?*"

Shakespeare was holding the plate of mussels in both hands and sniffing them.

"Lucky guess?" he said, coolly, and the very coolness sent a further chill down Fisch's spine.

"Am I being played with, sir?" said the critic.

"And are you indeed?" Shakespeare replied.

Then he slurped down the first mussel, breathed deeply, and whispered: "The *mooooooooons* of Neptune...*Shall I compare thee to a winter's eve?*"

Dr. Fisch rose, excusing himself to go to the bathroom. Passing Molly, he gestured with his finger, pointing towards an alcove, hidden by the kitchen-wall.

After a moment, the waitress appeared.

"Miss Moluskiewicz," Fisch whispered, and pulled out his wallet. "Here are five hundred Tremors. And my holo-note. *I want you to find out who that man really is!* Both the Janitor and I must know, *as swiftly after your assignation*, exactly what you have learned."

Frowning, Molly turned towards Shakespeare:

"But I'm not having any assignat---"

Dr. Fisch put a finger to his lips:

"The future of *Noye-Erdkelle* depends upon *you*, Miss M. *Please*! If that man is not who he says he is, we could well kiss this satellite goodbye! You are our only hope. And let me assure you, if I'm proved right, there are plenty more Tremors where this came from."

Molly frowned, but nodded.

"Call me this evening," said Dr. Herschel Fisch. "I bow – we all bow – to your prowess. Ply him with *moules* until he cannot move. Then take him to---"

It was Molly's turn to put her own finger to his lips.

"Depend on it, darlin'," she said.

Dr. Herschel Fisch went to the men's room, and found himself trembling.

It was not Shakespeare, this second time, who caused him to piss on his own hands.

It was something altogether different and more terrifying:

That mind-reading, ale-drinking mussel-slammer was not William Shakespeare at all.

He was...*a shape-shifter!*

The twenty-fifth canto

As you must know by now, thanks to popular fiction, popular cinema, and the shouts and yells of bloggers, World Prophecy has defined the destruction of the moon colony by the appearance of Three Warning Signs:

FIRST SIGN: the invasion of the moon colony by earthlings;

SECOND SIGN:

a) the discovery of the mystery of the Jews, the purpose of which is to save the cosmos, through the recognition of Paradise Now;

b) the key to the mystery of the Jews, which is that everybody's a child of Israel, including *some* Jews - those who are descended from the tribe of Judah.The rest aren't real Jews at all. They're children of Israel.

Even the Christians.

Even the Moslems.

Even the primal peoples.

Even the Asians.

The whole pluriverses are filled with children of Israel.

Everybody who has ever prayed to or asked a question of God or questioned His or Her Existence, is a stiff-neck! That is to say, a Child of Israel.

THIRD SIGN: the appearance of the Shape-shifter, who exists to call into question the meanings of existence --- by reflecting existence to itself comically, and tragically, and farcically, and comically-farcically and tragically-comically, farcically-tragically, etc etc. in literature, the media, politics and society.

The danger is this: ***anti-semitism,*** (which means hatred of humanity); ***greed,*** (which means Theft of Everything***); sociopathy (****which means the inability to identify with another human being)* could eventually destroy everything and everyone in the universe.

And the Shape-shifter could reflect those exaggerated states in his work, causing a pluriversal panic.

At the very least, Shape-shifters are disturbing because their artful theatricalizing in politics, society, literature, the media, makes us face different truths of our existence.

Shape-shifters force us to think.

The horror, the horror...

Moreover, we never know where the Shape-shifters themselves personally stand, or why.

Not that it matters. Their personality or belief-system *is not the reason for their existence.*

Their actions or works have been known to bring about revolutions.

They are not only the enemy but, worse, they are the honorable adversary.

Without their shape-shifting, we'd never know our weaknesses or strengths.

In the first book, "*Jews On The Moon,*" Newman Fears, the last Jew on earth, crash-landed onto the moon and then had spent much of his time traveling throughout the universe to discover the mystery as well as the key to the mystery of the Jews.

Once discovered, he learned that nobody really gave a shit about his answer.

Thus, TWO SIGNS of the THREE-PART PROPHECY already had been fulfilled; a single earthling had crash-landed on the moon; though not constituting an invasion, he had discovered the mystery of the Jews, as well as its key.

The THIRD SIGN, the appearance of the Shape-shifter, might well be occurring right now.

On these very pages.

This is why this the four books constituting *Jews On The Moon* are such a potentially dangerous and paralyzing work.

The twenty-sixth canto:

In "*Jews Beyond Jupiter,*" Dr. Herschel Fisch is faced with the dreadful problem of Shakespeare's true identity, which – once it is revealed - not only could destroy many academic careers, but also might very well produce devastating consequences for the moon-colony, and thus for the cosmos itself.

If you find this prophecy disturbing or terrifying, you might prefer to purchase more popular expressions of this dramatic theme: for example, Tim Lahaye's and Jerry Jenning's, "What a Blast: God's Final Destruction of the Hebrews"; the Spielberg-Lucas manga trilogy, "Indiana's Jews and the Temple at Shaker Heights," and, of course, the seminal work dealing soberly though anxiously with this very theme, published as: "Why Jews are Liberal," by the forward-looking antique radical and neo-conservative, Norman Podhoretz, whose economic system "Plus One *plus* Minus One equals Nothing" laid the very foundation not only of Reaganomics, but also led to the eventual buyout of the America's Empire. And yet, it earned Podhoretz the first Nobel Prize in Stand-up Comedy.

The twenty-seventh canto

But let us understand two things:
ONE: William Shakespeare is nobody else but William Shakespeare.
He always was, is, and always will be.

TWO: Dr. Herschel Fisch is misreading the events in the *Boite Lunaire*. His misreading is going to have nasty consequences in "*Jews Beyond Jupiter*." As perceptive as the critic may be - and Dr. Fisch is certainly more perceptive than most every else - a misreading of sign and text is the greatest failure of criticism. Even with as cogent, supple, and magisterial a mind as Dr. Fisch possesses, it is equal capable of magisterial failure.

Am I spoiling the story for you?
Quite the opposite.

I'm making it easier for you to bear witness to the interplanetary mussel itself as a major plot point, and one with miserable consequences not only for Dr. Hirsch, but also for this second book, which means: the cosmos.

The twenty-eighth canto

To some of you, the two cantos which follow may resemble the Etiology of the Whale chapter from "*Moby Dick.*"

They are informative, yes, and while themselves not incongenial to botanical and gastronomical speculation, they also possess both narrative and thematic bearing upon our world. Therefore, do not skip the twenty-fifth and twenty-sixth cantos, for they are critical to an understanding of certain major aspects of "*Jews Beyond Jupiter*."

Attend:

The twenty-ninth canto

The interplanetary mussel is not only an aphrodisiac, but also it is also a creator of altered states of consciousness.

Each mussel family, from each different planet or its satellite, produces a specific psycho-sensory pattern: because of the different geological, atmospheric and planetary zoologies in our solar system, each mussel family also possesses *dramatically different physical properties*, and which are reflected not only in the gustatory patterns but also in the psychic palates of the diners themselves.

I will describe the specific mussel families found in our universe: their size; color; weight; texture; sexual stimuli capabilities; psychological distortion, defined in traditional terms. (A more fully-informed catalogue can be purchased in any Barnes and Noble holo-shop, or at any spaceport in the pluriverse.)

A General Description:

First, all mussels discovered thus far throughout the universe are bivalve, but cannot be considered oceanic or freshwater, since each aquatic disposition varies according to the geological nature of each planet or satellite. However, aquatic or flowing chemicals, of whatever composition, seem to be the proper growing medium.

The mussels are found in a variety of settings: at great depths; along under-aquatic volcanic ridges; on water-floors; at media borders. All are attached to each other by tiny hairs, which appear to be the same "beards" as former terran varieties possessed.

It is difficult not to imagine these bivalves as "ocean cleaners," although we do not know *what* they clean, or if the acquatic medium actually fulfils the definition of an ocean at all.

As of this writing, Benschl, Keyes and Porchnik have presented "*Mussel Language Linguistics:Vols. 1 & 2*," (Liberty Press, Selva, Titan), and whose experiments in linguistics, semiotics and communication are still ongoing.

At present, all Outer Planet mussels have been known to signal the following three messages:

1: "This feels good."

2: "That hurts."

3: "Watch that one suck it."

This may not seem very conclusive, but its possibilities are enormous. It demonstrates that the mussel possesses grammatical variancy, emotive response, and descriptive logic, as well as the psychological capacity to choose among a variety of stimuli.

Those three known phrases, in fact, may reflect their most ancient history.

I am taking the following data from the other landmark study by Benschl, Keyes and Porchnick, "*The Psychodynamics of Interplanetary Mussel Ingestion*," and which has led to the authors' most recent experiments in communication with the bivalve. Whether their present work is a result of the mania and misapprehensions which accompany the eating of too many mussels on the part of its authors, or is, in fact, a psychological breakthrough of historic proportions, time alone will tell.

I will begin with a description of the exact mussels Shakespeare has eaten, and will add several descriptions of what he might well eat in future cantos. (Perhaps he won't eat them, but the information, nonetheless, may prove instructive, unless it doesn't, and therefore isn't).

The thirtieth canto

1) The Crab Nebulae Mussel: a general description

Size: 14-22 inches

Color: Steel grey-deep blue

Weight: 1/8 to ¾ lb.

Texture: Smooth but granular

Sexual Stimulus Capability: In most instances, fellatio of both sexes, lasting for several hours.

Psychological distortion: Laziness leading to sloth; long sleeps with dreams of fellatio of both sexes, lasting for several hours, and ending with the desire for a long and cold shower. Great sense of accomplishment and euphoria after shower. Also extensive if not manic use of lip balm for several months.

2) The Saturn Mussel

a) Jovian Mussel:

Size: 7-11 inches

Color: brown and black, mottled

Weight: ¼ to 1/3 pound

Texture: solid, with gelatinous coating

Sexual Stimulus Capability: immediate erection of both penis and clitoris; senses heightened; tendency to scream with each movement.

Psychological distortion: loss of control; adoption of fatalism; universe seen as impersonal; too many Jovian mussels eaten leads to the subject starting purposeless fires.

b) Rhean Mussel:

Size: 4-6 inches

Color: multi-colored

Weight: 1/10 lb.

Texture: gummy but with solid center

Sexual Stimulus Capability: subject given to love-biting and scratching.

Psychological distortion: happiness leading to mania; too many consumed Rhean mussels leads to the subject starting purposeful fires.

c) Enceladian Mussel:

Size: ¼ - 1/2 inch

Color: light blue-green, mottled

Weight: 1/16 lb.

Texture: soft and chewy

Sexual Stimulus Capability: tonguing and sucking;

Psychological distortion: infantilism; everybody is mommy; crying for no apparent reason; enuresis; people unused to Enceladians should put rubber sheets on beds before sleep.

d) Dionian Mussel:

Size: 1-2 feet

Color: bright green

Weight: ¼ - ½ lb.

Texture: creamy and soft

Sexual Stimulus Capability: rapture with touch alone; sexual penetration rare; subjects simply stroke each others' faces to achieve orgasm.

Psychological distortion: sense of astonishment and wonder with every breath; eventual inability to speak or to reason; ingestion of too many Dionian mussels often leads to cradle-cap.

3) The Neptunian Mussel

a) Naiad Musssel

Size: pea

Color: gradations of green

Weight: 1 to 2 lbs.

Texture: dense

Sexual Stimulus Capability: rapacious, regardless of sexual differentiation.

Psychological distortion: high excitability; mild paranoia; focus on one event to the exclusion of all others; loss of speech; two people eating Naiads together begin by wrestling and end up enmeshed in all possible aperture combinations. Extreme quantities of Naiad mussel ingestion demand hospitalization, or intense washing by a high hose.

b) Thalassa Mussel

Size: 2/3 inch to 1 ½ feet

Color: light blue to midnight blue

Weight: ¼ to ½ lb

Texture: smooth, with tiny grain-pocks on the surface

Sexual Stimulus Capability: normal sexual activity, with slower but longer, deeper expression of movement; uncontrollable smiling, for no conceivable reason;

Psychological distortion: loss of ego; growth of cosmic identity; saint-like tendencies, without martyrdom.

c) Galatea Mussel

Size: ¼ to 1/2 inch

Color: transparent

Weight: 1/16 lb.

Texture: knobby and tasty

Sexual Stimulus Capability: nearly instantaneous and constant orgasms of tiny expression and duration.

Psychological distortion: the eater develops into a God at swift incremental stages; he or she believes he has begun to see through matter and into the soul of things; demands atonement of self, and often ends up committing suicide in strange and interesting ways.

4) The Jovian Mussel: a general description

Size: 2/3 – 4/5 inch.

Color: Deep blue to celeste

Weight: 1/10 – 1/4 lb.

Texture: varies

Sexual Stimulus Capability: generally orgiastic, which is why they're the party-goers' favorite; the entire body becomes a sexual object, and stimulation begins with a glance, ends with penetration, continues with another glance, etc. Excessive Jovians have been known to have such orgiastic capacity that all eaters have had to have their sexual organs eventually removed.

Psychological distortion: Mania; the ability to monologize for days and to say nothing, but with gusto, while having sex. Dr. Herschel Fisch is convinced the first interplanetary edition of the Oxford English Dictionary was compiled by its editors while on Jovian mussels. He explains this by its capacious and lively illustrations, its meaningless definitions, and thoroughly inappropriate quotations.

5) The Uranian Mussel: a general description

Size: ¼ inch to ?

Color: invisible, save for presence of "beards."

Weight: 1/10th to 2 lbs

Texture: impossible to describe

Sexual Stimulus Capability: Quixotic. Putting it around revolving windmills.

Psychological distortion: Only three have been able to describe the event: each mentions a long tunnel leading towards a "black light," and then each is eased into that "black light" until absorbed by it; then, before them, each is faced with a myriad of similar tunnels, but with white lights appearing at their end. A Strange Being, who resembles a Powder-puff, tells them strange things, which they cannot remember, but which they know will change their lives.

6) The Plutonian Mussel: a general description

Size: ½ inch

Color: deep gold

Weight: ½ lb

Texture: hard, solid.

Sexual Stimulus Capability: bowel movements produce far greater pleasure

Psychological distortion: loss of affect towards self and others; grim need to lead; extraordinary capacity to browbeat and to enslave self and others; Often repeated phrase, the Sondheimian: "We serve a dark and vengeful god." Thirteen days of hospitalization and pharmaceutically-induced sleep may break the Plutonic pattern. Before the patient is hospitalized, however, he or she may well have changed the history of the world.

CONCLUSION: unless you are William Shakespeare, don't eat interplanetary mussels.

A fifth riff to Mnemosyne,
Before we hit thirty-first canto

The most surreal and impossible thought for a child: parents as sexual beings.

When my mother first explained to me how children were born, I exclaimed: "That's impossible! Nobody could have thought of that! Putting your penis in a vagina? You're making it up! That's ridiculous! Go stick your penis in a vagina and out comes a child? Do you think I'm stupid?"

She was laughing at my chagrin, which laughter I mistook as definitive proof of a put-on.

"Why would I make up something so strange?" she said. "Do you think all mothers make up such things? No. All mothers have husbands or sometimes friends who put their penises in their vaginas and leave their seeds there and the seeds become babies and after nine months, out they pop!"

I thought about that.

It was probably true.

She'd have to be incredibly odd to make up something like that, and to consider it a joke.

"Why are you telling me these things?" I asked. "I wanted to go to the library."

"Because it's time you knew," she said.

"Why?"

"Because I want you to hear it from me, and not from any of your friends, who may tell it wrongly."

"None of my friends ever said anything about putting penises into vaginas."

"Listen: this discussion is between you and me, all right? Your friends' parents have to tell them this. *Not you.* Okay? Now are you ready to go to the library?"

"Not yet. I think I want to throw up."

I don't remember throwing up, but I do remember the nausea that overcame me as I thought of all the girls I always played with – Joanie and Barbra and Jessica and Paula and Louise. I couldn't imagine putting my penis into any of them, although I liked to cuddle with Jessica and pretend we had just robbed a bank or had blown up a Japanese U-boat, and were hiding from the police or kamikazes. But Jessica and I couldn't rob banks or blow up U-boats or hide from the police or kamikazes if my penis was jammed into her vagina. Movement, I must assume, would be awkward. Besides, it would interfere with our imaginations!

"I want to know about seeds," I said. "When I pee, do I pee *seeds*? I don't ever remember peeing anything except pee."

"You don't pee seeds."

"So how can seeds come out of my penis if I don't pee them?"

"We can talk about that later."

"I want to talk about that now."

My mother was in over her head, and I knew it, though I didn't know why, and she knew it, and knew why very well.

"Okay. Supposing when you kiss girls?" she began.

"Yes?"

"They kiss you back? Well, when they do, sometimes your body makes seeds."

"I kissed Joanie Goldberg and Paula and I cuddle with Jessica. I don't think my body makes anything."

"Oh, but I mean, kiss for a long time."

"Kiss for a long time?" I asked. "Why would you want to kiss for a long time? Doesn't it get boring?"

"If you love someone," said mom, slowly, "it doesn't get boring, and you don't mind kissing for a long time."

"*Really?*" I wondered, growing bored by the odd and awkward nature of the discourse, and of the impossibility of imagining such strange goings-on. "But I love Paula and Joanie and Jessica, though I can't stand her parents. I don't kiss any of them for a long time. Well, maybe Jessica and I hug---hmmm---do you make seeds when you hug?"

"One day," said mom. "One day your body will make seeds lots of different ways. And when that happens, we'll talk again."

"Let's talk now."

"No."

I never thought any more about seeds until my friend Joe Miller called me, eight years later, when I was fourteen, and told me how to have an amazing experience:

"Go into the shower and take some soap and put it on your penis and scrub it and scrub it and scrub it. Then after it happens, call me right back."

"After what happens?" I asked.

"After the amazing experience I just mentioned," said Joe.

I did what he said. I had the amazing experience. Joe Miller was right. My life hasn't been the same since.

The thirty-first canto

To their left was an endless desert.

To their right was a path leading to the ocean.

Before them was an oasis and, surrounding its small pond, seventeen palm trees and a caravansery.

"*Now what*?" asked the three, in unison.

"Clearly a choice has to be made," said Moses.

"And a good one," added Moshe.

"And rather quickly, too, before we're spotted," Moussa replied.

"We have six pieces of gold and ten pieces of silver," said Moshe. "They will be useless in the desert; it probably will lead to our deaths, at the oasis; by the ocean, however, we could hire a boat, although we do run the risk of being caught by the Crusaders and having our throats cut."

"I have no doubt that we could talk our way out of any ill will at the oasis," Moussa answered.

"Yes, but I can find out more about my own people, if we go to the ocean," said Moses. "Perhaps I will discover someone who is sailing to England, and who will take us there, and from thence to Wales."

For a moment nobody said anything.

All stared at the sand.

Then Moshe sighed:

"What is our ultimate intention?" he asked.

"To find a woman and be happy," said Moses.

"To be happy and find a woman," added Moussa. "And to raise a family."

"We can find that in the desert, in Wales, and even at the oasis," replied Moshe.

"If we can find that anywhere in the world," said Moses, "then why be worried?"

"He's right," replied Moussa. "I suggest we take the gold piece and flip it. If it lands with the emperor's face staring at us, then the answer is yes."

"Yes, what?" said Moshe.

"Besides, there are *three* choices," nodded Moses. "Not two."

After a moment of reflection, Moussa replied:

"We will use a negative to determine the answer. Thus: we should *not* go to the desert. Flip the coin," began Moussa.

"Wait" said Moshe. "What if it says: Go to the desert, and therefore we don't ask if we should not go to the ocean or to the oasis. We will be denying ourselves two more possibilities."

"I've never crossed a desert," said Moses.

"Nor I an ocean," said Moussa and Moshe.

"I've never been to an oasis," said Moses.

"I have," said Moussa, and Moshe.

It was Moussa who thought aloud: "Moses wants to go to Wales. I would agree to cross the ocean with him. But we run the very real risk of being taken as slaves, or of being murdered as Moslem and Jew."

Then Moshe started to laugh, and the laughter would have the effect of changing their lives.

"I have a magnificent idea," he said. "Let us go to Wales as holy men, who are neither Christian, Moslem or Jew."

"But we *are* Christian, Moslem and Jew," Moses replied.

"No," said Moshe. "We are Joslians, which are Jewish Christian Moslems who follow the Teachings of the Great and Grand Lady-Lord, the Beautiful Joslian."

After a moment, Moses said: "That is very foolish."

"Precisely," grinned Moussa, giving his friend Moshe a hug. "That is Moshe's singular and instructive point. Joslian is our Shield, and we three are Her Prophets. In fact, we are the only ones who ever saw Her alive, before She was..."

"---Eaten by a lion?" said Moses.

"Exactly," replied Moshe.

"I couldn't have said it better," Moussa added.

"To the ocean," said Moshe, encouragingly.

After several moments on the path leading down to the sea, Moses said, "You know? I've been thinking about Joslian, and I truly believe they're going to love us in Wales."

The thirty-second canto

But before they had the opportunity to see if Moses' thought was correct, they would have to find a boat returning to Europe.

Moreover, It would be essential to try out their tale of The Beautiful Joslian upon Moslem and Christian and Jew.

And because there was a great deal of ocean between the coast of Africa and Europe for three who could not swim, certainty of presentation would become, therefore, all the more compelling.

The thirty-third canto

The port and its town had been seized by the Crusaders, and presented all the goodwill of such an undertaking: the dead were still in the streets, food for dogs and ravens, even desert hyenas and lions.

The luckier Moslems and Jews had gone into the desert, to face starvation, banditry, and slave-traders.

It was, therefore, all the more surprising for the marauding Crusaders to spot three extremely hairy and odd-looking men, appearing on the path descending from the mountain, and crossing with purpose to the largest tavern in the port.

The tavern was owned by an infamous Spaniard named Don Gesualdo. Nobody knew if Don Gesualdo was a Christian or a Moslem or a Jew or even a Spaniard. He spoke Spanish, Arabic, French, English, Italian and Hebrew.

Don Gesualdo's principal job was to ensure that the traveler parted with as much money as he possessed or, if there remained *scudi* in his purse, that he lost the rest at gambling and whoring. If neither activity was possible, the simple thefts of Don Gesualdo became, even more simply, murderous.

Don Gesualdo's wife, Donna Estrela, was as large as he, and managed the kitchen and the sleeping quarters.

Donna Estrella and Don Gesualdo had four children: three daughters, and a son. Collectively, the progeny weighed over twelve hundred pounds. They spent a great deal of time trying to evade performing all chores which came at them with blows from mother and father. The rest of their day was spent slapping and kicking at each other.

The thirty-fourth canto

As soon as the rag-tag trio of Moshe, Moussa and Moses entered Don Gesualdo's tavern, the son cried out to his father: "Papa, do you want me to throw out these smelly beggars?"

Magically - or so it appeared to all - Moussa held up a gold coin.

"Fat boy," he said. "With this coin I will conjur up eighteen of us. Show us to our rooms before we turn into a dozen more, plus six followers."

"Followers of what?" stormed Don Gesualdo, rushing angrily and noisily from the kitchen, his hands still wet from slaughtering a goat.

"The Saintly and Beautiful Joslian," added Moshe, "who knows no man, yet has known every man, though She Herself belongs to none!"

Moshe suddenly produced a gold coin as well:

"This is Her own emblem," he said. "Whoever follows Her must always proceed with this shield, for it possesses all the powers of the skies, and the depths of the seas. By the way, do you know if there are any ships bound for England or the Italian or Turkish shores, tomorrow?"

"The Venetians have a caravel loading now," said Don Gesualdo, frowning, and staring thoughtfully at the gold coin. "They leave some time later this week. Let me see that coin."

"Only followers of the Saintly Joslian are permitted to hold it," Moshe inveighed. "Unless you fear going blind. And then, Goddess forbid, only one blessed in secret ceremony by the saintly Joslian can cure you."

"Pablito!" shouted the tavern-keeper. "Take that coin and hold it. If you don't go blind, you may keep it while I kill these stinking bastards."

"Please, gentle sir," said Moses. "If you love your son, do not order him to touch the coin."

But the fat boy grabbed it out of Moses' hand.

Immediately Moussa stood before Pablito and said, "Your eyes are as pale as a donkey's pizzle. Watch what happens to them as you stare at the coin! How they will start to sweat, and the sweat will become as a gum, and it will close your lids, and you will be unable to open---"

Immediately the fat boy dropped the coin and began to cry "Papa! Papa!" and his father moved forward, but Moshe held up a hand and cried: "O Lovely Joslian, return the sight of the young and sweating Fat Boy so that he will see only goodness and beauty. Cause him to obey his father and mother each time they have good and beautiful orders to give him. Otherwise, may the parents themselves go blind if they scream at the young sweating Fat One, and make him do horrid things."

Don Gesualdo glowered, and Donna Estrella, who had appeared behind her husband, stared with dread at her son. Moussa clapped his hands three times, then Moses spit in the boy's eyes twice.

"Wipe your eyes, O Young Fat One," said Moshe.

Trembling, Pablito did as he was told.

"I---I can s-s-s-see now---Mother!," he said, crying like a calf.

He reached on the floor for the coin, then handed it to Moses, sniffing, "I'll never grab money again, even if papa and mama tell me to, and if they do, it will be *their* turn go blind."

"Give the gentlemen a room," ordered Donna Estrella to her husband.

The thirty-fifth canto

Before an abundant table, groaning with meats, cabbages, and honeyed tarts, Donna Estrella turned to the three happy priests:

"And do you know the lovely Joslian, magical sir?" she asked Moussa, in a respectful tone.

"They *said* they did!" spat Don Gesualdo.

"Shut your fat face!" replied Donna Estrella. "I'm asking *them.*"

"I do the speaking here!" countered the red-faced husband. "What could *you* possibly know of the lovely Joslian, woman?"

"More than you do!" shouted the wife.

"I've heard more tales about her than you have hairs on your cunt, *diabla!*" yelled

Don Gesualdo. "Only last night, three Frenchmen were speaking of a miracle she had performed in their own home town. Did *you* hear that? *Did* you? You didn't! Because *I did!*"

"I know all the Catholic saints," said Donna Estrella. "And nowhere is the lovely Joslian even mentioned!"

Surprised, and expecting support, Don Gesualdo turned to the three odd men, with a questioning expression.

"The lovely Joslian is not Catholic," said Moshe, shaking his head, then nodding quietly, and cutting into a shank of roasted and tender lamb.

"She's more than Moslem," Moses added, stuffing his mouth with cabbage and carrots.

"The Jews hold her in high regard, though she is not a Jewess," added Moussa, scooping a mound of saffron rice onto his plate.

"*Exactly*!" said Don Gesualdo, nodding hard and staring with anger at his wife. "That's exactly what those Frenchmen said last night. Don't tell me I don't know these things. She's all about miracles. The blindness was nothing. Not only can she raise the dead, she's also been known to raise the unborn!"

"We saw that as well," said Moshe, politely. "And believe me, senora, it is no easy feat."

"Twice we have seen it, in fact," Moses added.

"And, still, the first little girl came out speaking the language of the Turks, though she was as fair as a Viking," nodded Moussa. "As is the lovely Joslian herself."

"Give them more food," shouted Don Gesualdo to his daughters. "They are my guests. About time this tavern had serious people staying here. You don't gamble or use whores, do you? Because if you do games or women, all of it's on me."

"We spend our evenings in prayer and communication with Lovely Joslian," said Moussa.

"Food, damn you!" yelled Gesualdo, then pointed to a table near the window, and which looked upon the sea. "Pablito, go to the Venetians and tell them Don Gesualdo wants to purchase three berths for his friends, the Prophets of the Saintly Joslian. Tell them these men will bless the ship and provide a safe crossing----I assume you *can* do that?"

"We do it all the time," said Moshe.

"That goes without saying," added Moussa.

"Tell me," said Don Gesualdo, after Pablito had gone, and he began to speak with the expression of a young and loving girl. "When did you last see the Lovely Joslian? Is she actually as lovely as everyone says?"

Moussa smiled, shyly.

"She calls me My Prophet," he whispered, then pointed at Moshe. "She calls *him* My Voice." Then he held out a hand to Moses. "But *him* she calls... My Eternal Lover."

Both Don Pedro and Donna Estrella stared in awe at the Welshman.

Even with all that hair, his dark green eyes seemed to glow.

"Indeed," they whispered. "Certainly, one can see that..."

Moshe nodded politely, then turned to Moses, whispering wistfully:

"Tell our new friends what it is like to make love to a Goddess."

The thirty-sixth canto

Shakespeare was so mussel-bound that Molly Molluskiewicz had to call two friends to take part in the growing miracle.

One of the girls, yclept Molly Malone, was afraid Shakespeare was going to have a heart attack.

The third, called Molly Bloom, admitted that she had never seen a man fellated three times in succession, and *still* cry out for more!

The playwright appeared fatter, more awake, and keener for pleasure.

He took them on one at a time, then two at a time, then three. Finally, the women had to tell him to cease and desist.

"Now comes the gentler moment," he sighed "When you lie beside me, hair on my chest, hand on my fundament or my cave's entrance, and your breathing's slow, and your Venus-breath is moist with the smell of violets and dew, and eglantine. Do you know how much we've lost on our savaged Earth? Here we are at rest, below the surface of a moon marked by the dull fall of meteors. Yet I would give the greatest falling of the Heavens for a vision of Ophelia's sweet and watery bower: "*There is a willow grows aslant a brook,/That shows his hoar leaves in the glassy stream;/There with fantastic garlands did she come/Of crow-flowers, nettles, daisies, and long purples/ That liberal shepherds give a grosser name, /But our cold maids do dead men's fingers call them;/ There, on the pendent boughs her coronet weeds/Clambering to hang, an envious sliver broke;/When down her weedy trophies and herself/Fell in the weeping brook./Her clothes spread wide;/And, mermaid-like, awhile they bore her up.*'"

"That's terrible," said Molly Malone. "Falling in a dress, was she? What did her mother say when she come home all dripping?"

"She drowned, stupid," said Molly Bloom. "I know that speech. It's from a play by William Shakespeare. It's called *Hamlet.* We had to memorize it in school. I hated the bloody thing."

"You hated the play?" asked Shakespeare, with quickened interest.

"With a dirty great passion," said Miss Bloom.

"And did you hate Shakespeare as well?" asked the playwright.

"Aye, him too," said Molly Bloom. "It was he wrote the bloody thing."

"Odd," muttered the playwright to himself. "For someone who hated Shakespeare, you blew him ferociously well."

Molly Bloom sighed, and started to laugh, and tickled him playfully on his balls.

"If I ever met him, I'd do more than blow him," she said. "I'd strangle him slowly and make him to know it, for all that misery he caused me as a lass."

"Mmm, I think I'd like that well enough," said Shakespeare, ruminatively, then turned to Molly Moluskiewicz. "And what would *you* do, Mistress Moll?"

"Isn't he a strange one?" Bloom asked the Mollusk.

"Anyone who eats as many mussels as he does, one expects to be peculiar," the waitress whispered, gazing down reflectively at the playwright.

"Still," said Molly Bloom. "I was hoping it was I, and not the mussels, that took him on love's randy grand tour."

"It was all of you and my own muscle did it," replied Shakespeare. "The mussels merely came along for the ride."

"Good," said Molly Bloom, watching him rise. "We'll try it *in* for size this time."

The thirty-seventh canto

Why am I telling you this?

Because sex for Shakespeare was as juicy and as sloppy as a tavern meal, while love gave birth to memory and hope, and a sweetness that was worth savouring.

It was Time that ground you down.

You could never defeat it.

Or could you?

If you were aware enough and awake enough, sex and love produced such greatness in your art that you transcended Time. Your work rose above Time, as all great art transcended Time's grave watch:

"I know a bank where the wild thyme blows,/ Where oxlips and the nodding violet grows,/Quite over-canopied with luscious woodbine,/With sweet musk-roses and with eglantine."

He'd made love there, and also where the willow sits aslant a brook.

"These trees shall be my books."

Something about the three women, his Mollies, brought back so many memories of so many other women giving birth to and being born to so much art:

The Princess of France and her ladies-in-waiting.

Mistress Quickly and Doll Tearsheet.

Juliet's Nurse; Cressida, and their smarter sisters, Paulina and Bianca.

Poor Ophelia (that younger Desdemona), and Juliet.

Comic and attractive harridans, such as Beatrice and Kate the Curst and even Celia.

And the cold, sexy nasties: Tamara the Queen of the Goths, Lady Macbeth, Goneril and Regan.

And the sad Queens, so many of them: Cordelia, Hermione, Elizabeth, Margaret, even young Perdita and Marina.

And the women of magic: Titania, whom Shakespeare loved almost as much as he did Oberon, and Hippolyta, who had so few lines in the play because she was the Queen of the Amazons and he knew she could have struck his fancy so violently she would have dominated the work. In her case, less indeed was more. (Still, the boy-girl playing her probably also doubled as Titania).

Olivia.

Rosalind.

The brilliant and cunning and probably the most tragic and human of all his characters, other than Hamlet: Cleopatra.

What pretentious prig had said or opined that Shakespeare had never written good women's roles?

You could never write about such a stunning variety of women without having known them.

And having known them, you would have known enough, by then, never to judge them. Most of all, you would always love them, sometimes sleeping with them, but always *looking at them* and *listening to them* as a lover and as a poet and as a horned man of science.

If you were lucky - and Shakespeare was very lucky - you'd have a wife like Anne Hathaway who knew what a man wanted, and who listened well enough, even if she didn't understand half the matter in his hand, and he knew she was the very country of his youth, and had shared the first and second best beds of his life, and the final truth of his Time.

Having an Anne waiting at home and keeping the sound of his deepest and truest nature alive, the other women appeared to him for his listening, and his theater, and sometimes even for a sonnet.

While he fell in love with boys.

The thirty-eighth canto

Shakespeare was telling Dr. Fisch --- because the playwright was now in the mussel's manic phase, and the women were asleep, all three, in each others' arms, wasted, until Molly Malone had slipped off the bed and onto the floor and remained asleep, and so the playwright had decided to go for a walk, to get some forced air, and had bumped into Fisch at Sholem Aleichem Park, where an octet was playing Mendelssohn's *Octet* brilliantly, even though the oldest player couldn't have been more than eleven years old.

Shakespeare was telling Dr. Fisch that he'd a simple formula for his comedies: get the boys into ladies' clothes quickly, and the boy-ladies into men's clothes even more quickly. The illusion of boys playing ladies playing men - Rosalind, Viola, Portia - was a comedic *tour de force.* Nobody had ever beaten that, before, during and after the theater of Elizabeth's time.

He was reminiscing about---well, there were two boys in his company who were fetching, but he'd usually tried to avoid professional romance - except for one of the lads, and he couldn't help himself, he was such a fabulous and funny bitch, with a wonderful pitch to his voice, and the kind of self-mockery that comes from being buggered so often that he no longer cared about sex but instead gave himself over to observation and laughter; he could have been a wonderful writer of comedies himself, but he was too lazy, the silly sod; still, he could give you the most fabulous handwork as he told such harrowing stories about his life, as he produced That Look for you; in fact, Shakespeare wrote Rosalind for the little grub, and Portia, too, and eventually Cleopatra.

"Because of the sobriety with which those works have been greeted," said Will Shakespeare, "it's so easy to forget that all of those ladies were the biggest cockteasers I'd ever created."

"In all of literature," added Dr. Herschel Fisch, but Shakespeare wasn't listening. He was on a roll, due to mussel-bringing memories.The boy-actor had also played Miranda, to such laughter, and the horrible thing now is that Shakespeare has forgotten his name; the worst of it was that the darling had left their theater to become the mistress of – was it Oxford or Wriothesley? The poet couldn't remember!– but within a month the saucy bitch had been murdered by the acquaintances of one of those noble lords, probably because of jealousy, or perhaps they were right after all and the boy was nothing but a thief; his death the best thing ever happened to him - other than playing Rosalind, Portia and Cleopatra.

Herschel Fisch listened with horror and fascination.

The Elizabethan Age had come alive, for a moment, and the stinking excess of it struck terror in Fisch's heart.

"Yes, well, of course, it has always been *assumed* you were bisexual," said Fisch, slowly, for lack of anything better to say.

"You are such an ass," Shakespeare snapped, and clucked his tongue. "Everybody was 'bisexual,' as you call it. Or *nearly* everybody. It wasn't a crime, you know. The only crime was raping a child or a horse. If two people enjoyed playing the hornpipe or dancing the death of the bear, what did it matter? 'Did Shakespeare love Anne, or was it merely a marriage of convenience?' 'Was he in actual fact a lover of men?' 'Did he become a Puritan?' I cannot understand how anyone can consider such questions as a means of earning a living, or as the subject of teaching. It's even worse than the journalists because it smacks of such dizzying self-regard and pretension. The simple answer, Fisch, is that we loved magic and illusion and were terrified of it as well, that's the truth of it, and there's nothing more magical than a young boy who can portray a young woman while remaining a boy. Have you never found yourself attracted to such a creature?"

"I can't remember," said Dr. Fisch, simply, frowning. "Perhaps. But my fear of arrest and scandal is doubtlessly greater than any attraction I might have felt, or feel, if I feel anything at all. Actually, I do not care for scandal. The thought of prison has always been, for me, a great dampener."

"Always?" grinned the playwright. "Though you're an imaginative vandal, Doctor, a literary Pandarus, living off other people's art? Listen to me: you'll never be alive until you find yourself stung by the ambiguity of the sex of the bee."

"What does that mean?" asked the critic, grumpily. '*Ambiguity of the sex of the bee?*'"

"'*Most mischievous foul sin,*" smiled Shakespeare, "*in chiding sin!*' A pander of another's art, and high-degreed, if only to insulate yourself from the pox of mortality."

"That's most unfair," said Dr. Fisch. "If anything, I am a literary docent who takes pleasure in introducing the young wanderer to the world's collections. I honor you, sir. I don't exploit you. If I exploit anyone, it's those *soi-disant* academic critics, whose idiocies I submit to general laughter."

"O rare Herschel Fisch," smiled Shakespeare. "But now I must leave you."

"Of course," said the Doctor, frowning. "Weren't you supposed to be having a tryst with Molly, the mollusk-woman?"

Shakespeare held up a finger, smiling coldly:

"Careful, doctor. Your pimpery is showing."

Then the playwright turned to the band-stand and said:

"I find Mendelssohn adorable, yet he hates me, still, for his "Midsummer Night's Dream." He says that piece of music destroyed any appreciation of the rest of his *oeuvre* for future generations. How stupid. Here we are on the moon, and little children – children! – are playing his "Octet," many hundreds of years later."

"If you're free this evening---"

"I am always free," said Willliam Shakespeare. "I am no one's slave. Until this evening, Doctor."

No one's slave? Thought Dr. Herschel Fisch, grimly, to himself. We'll soon see about that!

With a cold nod of his head, he moved toward the gazebo and, as if Shakespeare had given him an assignment, he began to eye the boys in the band.

A quickie sixth riff to Mnemosyne, before the thirty-ninth canto

The redheaded woman with the blue-green eyes, lovely smile and light purple cotton turtleneck almost busted my piggy-bank.

I was seven years old, and achingly in love.

I always had an excuse to ride my bike to Neff's Department Store, on Riverside Drive, next to the Toluca Lake Drug Store - which had the great perfume smell and the super signed photographs of all the singers and actors and dancers and comedians who lived in the area - to find something to purchase.

I began having dreams about the redheaded woman with the light purple cotton turtleneck, and somehow my pajamas and my sheets became steamy.

One Saturday morning, my mother found me trying to break my piggybank, and asked me why.

"Oh, there's just a new Bugs Bunny comic that I have to get, and I didn't have enough allowance, so---"

"Is it *this month's comic*?" asked mom.

"Yes."

"You bought that yesterday."

"Oh, right, but there's also the *Classics Illustrated*, 'Uncle Tom's Cabin," I really want to get that."

Mom crossed to my desk, and pulled up the *Classics* comic.

"Here it is," she said. "Now tell me: what's going on?"

I mumbled:

"I like the redheaded woman at Neff's, and I just wanted to see her again, that's all."

"Molly? She's very nice," said mom, politically pleasant. "I love her hair, don't you?"

I had begun to grow steamy, once again, and turned away.

"And she has such pretty eyes," continued my mother, quietly, watching. "I have to go to the market in about an hour. We can go there together, and while I'm inside, you can go to the department store and say hello to your friend."

I shrugged, frowned, nodded seriously.

"Just don't buy the same comic book over and over again, okay? I'll advance you a dime against next week's allowance, if you'll straighten your room."

After she had left, I swore to myself.

This was *my* secret, and now mom knew it, and - well – but – it didn't seem to matter. As I cleaned my bedroom, I heard her speaking on the phone.

Toluca Lake was a surprisingly cozy area, a wonderful place in which to grow up, before the city put in the freeway.

The Toluca Lake Golf Club hadn't wanted the freeway to destroy its eighteenth hole, so they smarmied with their members and the politicos. They got the freeway to ram through at least sixteen *blocks* of sweet houses instead.

Besides their policy of segregation against Jews, blacks, Hispanics and Asians, diverting the freeway from the eighteenth hole and into the residential streets of Toluca Lake was yet another reason for hating the Toluca Lake Golf Club.

Toluca Lake was a small village, wedged between Burbank and North Hollywood. Most of its residents were craftspeople and performers in film, radio and music. The village was five minutes away from Republic,

Universal, Disney and Warner Brothers studios. When you crossed hilly Barham Boulevard, you were soon in Radio-land, on Sunset and Gower, where NBC, ABC and CBS gave their national broadcasts. You were also near Paramount.

Most of the people living in Toluca Lake were *slightly above-the-line* to *below-the-line* in film and radio credits: character actors and actresses; singers and musicians; composers; arrangers; radio and film-writers; publicists; sound and film editors; grips and set-builders; wardrobe and make-up artists.

Our neighbors were Gordon McCrae, William Holden, Billy May, Huntz Hall, Wendell and Ken Niles, the radio announcers, Ivan Ditmars (who played organ on all the radio soaps), the agent Berle Adams, David Robison, the radio writer and father of the girl I kissed, Paula Robison, and who now kisses a flute almost better than she'd kissed me. And that was *only* two blocks around our house.

You could go to Du-Par's, in North Hollywood, at any time of the day or night, and learn who was working where, whether in film or radio and, later, tv.

Most of the tv studios were, at first, in the Valley as well.

I always saw Lon Chaney, Jr. at Du-Par's. His hair was always brillantined. Even with his sad and droopy eyes, he looked as if he'd just come out of an Olympic pool. For a man playing the world's worst nightmare, he always seemed sad and sweet, as if he needed a friend.

You could eat with your family at Alfonse's, the only restaurant in Toluca Lake, and see all your friends. Later, in the early 80's, Alphonse's became one of the best jazz clubs in L.A.

With the exception of Walt Disney, the heavyweights in the Industry – *those with credits miles high above the-line* - lived in Beverly Hills, Brentwood, or had estates in the Pacific Palisades. They were also closer to 10th Century Fox, MGM, and Paramount, the three major studios.

Crosby, Hope and Disney, however, were Toluca Lake mainstays.

Dad built our house, in 1939, in Toluca Lake, when he was with the Artie Shaw band.

For nine thousand dollars.

It sold several years ago, for $450,000, which is beyond ridiculous.

As children, we biked around three blocks – from Ledge to Biloxi, to Strohm and Sarah Streets; onto Riverside Drive, and to Neff's Department Store, the drugstore, or to the market.

In the fall, the sycamores dropped their leaves, and were raked into piles and burned in the street. The smell of the leaves was dreamy.

When I entered Neff's Department store, later that day, Molly the redhead - this time wearing a light-green turtleneck - came over to me and kneeled down, took my hands and pulled me to her. She gave me a nice hug, then straightened my hair, and kissed me on the cheek. She said, "Here's my favorite pal."

She'd never done that before. I pretended that I didn't mind, but I couldn't smile, because my body was very busy, evidently, making seeds. I started to get teary-eyed, and so she held me once again and said, "Hey, kiddo, you have a fever, are you okay?" And I felt her breasts against her sweater, and she was so soft and cool, and I leaned in and nodded, and her perfume was so crisp and lemony and refreshing, and when she asked, "Where's your mom?" I could only point towards the market.

She took me by the hand, and in truth I don't remember the rest, except that mom drove me home and I went to bed and did indeed have a fever, but I slept through it, and it broke, and that evening I learned that Molly was getting divorced or remarried or something, and would be leaving Neff's, in a week.

It was impossible to concentrate in school.

I didn't want to play with any of my friends.

I wanted to spend every minute with Molly at Neff's, and hold her hand, and be kissed, and feel the softness of her breasts within the sweater, because all of it had happened so swiftly, the softness of her lime-green turtleneck embrace, her kiss, her holding me, her perfume, the sweep of her hair upon my face, the dimples in her cheeks, her smiling eyes, and her wide and generous mouth, it had given me a fever, and a wonderful feeling of confusion.

I wrote her a letter.

I snuck into the store and saw her helping an elderly lady, so I ducked around the counter and left the letter at the cash register, with her name on the envelope.

I crept back outside, and then rode home as swiftly as I could, I didn't even stop at the Drugstore to look at the photos of actors and actresses, which I thought were very funny, and still do: *"Best wishes, Bing." "Happy trails, Roy." "To my best pal, Bob Hope." "Love you, Jack Carson." "The only human I ever loved, Charlie McCarthy." "I so much crave those lipsticks! Liz Scott." "Thanks for everything, your friend, Veronica Lake."*

Veronica Lake and Liz Scott looked like twins.

I imagined both of them in light purple turtlenecks, each with their blonde hair over one eye, and how they would hold me and would sweep their hair upon my face and give me an embrace and a kiss.

Soon I found myself standing in the drugstore with my penis high and pushing against my pants, and *that* was a first.

I wondered if that's what happened to your body when seeds were being made. But I hadn't kissed anyone. I'd merely thought it. And now my penis was getting into the act, and on the strength of a single thought!

As much as I hated to admit it, mom had probably been right.

I wondered what would happen if I put my penis into the vagina of Molly at Neff's. Would I even know where to find her thing? I knew it was somewhere between a woman's legs, but what did it look like? And once you put it in, what did you do with it? Look at it? How could you even see it? Did you talk about other things, drink some juice, and wait for it to make seeds?

I knew that my fever had something to do with the process.

In fact, it probably had everything to do with all those confused and rushing feelings.

There are times when Bugs Bunny comics are a necessity.

And this was one of those times. This experience with Molly was becoming too mysterious.

With my penis sticking up hard in the air and pushing against my pants, I managed to ride my bicycle home, Bugs Bunny tucked hard under my arm.

Further Sexy Adventures of the Sixth Riff

What had my letter said?

"Dear Molly: I will miss you very much, and think you are very nice and beautiful. I especially like your hair and the way it swings near your purple turtleneck. You should always wear purple turtleneck sweaters, even though you also look very nice in the light green turtleneck.

I hope to see you again sometime."

Two days later, a letter arrived in the mail:

"Dear Stephen: I will miss you very much as well. You are the sweetest boy. Thank you about what you said about my hair. I will take your advice and will always wear purple turtlenecks, and will think of you every day. I hope we will meet again.

Love, your friend, Molly."

A year later, my mother told me that she'd spoken with Molly about my feelings, and that's why the woman had kissed me at Neff's, and had thought my infatuation was "so cute."

I was furious, and ran to my bedroom and tore up Molly's letter. How perfidious girls, mothers, and their lady friends could be! Boys would *never* do that. If they did, they weren't boys. I realized then that boys were much nicer and far more honorable than girls.

And also far more stupid, and, as a result, far less interesting.

I attribute the event with Molly, and the insight it produced, as the principle reason I eventually became a writer.

The thirty-ninth canto

Mollusk Molly was the first to hear Shakespeare return to the hotel-room and piss in the bathroom john. Bloom herself was snoring, and Malone was thoroughly asleep, curled in a fetal position, on the floor, like a Siamese cat.

Shakespeare flushed the toilet, washed his hands.

Then the Moll heard him start the shower, humming to himself, and then the scrape of the curtain against the rail. She thought: He said he was a writer. That's all I've learned, other than the very solid fact that he loves to make love and have love made to him and, strange, he's the best listener I've ever known, one of the few men who doesn't eat, or be eaten, and run. I found myself within three minutes of a dirty great blow telling him of my sister's horrid death, then Molly Bloom told him about her affairs, and how she hated to cheat on her husband, but that she had to, for he seemed to encourage her, which meant he'd probably a quiff in the closet somewhere himself; Molly Malone shocked us all by telling of her wasting disease, and how her doctor had said eventually she'd "die of a fever," although Will said she probably meant "favor," implying she'd a sex disease. But he wouldn't speak of himself, nothing at all, so I've nothing to tell the Doctor, or the Janitor, not that I'd tell them anything, anyway, even if I didn't *like* the man. Jews don't talk, and Herr Doktor Fisch-hook should have known it!

Shakespeare came out of the shower, dripping, still, and with a towel about his waist.

"I think we should find a place that makes an art of roast beef or venison," he smiled. "Are you game, Mollusc?" and wiggled his eyebrows.

"How can you be hungry, Will?" she asked.

"Appetite breeds greater appetite," he smiled. "Shall we wake the ladies, or let them sleep?"

That was a good question, thought Moll. She wouldn't mind having the writer all to herself, though she was talked out and fucked out; still, she did enjoy his company. How many men really *listened*? She thought to herself. Rare, indeed.

"Who wants to go to the Natal Nosh?" she called, loudly.

Molly Bloom stirred.

Molly Malone remained serpentined, in her position, on the floor.

"Mmm, I wouldn't mind that," yawned Molly Bloom. "I could do with some matzah ball soup and corned beef on rye."

"Excellent," said Shakespeare. "And what about our friend - Miss Malone?"

"She'll sleep another twelve hours, if I know her," said Molly Bloom. "Throw that comforter over her. I'll leave her a note."

The fortieth canto

On the Kurfurstendamm, the elegant half-hour Berlin shopping street of the colony, Shakespeare strolled between his two Mollies. He was happy, pleasantly bored, and ready to return to the Higher Plane – after a pot roast, perhaps, and a shank of lamb, mashed potatoes and – he couldn't help himself - noodle kugel, and two more lively blow-jobs.

"Where's home when you're back home, Will?" asked Molly Bloom.

"And when you're home," added the Moll, "where's *Mrs.* Will?"

"Home is far away," said Shakespeare. "And Mrs. Will has become a witch, as you would call her. Though we are the best of friends, we do live apart."

"Do you have any children?" asked Molly Bloom.

"Indeed I do," said Shakespeare. "Every playwright who ever held a pen. 'Every dreamer who e'er awoke in wonder.' Every poet who invoked a Muse, and who received an answer."

"What does that mean?" asked the Moll.

"It means that you ought to learn how to read, Miss Bloom, or to go to the theater more often," Shakespeare yawned, in spite of himself. Then they entered the largest and most exclusive delicatessen Shakespeare had ever seen.

The forty-first canto

The Natal Nosh was nearly one square mile of tables. On its walls hung enormous photographs of every Jewish entertainer who had ever trod the boards or flit on screens, both two-, three-, and four-dimensional.

On the photos each luminary had written "To Nate----Great meal! Thanks."

"'*If this be error and upon me proved,*'" whispered Shakespeare to himself, "'*I never writ, nor no man ever loved.*' Such magnificence here! Between the three Mollies, the *Boite Lunaire* and the *Natal Nosh - Some Body -'teach me to repent*!'"

"You sound like someone about to leave town, Will," said Molly Bloom, smiling at his pleasure and awe.

"I might very well reconsider my departure," said Shakespeare," after I peruse the menu. Incidentally, what time is it? I must be at Shakespeare in the Park before seven. I promised the cast a few words of encouragement."

"Are you a director?" said the Moll, surprised.

"I have directed, yes."

"I thought you said you were a writer," Molly Bloom replied.

"An actor, too," shrugged Shakespeare. "Come. What are we to eat? Let us order all we wish, and do to this restaurant what we did to the bed."

"Tell me what we did to the bed," said Molly Bloom, taking Shakespeare by the arm, with a slight toss of her thick raven-colored hair and a side-glance of her grey eyes, and leading him to a table.

"'*Lay on, Macduff!*'" said Shakespeare, staring at the cold cuts, and intoning without missing a beat, "'*And damned be him that first cries 'Hold, enough!*'"

The forty-second canto

The minute Moshe saw the Jesuit scholar, Fulvio Tagliacazzo, he knew there would be trouble.

Moreover, the caravel had not even left the port, when Moshe and Moussa became violently ill. Both leaned over the wooden railing and emptied the contents they had ingested, from Don Gesualdo's tavern, into the ocean.

Tagliacazzo stood at their side and called to the Captain, Ser Lorenzo, "Are these two-thirds of the saintly trio, who are meant to protect us, in this our earthly voyage?"

Moses bowed politely and said, "They are doing so, even now, sir."

Tagliacazzo, who was short, dark, with thick, matted hair and a greasy smile, hissed: "And how is that possible, learned sir? I am at your disposition, and anxious to acquire knowledge of this woman – and what do you call her? –The Lovely Joslian?"

Moussa looked up, gravely, wiped a piece of vomit from his sleeve, then flicked it off, in Tagliacazzo's direction:

"In a moment, sir," he gulped. "We are emptying ourselves of the liberties the occupants of this ship have taken during their time ashore. When we are finished, Ser Lorenzo may consider his caravel cleansed of sin and moral turpitude."

Moussa turned back to the railing and continued to heave even more stomach-churnings into the sea.

"The Lovely Joslian taught us many things," said Moses, sweetly, to Tagliazzo. "And this sea-cleansing was one of the first, since she herself was born of the sea."

"Like Venus, or Aphrodite, I suppose?" said Tagliacazzo, snidely. "I suppose she was half-mortal, and her father a God of the sky, such as Zeus?"

Moshe turned around and let loose such a projectile vomit upon Tagliacazzo that the latter fell backwards, and slipped on a rope, knocking his head against a barrel of ale. Instantly, he became silent.

"An interesting question," said Moses to the unconscious Jesuit, "but irrelevant. She was merely born in Alexandria, which is a great city by the sea."

The Captain, Ser Lorenzo, snapped his fingers, and two sailors took the body of the Jesuit and laid him away from the activity.

"I thank you for your vomit," he said to Moses. "I know you to be true prophets and miracle-workers, for nobody ever is sick while the ship's still at anchor."

Moshe waved a grateful wave, and returned to his sickness.

Neither Moussa nor Moshe had ever been on a boat before, and the experience, even before the ship had been un-roped, had proven, to their stomachs, most unsettling.

Yet all three were following the First Spiritual Life Law of the Lovely Joslian:

Rule the First: When things are bad, it would be good to make them better.

The Second Spiritual Life Law of Lovely Joslian, as we will see, would prove, however, more difficult to enact:

Rule the Second: Break the rules quickly, before the rules break you.

Facing them, in the form of the Jesuit, Tagliacazzo, was the rule of the Holy Church.

More particularly, the rule of the newly formed Inquisition.

And, most specifically, the grim dedication of one Jesuit scholar, Fulvio Tagliacazzo, who would awaken from his unwitting sleep with more rules in his head than vomit on his cloak. For him, suspicion soon would give rise to vengeance.

The forty-third canto

The captain of the caravel, Ser Lorenzo, was rare.
He was a happy Venetian.

Most Venetians were not happy; rather, they were filled with damp thoughts. Thoughts, as Erasmus of Rotterdam has written elsewhere, breed great unhappiness, and put lines of stress on one's otherwise unblemished features. Thoughts do not contribute to the fantastic possibilities contained within a mind at ease.

Within two hours after the caravel had set sail, Ser Lorenzo was happier than he'd ever been, for the sailors were singing, and laughing, and merrily going about their chores, without any grumbling.

When a pissing contest began in the aft-deck of the caravel, Ser Lorenzo put money on his second mate, known as Giovanno 'Er Lungo', a Roman with an enormously long penis and a urinary projection of seven feet six inches.

Ser Lorenzo crossed to the three Moses, and grinned, nodding happily:

"You have certainly cleansed my men and the ship of all known foulness," he said. "On the first day seaward, usually they're still drunk, or living with heads the size of zebras, or suffering from a pox given to them by one of the whores at Gesualdo's. But you've cleaned 'em thoroughly, and we've unnaturally fine weather, and the wind's at our back. The only one who's under the weather appears to be the priest, and he's told me he wants to talk to you before the crew, because he's convinced you're the work of the devil. I told him you'd all agree, and why not, good sirs? A splendid fight of the spirit is better than being becalmed in the doldrums! I'm sure you'll put an end to his wailing, once and for all. My only fear is that he's well-attended in Venice, and powerfully so. Therefore I'll put you down in Bari, before he has a chance to martial his forces. From there you can slip off to Greece or even to Rome, and none's the wiser."

Moussa replied, "We would be most happy to discuss his credence with our own, and at any time, good captain."

"And thank you for considering Bari as a point of departure for ourselves, Ser Lorenzo," added Moshe. "But let us first see how our dialogue develops, before we leave your graceful caravel."

'I'll tell him, then, you'll speak before the crew this evening?" asked the Captain.

"Whenever you wish," said Moussa. "We are at your disposal, and are delighted you have the confidence in us to allow us to speak for ourselves."

Ser Lorenzo nodded, and left the trio.

"*Now* what?" asked Moses, quietly.

"Simple enough," Moshe shrugged. "Whatever he says, we reply in triple. And we do not say the opposite. Only half of the opposite. Thus, the mathematics become even more confusing."

"If I cough," said Moussa, "then you speak, Moses."

"And if I cough," said Moshe, "then you speak, Moussa."

"And if I cough," said Moses, "then either of you, please, speak immediately."

"But what if he begins to talk of Catholic doctrine?" said Moussa. "I know nothing of that."

"We reply that we are not scholars of the Church," said Moshe, "and that such scholastic thought would be useless to argue. Instead, we ask him about various Doctrines of the Lovely Joslian. He will not be able to answer, and so we will arrive at a stalemate. Until we perform a miracle."

"I'll do the miracle," said the Welshman. "In fact, I'll speak Welsh. That's been known to frighten most Englishmen, and they're not easily given to fear."

"Excellent," said Moussa. "However, the priest is an Italian."

"Still," considered Moshe. "To my mind, the only thing that can happen is that he makes us all become tongue-tied, and they toss us into the sea."

Since this was a very real possibility, there was nothing else to say - until the arrival of evening, on the main deck, and with all the sailors seated by the railing, and the scholar Tagliacazzo standing before them, prepared, as only a scholar Jesuit can be:

Waiting for the kill.

The forty-fourth canto

For Shakespeare, *The Natal Nosh* had provided a series of tastes as varied and as unusual as any Bankside tavern. The quantity of fare, however, made the playwright nostalgic for a London which no longer existed.

No one spoke.

Rather, they gave themselves, noisily and happily, to food and drink.

Shakespeare's gustatory enthusiasms seemed to spur them on, so much so that, at first, none noticed Ahasuerus, Dr. Fisch, and a special team of the Universal Forces of Order enter the restaurant, with the latter group taking up strategic positions at its four entrances.

Mollusc the Moll was about to order the cheesecake sampler for three when she spotted Herschel Fisch and the Janitor making their way towards their table. Shakespeare caught her glance, and looked up.

"Isn't that the guy you came with a couple of nights ago to my restaurant?" Molly asked, a bit too quickly for her own good.

Shakespeare watched Fisch and Ahasuerus moving steadily and darkly towards their table.

"Indeed," he said, "and the Janitor as well."

"Do you know him?" asked Molly Bloom, licking strawberry cream cheese from her index finger.

"I met him once," said Shakespeare and, seeing that both men were now staring hard at him, he waved coolly and made a circular gesture about his table.

"They appear to be very serious, don't they now?" said Molly Bloom.

Shakespeare did not reply, but noted that the Mollusk was looking at her plate, fretfully. He recognized her gaze, at once, as the look of an actor who had just accepted the lure of another resident company, and had told no one.

He thought:

Is she a spy?

If so, why?

To what end?

He'd merely dropped down to watch the first production of "*Merchant of Venice,*" on the terrestrial moon, presented by the JAP. What did they have, he wondered, that was worth spying for?

"Interesting," said Shakespeare, then caught Fisch's eye, and pointed at the young women. "Doctor Fisch and S'ior Ahasuerus, come join us. Let me introduce you to the Misses Bloom and Moluskiewicz, my pair of Mollies. There is a third, a Malone, making up our trine, but she's busily dying of a favor at the moment and does not wish to be disturbed."

"There's only one seat available," said Ahasuerus, and looked at Doctor Fisch, who promptly turned about, in search of a waiter. "It is more than evident you have been eating here for quite a while."

"Thirty minutes," said Shakespeare. "Give or take an hour."

"And what does that mean?" smiled Ahasuerus, picking up the menu and opening it with a quick flick of his wrist.

"It means you've something on your mind, sir," said Shakespeare, quietly, "and have been following us to assuage your curiousity. Or, would you rather speak, or order first?"

Ahasuerus did not look up from the menu.

"Their Leo is excellent here," he said. "The lox eggs and onions. I think the addition of a bit of cream cheese gives it more body as well."

"What about their Sagittarius?" asked Shakespeare, with eyebrows raised.

Ahasuerus blinked, then frowned, looking up:

"I see no Sagittarius here," he said, and pointed to the menu.

"Salmon and gefilte fish in two tomato rarebits, integrated under sesame bagels," Shakespeare replied. "There's also a Virgo, which is Virgin roasted garlic oil. I had it, once, in California, before the big quake, at a boutique restaurant in Malibu. They put it on *mozzarella di bufalo.* At that time, you could see the *bufalo* on the mountainside, across the highway. Not your prairie buffalo, which they were making into burgers, before that National Park blew up and started a national landslide. These *bufalo* were gigantic horned beasts that gave wonderful milk for *mozzarella.* Can you imagine what the history of the American West would have been, had *bufalo* roamed the plains, and the Plains Indians had used them for making *ciliegi, ciliegini* and *mozzarella?* Once wheat was planted, the possibilities would have been infinite. Not only for making *croissants* and *cornetti,* as well as *foccaccia* and even stone mill rye, but also for the various kinds of pasta: *tortellone verde, linguine fine, papardelle* for venison, of course, and the *lasagna* noodle, with *mozzarella di bufalo* as a filling. Were I an aboriginal, I never would have left home, knowing that a meal was waiting for me, provided by the *bufalo,* and Ceres herself. What a masque I could have written! I believe General Custer and – was it Geronimo? Sitting Bull? I can't remember – together they would have opened the largest *ristorante* in all of the Dakotas. Nobody would have died, except by over-eating! Come. Here's your waiter, and – excellent man! - Dr. Fisch, at last, has found a chair."

Fisch was in fact carrying the chair, yet having a dreadful time finding a simple passage around the other diners to their table. By the time he had arrived, and seated himself beside Ahasuerus, he was sweating like a drain.

"Poor fellow," said Shakespeare," and pushed his glass towards the scholar. "Have some water. Being dehydrated on the moon must have serious repercussions."

The waiter stood before them, pencil on pad. His eyes were brown, bleary, and his skin wrinkled; he had neither shaved his stubble nor washed his grey-striped outfit in several weeks.

"I'll have the Sagittarius," said Ahasuerus, calmly, but with authority.

"*The what? Whaddayoutalk?* The *Sadgey-what?*" asked the waiter, with a thick Hungarian accent. "Listen here, you trying to be funny?"

"The *Sagittarius*," said Ahasuerus, blushing slightly, and pointing to the menu. "It's somewhere here, on the menu."

"We don't got no Sadgey-shmadgey. I'm busy, go figure what else you want, then next winter sometime I'll come back for your Sadgey-shmadgey, after they turn me into a *latke-shmatke...*"

Muttering to himself, the waiter whipped about, and shuffled away.

"Odd," said Dr. Fisch, staring after the former Hungarian.

"Indeed," said Shakespeare. "And swift-moving, too. Why ever would he have an Hungarian accent, after all these generations on the moon?"

"Are you sure they've such a thing as a Sagittarius here?" asked Fisch, politely. "Actually, the fellow's right. I don't see it on the menu."

Molly Bloom started to laugh.

"Don't listen to him," she grinned, pointing at the playwright. "He's a trickster, that one."

Dr. Fisch looked over at Molly Moluskiewicz, who shook her head, slightly, and shrugged – which gesture was not lost upon the playwright.

So, thought Shakespeare: it's as I'd imagined.

A bit of villainy.

"You're *supposed* to be Shakespeare, if I'm correct," said Ahasuerus, suddenly very serious, if not grim.

"*Shakespeare*?" laughed Molly Bloom. "*He's* not Shakespeare. Shakespeare's been dead for centuries!"

"He *says* he's Shakespeare," replied Ahasuerus, lugubriously. "And according to Dr. Fisch, he reads minds. We fear that he may well be a shape-shifter, and not Shakespeare at all."

Molly Bloom continued to laugh, shaking her head, but her expression was no longer amused.

"What's the difference between a playwright and a shape-shifter?" asked Shakespeare, quietly.

"You don't know?"Ahasuerus replied, measuredly, "or prefer *not* to know?"

"What you will," replied Shakespeare, and turned coolly to Dr. Fisch, as if expecting a further commentary on shape-shifting.But Fisch stared coldly at Shakespeare, wrinkling his brow and puckering his eyebrows:

"You told me you came here to see the first production of "*Merchant of Venice*" that had been performed in our moon colony of Jews and children of Israel," began the scholar-critic.

"Precisely," said Shakespeare. "In actual fact, because of the performance, I've won a rather large bet."

"What kind of bet?" asked Ahasuerus.

"Voltaire said that your company would present Portia as the sweetest virgin who'd ever lived," answered Shakespeare. "I replied that it would be quite the opposite, and I was correct."

"And how were you so certain?" asked Ahasuerus, coolly.

"Because a Jew would know a racist within a second of meeting her," Shakespeare replied, simply. "Why do you think I made Portia's suitors

Outsiders who would be rejected? A Jew would understand Portia immediately."

"And what did you win?" asked Dr. Fisch, coldly.

"Ahh, the question is: what *will* I win?" Shakespeare smiled. "A secret known only to Voltaire and myself. He will be most unhappy...Still... Because he is my friend, I may very well have to lie and say he was right...but then, if I do, he will monologize about the perfidy of Jews, and how they have always pretended to be Christians...So I might have to tell him he was wrong, and break his Gallic heart."

In spite of himself, Dr. Hirsch asked, "Voltaire's not been cured of his anti-semitism then? Even on *your* plane?"

Shakespeare laughed:

"Muses also have their off-days, Doctor. Now here is your waiter once again. Be nice to him this time. Perhaps he'll drop his accent, instead of a plate."

Immediately, Ahasuerus told the man, "I'll have a Leo."

"Make that two," added Dr. Fisch.

"Three," said Shakespeare. "Ladies?"

"I'm full up, I am," said Molly Bloom.

"What about you, Miss Mollusc?" said Shakespeare politely. "Have you anything you wish to add, or do you want to wait until I've gone, to speak with the doctor?"

The Moll blushed, embarrassed.

So did Dr. Fisch.

Quietly, Ahasuerus said, "I'm afraid I'm going to have to ask you to leave as soon as possible, Mister Shakespeare. It's not only for the greater good, but also for your own. If others find out or believe that you're a shape-shifter, your life will be worth very little."

"I'm a playwright," said Shakespeare. "I'm not a shape-shifter. I haven't acted in centuries. Unless you count making love to Miss Mollusc a performance."

"Here, what about me?" said Molly Bloom, grinning.

"You sent me to the stars," smiled Shakespeare. "This other one was too much the watcher. The perfect critic or spy. You, on the other hand, Miss Bloom, were an artist, as was Miss Malone."

Shakespeare turned to Ahasuerus and said: "Let me tell you about what you call the greater good, sir, and which is nothing but a platform for your own vanity. You forget what *this* Shakespeare once wrote: "'*Within the hollow crown/That rounds the mortal temples of a king/Keeps Death his court; and there the antic sits,/Scoffing his state and grinning at his pomp, /Allowing him a breath, a little scene, /To monarchize, be feared, and kill with looks,/Infusing him with self and vain conceit,/ As if this flesh which walls about our life/Were brass impregnable; and humoured thus,/Comes at the last, and with a little pin/Bores through his castle wall; and farewell, king.*'"

He looked long at Dr. Fisch and said:

"'*Throw away respect,/Tradition, form, and ceremonious duty,/For you have but mistook me all this while./I live with bread, like you; feel want,/Taste grief, need friends. Subjected thus,/How can you say to me I am a king?*"

"Because you *are,* dammit, or *Shakespeare is,*" whispered Dr. Herschel Fisch. "And we can never be what *he* is, or what *you* are..."

"Voltaire doesn't think I'm a king at all," smiled Shakespeare. "Nor Tolstoi. Shaw had to admit I was, however, and Joyce. In fact, when the Irishman was asked what book he'd take to a desert isle, he said that although he might prefer Dante, he'd have to choose the rich plays of the Englishman. But to myself, *what am I, doctor*? Exactly what Richard said. I simply like to listen, and to look, and to dream. That's what any artist does. Neither of you were present, during the last days of our earth: the vanity was so great, there were so many self-styled artists who made no art at all. People too stupid to feel and to think were simply busy declaring that it was too stupid to feel and to think, that art was a fart, and nothing more. *Reaction was everything.* In America, as I witnessed, such savagery was defended by the idiotic notion that everyone 'had a right to an opinion,' though no distinction was made between opinion and considered fact. When I was a lad, *an opinion was earned* before one had the right to express it. But in those last days of earth, having an opinion was considered the same as having a thought - which at best is stupidity; at worst, madness. And now, because I have always observed how people move and speak and think, you characterize me not as a writer, but as a shape-shifter. A trickster. A mythic beast which will bring about what? The destruction of this culture? How wit-less."

"And if you *are* a shape-shifter?" said Ahasuerus.

"What will happen to us?" continued Dr. Fisch.

"You will never know," Shakespeare replied, coldly, then called, "The bill, please."

Shakespeare stood up, took Molly Bloom by the hand, and whispered, "You were adorable. So was Miss Malone."

He turned to the Mollusc, and it was as if he were addressing the restaurant itself:

"As for you, Dame Moll, I bear you no ill-will, but I am dismayed by your foolishness and most *sophisticated* lack of judgment."

He nodded to Ahasuerus:

"And to you, sir, may I remind you: "*Uneasy lies the head that wears a crown.*"

"I'm merely a Janitor," said Ahasuerus, frowning. "With a closet and a broom. Hardly a crown at all."

"*Ah, what a life were this!*" whistled Shakespeare, ironically. "*How sweet! How lovely!/Gives not the hawthorn bush a sweeter shade/To shepherds looking on their seely sheep/Than doth a rich embroidered canopy/To kings that fear their subjects' treachery?'"*

Then he called, even more loudly still: "The bill, I say!"

And before the United Forces of Order could move to surround him, Shakespeare, or the Shape-shifter, or whatever and whoever he was, appeared to have disappeared.

Dr. Herschel Fisch looked wildly about, then, sighing like a deflating balloon, he slumped onto the table, his face falling, noisily, into a bowl of beet borscht.

When the waiters had revived him, the critic stared blearily at Ahasuerus; his eyes began to roll as he simpered, "It was so absurd, all he talked about was food, and sex, and sometimes his craft, though rarely his themes! Why, he's as dull as a dead zone!"

Dr. Fisch began to giggle, uncontrollably, and declaimed:

"*'Who says that fictions only and false hair*
Become a verse; is there in Truth no beauty?
Is all good structure in a winding stair?
May no lines pass except they do their duty
Not to a true but painted chair?'"

Furiously he turned to Ahasuerus and grabbed him by his lapels and pulled him to his nose:

"That's not *your* Shakespeare, you know! That's *my* George Herbert!

"Must purling streams refresh a lover's loves?
Must all be veiled, while he that reads, divines,
Catching the sense at two removes?'"

Then he turned to the other tables and, now sweating and spitting, he yelled:

"FUCK SHAKESPEARE! FUCK MARLOWE! FUCK MILTON! THEY'RE LIARS, ALL OF THEM!"

Further quoting Herbert and DuBose Heyward, he declaimed:

'"*I envy no man's nightingale or spring!" I's my own boss now--- now an' fo'ever! Look at me now, Bess! I killed Crown! Yo' got yo' man!*"

Everyone at the Natal Nosh, who bore witness to Dr. Herschel Fisch's outburst, realized at once that the great Shakespearean scholar and critic had finally become as mad as the playwright's own creation, Tom o' Bedlam.

The forty-fifth canto

A great portion of the crew was assembled and waiting gleefully for the debate between the scholar of the Christ and the three prophets of The Lovely Joslian.

"Which of you shall begin?" asked the captain, Ser Lorenz.

The three prophets of The Lovely Joslian pointed at Tagliacazzo, and bowed with gestures of good will, *politesse*, and *buon senso.*

"Very well," said Tagliacazzo, as politely as a determined Jesuit could be when faced with an argument regarding his life's thought and belief. "Let me commence with a few innocent questions, all of which I pose most respectfully," he added, nodding towards the crew. "Do you mind?"

All three prophets shook their heads, with various gestures of innocence, of simplicity, of rustic charm.

"Because I do not wish to begin this discussion with an argument against your persons or the perplexity of your beliefs," continued the Jesuit. "I beg you to please accept my sincerest apologies if I give you the impression that I mean to behave otherwise."

In unison, all three prophets held up a hand, and nodded with soft smiles.

The crew applauded them, as if already they had scored three masterful points.

"Yes," hissed Tagliacazzo, pretending to be in agreement with the crew's decision of preferment. "I too recognize the grandiloquence of your gestures, gentlemen, although I am *not* about to confuse public sympathy with religious considerations, as I am sure you yourselves would agree."

All three prophets nodded their heads furiously: of course they agreed.

"My first question is a simple one," began the Jesuit. "Our belief as Christians is of Triune: We believe in God the Father, God the Son, and God the Holy Spirit. Do you believe this as well?"

All three shook their heads: no. They did not.

"Ahh: then what do you believe?"

Moussa held up five fingers.

"I don't understand," said the Jesuit scholar-priest.

"We believe in Pentaplus, the five principles," said Moshe.

"You only believe in three," added Moussa. "We are, I believe, therefore more advanced."

"At least by two," interjected Moses.

The crew nodded to each other, and some began to applaud.

"And what are the five principles?" asked Fulvio Tagliacazzo. "If they are not God the Father, God the Son, and God the Holy Spirit?"

Both Moussa and Moshe coughed.

Therefore Moses stepped forward:

"They are God the Mother; Goddess the Father; God and Goddess the In-laws; God the Lovelier Joslian, and Goddess the Loveliest Joslian of all."

Many in the crew frowned, and began to stare at the Jesuit, hoping that he could explain the unexplainable.

"How can God be a Mother?" he asked.

"The question, rather, is: How could he not?" said Moussa. "Especially since the Goddess is a Father."

"Yes, but you said they are also In-laws. Of whom?"

"Of the God and the Goddess," Moshe replied, as if the answer were self-evident.

"But how can they be the in-laws of themselves?" asked the Jesuit.

"In the same fashion that God the Father can also be God the Son," said Moses. "It's one of those things we all of us call miraculous."

The crew applauded.

(A swarthy, bearded fellow said, "He's right, by the Cross of Saint Valience! I never thought of that!")

"And thus, I would assume, you would say that since *both* the God and Goddess can be their own in-laws, they can also be The Lovely Joslian," sighed Tagliacazzo, rolling his eyes at the crew.

"If you say so," replied Moses. "So be it."

"Do you have another question?" asked Moshe. "Clearly miracles are ubiquitous, don't you agree?"

"No, I don't."

"Neither do we," said Moshe. "I'm glad we all of us agree."

(The bearded fellow said, loudly, "A good man, by the Hilt of Saint DeVere!")

"I have a question for you," said Moses, and turned to the Jesuit: "Do you believe that Mary was a Virgin?"

"Mary the mother of Jesus?" asked Tagliacazzo.

"Oh, she was a Virgin, all right," said Moses. "He's speaking of Mary the daughter of the tavern-keeper. We thought you looked pale when you came aboard, and wondered if you'd spent too many an hour with her."

Everyone laughed.

"Please," said Moshe, holding up a hand. "We are not here to attack the Jesuit scholar about his personal life. Sir, what you do, and with whom, on your own time – as long as you hurt no one in the doing - provided neither child nor beast be part of your pleasure - then know that we are your champion and will fight any man who challenges your right to a fling with the tavern-keeper's daughter, who is well-known to many here, who have also flung themselves, for a farthing, upon her huge person! But to speak of Jesus' mother, Mary, as a Virgin, is to recognize that Saint Joslian's father did not----but *you* tell it much better than ever I could," he said to Moussa, who nodded, and continued, without missing a beat:

"It was during the time of Sardko the Pastrian," he began, "who had swept his buttery hordes through the swamps of Calumnia, long before the time of the Prophet, but shortly after King Saul had added the vowel of "u" to his name, for he would not allow himself to be known as Sal, which does not translate at all from Aramaic into English, being a diminutive of Salvatore, which is Italian for Savior."

"The Latin, of course, when referring only to the Christ, is *Salvator*," Moses added. "Otherwise it is Liberator, or Conservator."

"The Greek word is *Soter*," added Moussa. "And don't ask me how I know, because I simply know it."

"This is very true," said Moshe. "Such is the way of the *Liberatrix Dominatrixque Joslin Pulchrissimae.*"

"I can assure these gentlemen," said Fulvio Tagliacazzo, playing to the crew, "that I am well aware of both the Greek and Latin tongues."

"We were addressing these *remarks* to the crew," said Moses. "Can you translate what my colleague said?"

"And what was that?" asked the Jesuit.

"*Liberatrix dominatrixque Joslin Pulchrissimae.*"

"Joslin, the Most Beautiful Liberator and Dominatrix."

"Ahh, then you know her as well?" asked Moshe. "How is this possible?"

The crew began to smile.

"Do you know her as *Liberatrix* or as *Dominatrix*?" continued Moses.

The crew began to applaud.

("By the Blood of Martin the Gardener," said the bearded man, "If he says *Dominatrix*, I'll give him my own ship's rope for his pleasure!")

"I do not know her at all," snapped the Jesuit. "Now please continue with your tale, such as it is."

"Very well," replied Moussa. "Though you will not speak of the face of the Lovely Joslian you have seen, do not think it has gone unnoticed." He turned to the crew: "One of the chief eunuchs of Sardko the Pastrian, a certain Damian Kush who was a thief from the island of Kleptos, suddenly announced one day that not only were his testicles missing, but, during a thoroughly uneventful night, his penis had mysteriously disappeared. Sardko demanded a search, both high and low, of field and valley, of sea and sand, of *yurt* and *swunyik*. After two days and nights, Damian had a dream: in that dream, a lovely young woman came to him and said: "Father, I am of your seed, and one day you will worship me." The court eunuch was most perplexed. "But how can I be your Father, O my daughter, when I have neither testicle nor fundament?"

"What does it matter?" she replied "If God is Mother, and Goddess is Father, and both are in-laws, and I am Lovely, you can be Anything my Heart Desires – and which is why, in Pastrian, eunuchs today are called *Pashki Bollushki,* or "Anything My Heart Desires." I myself have known several Pastrian eunuchs, and it is extremely difficult to speak with them and receive a straight answer, since they all have the same name."

Moshe began to cough.

Moussa turned to him, perplexed.

All the crew were open-mouthed, sweating, leaning forward, waiting to see how the tale would end.

"Moses knows this part of the tale better than I," said Moussa, and nodded towards the third prophet.

"Indeed I do," Moses replied, "but I do not know if it will interest the Jesuit."

"It interests *us*!" yelled the crew. "Tell us the story of the eunuch and his daughter!" they screamed.

"Is it possible?" asked Moshe of Tagliacazzo.

"Is what possible?" replied the Jesuit, coldly. "That a eunuch can have a daughter?"

"Or a virgin a child?" answered Moussa, with a smile.

"Please. Tell them the rest of your tale," sneered Tagliacazzo.

"Excuse me," said Moshe, "but have we laughed at your religion? Have we sneered at your beliefs? Please do not laugh or sneer at ours. Remember: without the cleansing of this ship, we would have floundered in the sea, and you yourself might easily have been swept overboard."

("A prophet and a mage," whispered the man with the beard. "The man is a prophet and a mage!" and crossed himself three times, then twice more, then spit over his left shoulder.)

"I think, now, you might ask of us a different question," said Moses. "The tale you have heard has a very distinct rhythm, which is part of the telling---"

"And of our religion as well," said Moussa.

"Most of all, it is the essence of our belief," added Moshe. "Without it, the eunuch could not have given birth to the lovely Joslian. But by your interruption, priest, you have broken the rhythm."

"And how have I done that, sir?" replied the Jesuit, hotly.

"Would you see us grab the wafer during your Mass," exclaimed Moses, "as you hold it high? Would you see us break it in parts and pass it to our friends for a Sunday's meal? That is what you have just done to us. It is a shame, and shows spiritual malignancy and religious disrespect."

Immediately Moshe, then Moussa, then Mose began to chant:

"Goddess Goddess Goddess Goddess Goddess

Not us Not us Not us Not us Not us

God God God God God

He did it He did it He did it He did it!"

Then they began to chant in a round. After the fifth rendition, when Moses and Moshe had began to sing those words in a polyphonic fashion as well, Moussa joined in, with proper arabesque enthusiasms. The full *cantasmus* took five minutes and, at the end, the entire ship's crew, with the exception of Tagliacazzo, began to cheer, and offered them wine, but the three put it by.

"This was the first Hymn to the Lovely Jocelyn, and which was sung to her by her illegitimate child," called Moshe, with a small bow, and pointed at Moses. "*Him.*"

All stared.

"Yes. The young man before you is known as Her Greatest Lover, and is our first Prophet," Moshe continued.

"And second Greeter," added Moussa.

"And third Bread-maker, and fourth Yeast-pounder," continued Moshe.

"And fifth Bowl-licker," pronounced Moussa, "for which He is named, in hymn and in chant."

"Because Bread is her staple," said Moshe, "and Licking is her sign."

"Moreover," continued Moussa, "she is possessed of three vaginas, and that is why She is known by all as The Great Comforter."

"Tomorrow night we will bring to each of you her Bread, and that will give you sound sleep and sounder dreams," said Moussa.

The crew began to cheer.

"Hurrah for the Bread of the Lovely Dominatrix!" yelled the bearded man.

And the crew cheered him on with "Huzzzah—Huzzah----Huzzah!"

"*Extra ecclesiam nulla salus,*" called the Jesuit, portentously, over the shouts of the crew. "*'Outside the church there is no salvation.'*"

"Of course there isn't," said Moshe sweetly. "Salvation comes from all who are inside the church. On the other hand, we say: within the Lovely Joslian there is salvation – if you are one of the three who is lucky enough to be within her."

"Therefore," added Moses, "I think we all agree that each church we are speaking of has very well-defined responsibilities as well as clearly-defined limits."

"That *is not* what I am saying," snorted Tagliacazzo. "I am saying that unless you receive the rites of the Church, *you cannot be saved*!"

"That is precisely what my father used to say," said Moses.

"Your father was a good man, obviously," replied Tagliacazzo, darkly.

"He was also wrong," continued Moses. "Which is why he never stepped inside the church. Knowing that if he entered the church, he would be saved, he assumed that as long as he stayed out of it, *he had already been saved.*"

Moussa pointed a finger at Moses, while facing the crew as if he were a magician.

"Are you contradicting the Jesuit who didn't know your father at all, but who called him a good man, by saying your father *wasn't* a good man?"

"Indeed," Moses nodded. "He beat my mother and beat his children and bore seven illegitimates and never took care of them. How is it possible for this Jesuit, who didn't even know my father, to assume he was a good man? My father is still alive. What does the Jesuit know of

Jesus, who died over a thousand years ago? Did he ever meet him? Most importantly, what does he know of the lovely Joslian? Has he ever known her?"

"*Ignorantia neminem excusat,*" said Moshe, calmly, and slowly. "*Extra Ignorantiam nulla salus.*"

He smiled politely, and turned to the Jesuit:

"Shall I translate, or should you?"

"You said' *Ignorance excuses no one*'," replied Fulvio Tagliacazzo, glowering.

"Do you agree?"

"Of course."

"And then I what else did I say? Translate, please."

"'*Beyond ignorance no one can be saved.*'"

"Something like that," said Moshe. "So if no one can be saved outside the Church, and if no one can be saved beyond Ignorance, then Ignorance and the Church are one and the same."

"Brilliant," exclaimed Moussa. "Even I did not see that," and turned to Tagliacazzo. "A Greek construction, sir, which we had already translated from Arabic, long, long before you moved out of your cave."

"Answer me this!" called Moshe, turning to the crew and exclaiming, loudly: "will you have bread tomorrow?"

"Yes! Yes!" they shouted.

"By the inside thumb of Our Holy Gennifer!" cried the bearded sailor. "We will have bread!"

Above the exclamation, above the exultation, Moses held up his hands for silence:

"Then let us sing the second hymn to the Goddess, and retire now, for we must rise early to honor the Lovely Joslyn," he intoned, and then began to sing, in the deep, full-throating ecstasies of the Welsh voice:

"Bread bread bread bread bread
Eat it hot eat it hot eat it hot eat it hot
Her yeast is rising, so is mine, Her yeast is rising, so is mine!
O my O my O my O my O my!"

All three began to sing the Second Hymn, first as a round, then as a rondolay, and then as both a *finnochio* and a *cantabile*, sung this time *molto allegretto* but, nonetheless, happily and with great verve.

With an angry gesture from the bearded man, even Tagliacazzo was made to accompany the song.

"I am not finished with them yet," Tagliacazzo whispered to himself, then turned to the Captain, with a fixed smile:

"And have you enjoyed the discourse this evening, my Captain?" he asked.

"More than you, priest," laughed Ser Lorenzo! "More than you!"

The forty-sixth canto

Moshe and Moussa excused themselves, crept to the fore of the ship, and threw up over the rail, once again, but this time with exceedingly great spirit.

The bearded fellow, both surprised and awed, called the attention of captain and crew to the pair's dilemma.

"Yes," said Moses. "Now they are filled with the spirit of the lovely Joslian, for they are clearing the deck of the anger of the priest. So terrible, is it not, how the Jesuit has proved himself a poor loser."

The forty-seventh canto

Later, the bearded man sidled mysteriously up to Moses, took him by the elbow and whispered: "But tell me, honored sir: does She, the lovely Joslian, truly possess three vaginas?"

Moses looked furtively about him, then shook his head.

The bearded man gasped.

With a frown, then a cold stare, Moses held up five fingers.

"She is a *Pentaplus,*" he whispered. "She has five. The last two are placed most privately upon her person. This must remain a secret thought between us. I am telling you, signor, because you made manifest a certain devotion, with your question."

"I will be your slave, sir," said the bearded fellow. "I must see this woman before I die. I will worship her a thousand times and kill any man who speaks ill of her."

"I must ask my fellow prophets," said Moses, frowning.

"No," replied the bearded man. "This is my life I offer! Say yes to me now, or I will slay myself!"

"Very well," said Moses. "Kneel, and I will..."

"I'm not very good at such things," said the bearded man, ruefully. "My beard always interferes."

Moses blushed.

"I am asking you to kneel so that I can *bless you, and nothing more,* that I might invoke the spirit of the Lovely Joslian! Jesus Christ, man, who do you think I am?"

The bearded man kneeled, full of apologies.

As Moussa and Moshe came around the corner, wiping their lips, they spotted the strange event.

"You will be our protector," said Moses to the bearded fellateer. "From now on, until the lovely Joslian does otherwise, She will send you dreams, and answer your prayers, that one day you might be summoned to see her many parts."

The bearded man looked up, with tears in his eyes.

"I am her slave," he said.

"She doesn't take slaves," Moshe replied, moving with Moussa from out of the darkness. "Moses, what is going on?"

"This man, whose name I do not know---"

"Carliman the Dreamer, from the island of Ipnos," said the bearded man.

"—this Carliman wants to join us, and to follow the ways of Joslian."

"But Moses, surely you, of all of us, knows she never asked us to proselytize," said Moshe.

"He said he will kill himself," Moses replied.

"Not our fault," said Moussa. "His fate, not ours."

"What would the lovely Joslian do?" replied Moshe, stepping on Moussa's foot, for the bearded man, the fellateer, Carliman the Dreamer, suddenly appeared gloomy and ferocious. "She would say, 'Rise and follow me; but before you do, take a bath."

"Very well," whispered Moussa, darkly, to Moshe, "but don't say I didn't warn you."

"I will serve you as the eunuch served the Pastrian," replied Carliman. 'What must I do now, sires?"

"As he said," replied Moses. "Go clean yourself, and we will speak of this only when we set foot on land. Until then, this matter must remain a secret between ourselves."

"So be it," replied Carliman the Ipnosian. "Bless you, prophets."

When he had gone, Moussa said, "Moses, if you were in love with him, I could understand. But you're not. You're putting us in danger, and I don't like it."

"I do," replied Moshe, with curiousity. "He was sent to us for some reason. Let's see what it is."

"Besides," added Moses. "I don't think people will pick a fight with us, when they see him."

"There is no reason to be fighting," said Moshe. "We've relied upon ourselves thus far. Let him be our secret weapon."

"I still don't like it," said Moussa. "And those epithets of his: Martin the Gardener, Saint Cunt-lick the Prophet, by our bloody Saint Bologna---I don't know half the people he's talking about."

"Nor does he," said Moshe thoughtfully. "That's why I think I like him."

"That's very interesting," said Moses. "I didn't think of that."

"But why?" said Moussa, with frustration.

"*Why should his ignorance interest you?*"

"Because he sounds like us," said Moshe. "And thus I think he may be hiding something."

Both Moses and Moussa stared, surprised, at Moshe.

The latter smiled, and shrugged.

And in that shrug they realized:
Moshe was probably right.

Who was Carliman the Dreamer?
From the Isle of Ipnos.

Wherever that was?

First part of the seventh riff for Mnemosyne, Before we arrive at the forty-eighth canto

Charles Lamb's *Tales from Shakespeare* was given to me by Margaret, the older daughter of a neighbor. She had been visiting her parents, and would occasionally come to our house to talk about books or theater with my mother and me. She wanted to be an actress. She also drew pictures and wrote stories. She was sixteen.

Her book was from her own library, and she wanted me to have it – now that she was reading Shakespeare in the original.

Her favorite play was "Midsummer Night's Dream," which she read to me.

The illustrations, by Arthur Rackham, were magical and strange and rather frightening. But the world of the woods outside Athens: of fairies, changelings, lovers and, of course, of Bottom was extraordinary. Especially putting the different worlds together: of humans, mythical heroes, and spirits, all of it miraculous to me.

I wanted to hear Oberon and Puck's speeches in the original, so Margaret went to her grandmother's, brought back her book of the complete works, and began to read:

"*I know a bank where the wild thyme blows, Where oxlips and the nodding violet grows, Quite overcanopied with luscious woodbine and eglantine...*"

That was life-changing.

The magic of setting, the magic of words.

That evening I read through Lamb's book, and was especially frightened by and yet attracted to "Macbeth." When I mentioned the play at dinner, dad said he had a recording of Orson Welles' production somewhere, and it also had the text and Welles' own drawings of the play.

He located it, handed it to me, and I ran – "Walk or you'll break it!" – to my bedroom. Carefully, I put the first 78-disc on my record-player.

"John Houseman presents...The Mercury Theater production of...William Shakespeare's....MACBETH..." and swiftly there was wind, and a storm, and I was happily frightened, and then the witches began the scene at the end of their scene, and I kept playing that first scene over and over until I'd memorized all the parts, and could recite it with the actresses.

Imagine, beginning a play near the end of a scene!

I loved the confidence of the playwright – to be able to bring that off, while keeping the audience enthralled!

And then the second scene, "*What bloody man is that? He can report, as seemeth by his plight, of the revolt the newest state.*" The inversion of 'newest state' was confounding, and I kept wondering what was meant, until I figured out that "By the way he looks, he can tell us the latest news of the revolt." Why were words put in the order in which Shakespeare had placed them? I realized that there was a reason for it: He can report – pause – as seemeth by his plight – pause – of the revolt (breath) the newest state."

State is a hard sound. Revolt is a softer sound. (Later I learned that State is a masculine word, and Revolt has a feminine ending).

Shakespeare had wanted you to <u>hear</u> these words and phrases: *report – plight – revolt- newest state.* Besides telling us something about the character speaking, the sound of the words themselves, and their placement, were ways that Shakespeare had ensured that the audience understood clearly and emotionally what was happening. While the characters were speaking about *events occurring right now,* to each other, they were also telling the audience what to know, by showing them how to hear it.

Theatrical craft was extraordinarily exciting. Its vitality, which was Language, had been as magic to me then as it is magic to me now.

King Duncan, in the second scene, seemed to me rather stiff, and a bore.

But imagine the opening lines of the third scene:

"*So foul and fair a day I have not seen.*"

As an eight year old, it was already obvious to me that somehow the man who spoke those first lines in the third scene had some kind of unspoken relationship with the witches. Hadn't they ended their first scene with "*Fair is foul, and foul is fair, hover through the fog and filthy air?*" and he had begun his first scene with "*So foul and fair a day...*"

I kept playing that scene over and over, and memorized it as well. Shakespeare was speaking directly to me, and I was answering.

I liked Banquo. I thought he was a good friend.

Macbeth didn't say very much, but what he did say could be understood many ways. He didn't tell you any truths about himself. Shakespeare was also showing you and, more subtly, telling you, how people behaved with each other.

I went to sleep, thinking: "*How could one man do all that?*"

I've spent the rest of my life pursuing, as intelligently as possible, and as imaginatively as his best audience, everything that question implied.

Second part of the seventh riff for Mnemosyne, Before we arrive at the forty-eighth canto

The next day, at breakfast, my dad asked: "How did you like Macbeth?"

"So far I've heard three scenes."

"You were playing the records for over two hours," said Mom. "How long is the play?"

"I was memorizing them," I said, and began to recite.

After I had finished, out came dad's jazz musician:

"*I'm hip, son, but how did you like the play*?"

"I love it," I replied, laughing.

"Are you going to memorize the whole thing?" asked mom.

"The scenes I like, yes. He's so great," and I started to tear quietly, because my heart was so full of Shakespeare. My father became embarrassed and gave me a squeeze, and my mother began removing the plates, and I saw that she was starting to cry as well.

"That's what happened to you, in the pit at CBS," said Dad, "when I played the first measures of "*Rite of Spring,*" remember? I said to you, "I know Stravinsky's great, but don't become a musician.' Anyway, that happens to me every time I hear Debussy. It doesn't matter what the piece is. Immediately I think I'm going to explode."

My mom said, "Me too, the first time I heard 'King Lear' in English."

"What did you hear it in before?" dad asked.

"Come on, you know damned well. My uncle Sam did the first '*Lear*' in Yiddish, and that's the only Shakespeare I'd ever heard until we moved to the States. He did '*Lear*' and '*Hamlet*" in Yiddish. I think he was the first Yiddish Hamlet."

My father stood up, stuck out his belly, put his arms on his hips and recited: "'*Keyn zayn, oyder nisht keyn zayn...*'"

My mother answered, slamming her hand on the table: "'*...aher iz a onfreg*!'"

And the two of them laughed so hard, they began to cry.

"What *was* it?" I had to yell over their laughter. 'Come on, what's so funny?"

"'*To be or not to be*,'" said mom, between hiccups. "*Here is a question*!'" Then: "Let me---let me remember," she puffed, heaving with humor."What was it in *Lear*? The perfect Jewish line: "*Velkh of du, shall meir derzogn, lib hobn mir der merste?*"

"'*Which of you, shall we say, has love for me the most*?'" questioned dad.

"Exactly, almost! 'Which of you, shall we say, loves me the most?""

Once again they began to guffaw.

"How do you say, "Fair is foul and foul is fair" in Yiddish?" I asked.

"*Loyter iz*...I don't know what's *foul...Loyter iz* foul, *und* foul *iz loyter*, I don't know," said mom.

"Just do us all a favor," said dad, "and don't become an actor."

My mother, who had just given up acting, and my father, who was forever a musician, were handing useless advice to their eight year-old Shakespeare-smitten writer-son.

Needless to say, the advice, given to me by my parents, and to my parents by their own, never took.

How could it?

We all cried too much, and laughed too hard, all of us, to do anything else, or to be anyone other than who we were.

The forty-eighth canto

Dr. Herschel Fisch couldn't remember where he'd placed his Memory.

He knew It was somewhere between his bookshelves, and his holo-player.

Now he was hearing a great many voices, and witnessing a great many events, and he couldn't place them! He should know these people!! He should know this place!!!

Well-dressed souls were flittering about him, in the firefly-flickering lawn, with the great sycamores and potted ivy.

A hotel, he thought. It must be a hotel.

But *where?*

Several of the hotel's guests were speaking to him, but as long as he was without his Memory, there was nothing he could say to anyone.

On what shelf, and in what volume, had he placed It?

To himself, Doctor Herschel Fisch said aloud: "Still, knowing one has misplaced one's memory is something of a start, and implies one has had a memory, in fact, to misplace, and *somewhere*, and after all."

The problem was this: where had Fisch placed his bookshelves?

Earlier, in the hotel's library, by the stand of graceful potted palms, he had discovered a series of volumes: *The Hardy Boys and the Secret Tower; Nancy Drew and the Hidden Stairwell; American Poems Americans Have Always Loved; Six Profiles*, by Richard M. Nixon; *Profiles in Courage*, by John F. Kennedy; *Six Characters in Search of an Author*, by Luigi Pirandello; *Six Authors In Search of Courageous Profiles*, edited, of course, by Norman

Podhoretz, author of "*Why Jews Are Liberal,*" as well as "*Gidget Goes Jewish,*" based upon the Gidget series of novels, by Frederick Kohner.

"Frederick Kohner," said Fisch, to himself. "The name has a ring."

To those who cannot hear the ring, let me quote from the most recent edition of the Universal Wikipedia:

"Frederick Kohner, a Czechoslovakian Jew, worked in the German film industry as a screenwriter until 1933 when he emigrated to Hollywood after the Nazis started removing Jewish credits from films. Over the coming decades Kohner and his wife Franzie raised their two daughters by the beach while he toiled as a screenwriter for Columbia Pictures. As his children grew into American teenagers he noticed that his daughter Kathy in particular was drawn into a very specific, regional, contemporary slice of American teenage culture – the surf culture.

Surfing was a then minor youth movement that built its foundation around a sport, love of the beach, and jargon that must have proved a challenge to an Eastern European immigrant. The details fascinated Kohner, who was empathetic with his daughter's feminist intention to participate in a "boys-only" sport. A book was conceived and Kathy became her father's muse as he delved into the surfing world with his daughter as his guide. Over a six week period Kohner wove the stories she told into a novel, which he titled upon completion with her nickname, "Gidget."

In the original novel, Gidget gives her name as follows:

"It's Franzie," I said. "From Franziska. It's a German name. After my grandmother." http://en.wikipedia.org/wiki/Gidget - cite_note-novel-0

She does not give us her last name. In subsequent novels, her name is Franzie Hofer. In the films in which she appears her name is changed to a more English sounding Frances Lawrence, and the names of some other characters are changed as well. In the 1960s television series (episode 16, *Now There's a Face*) Gidget gives her full name as Frances Elizabeth Lawrence."

Dr. Herschel Fisch was now as mad as a rodeo bull and as crazy as its rider. Equally, he was as crazy as a rodeo bull and as mad as its rider.

He picked up a copy of the Gidget book in the hotel library, perused its contents, with jaw-dropping surprise and growing mental numbness.

"This tiny surfing German/Czech Jewess has become a *zoftik shikse* from Malibu," he said aloud, causing the travellers in the lobby to move to a different palm-lined area, far from the shelves of books. "Has that same metamorphosis occurred to *myself*?" he wondered. "Whoever they are, they tell me my name is Dr. Herschel Fisch. But could it not be Fisher Hart III, scion of the Philadelphia Harts, inventor of the sewing thimble, Gregorian chant and baseball bat? Had I not married the Princess Nep---Nep---Nep-Nep----"

His mind, now running on empty, continued to channel the sound "Nep-nep-nep," which attracted to him a great many historical events, from *Nap*oleon's retreat from Moscow, to the discovery of the planet *Nep*tune by William Herschel, to the origin of *pharmakon nepenthes, or* Nepenthe, the medicine of forgetfulness - explained by the ubiquitous Wikipedia as a medicament "given to Helen by a queen of Egypt."

Helen *who*?

Helen Hayes?

Helen Gahagan Douglas?

Helen Hunt Jackson?

Helen of Troy?

And which queen?

Nefertiti?

Cleopatra?

Latifa?

Douglas MacArthur?

"Nep-nep-nep" Fisch-Hart continued to say, until four hotel staff-members led him gently but firmly to the chief clerk, who said, "Bardo-4, gentlemen --- The dark-side."

The forty-ninth canto

They placed him in an elevator, which took him downhill, and then upcountry, and onto the etheric plane, where he was frozen at once, and his consciousness algorhythmically trimmed until he could assimilate a nonlocal state.

And, thus, his consciousness, moving towards that nonlocalized state, began to travel.

Here is what happened:

The fiftieth canto

This is absurd, thought the nonlocal consciousness, (and which will be referred to in this canto as DFNLC), of Dr. Herschel Fisch.

I'm in the eternal realm now, he thought, and I'm not even dead.

DFLC, (and which will be referred to as Dr. Fisch's local consciousness), lay frozen, crazed, and a bore to himself.

Well, what do you wish to do? asked a very sweet and concerned voice.

I certainly don't want to go back there, said DFNLC. *Fisch has so many complexes and responses he can't even breathe without some kind of analysis, analogy, literary example and, of course, projection of what such a breath might mean to the world of literature!*

He's a very bright man, though, sounded the very sweet and concerned voice, (which will be known as VSCV in this text).

No doubt, said DFNLC, *but it's the rest of him that bothers me. He has so many voices around and inside him that he's long forgotten I even exist! When we do connect, on those rare occasions, I feel like a librarian rather than an eternal aspect of the good doctor.*

Still, he does need you more than ever, said VSCV.
We're <u>in</u> ever, DFNLC replied. *How can he need me more than that?*
Just connect cleanly with him, said the VSCV.

He's nuts, pal! snapped the DFRNLC, with some acerbity. *How can I connect cleanly with him?*

Through analysis, analogy, literary example, and of course projection, replied VSCV, sweetly.

Very well, sighed DFNLC. *Should I take the O-O-B Metaphorical Tunnel, meet him halfway?*

It *is* fast, replied the very sweet and concerned voice, but I think a Dream might be the quickest way. He is, after all, in Bardo-4, and that's more a more appropriate field for your meeting.

Soon the odor of lime blossoms wafted in space, and Doctor Fisch's nonlocal consciousness swept within it and drifted into Bardo 4 - in the basement of the hotel where Dr. Fisch lay frozen - and began to permeate its dark side.

That was the easy part, thought DFNLC. *Now to connect with him:*

The act of connection was as easy as shaking hands on the space shuttle with a grasshopper.

Note:

For those of you who don't know the difference between local and nonlocal consciousness: think of local consciousness as the local subway or bus-line that takes you where you want to go every day.

Think of nonlocal consciousness as the space shuttle, which actually takes you where you need to go most any day, but your local consciousness doesn't know it, so you don't think the nonlocal consciousness even exists– or, since it does, it's only for astronauts, not for you.

You don't have to believe in God to accept what I'm saying.

You don't even have to have read Norman Podhoretz' "*Why Jews Are Liberal.*"

But quantum mechanics and a deeper study of the human genome, as well as a Weekend Getaway Vacation with Tibetan monks at Dharamsala, would help you to comprehend.

But if it doesn't matter to you, either way, that's just fine, too.

I'm telling you of one amazing moment in one amazing tale, so swing with it.

The fifty-first canto

Dr. Herschel Fisch-Fisher Hart's dream went like this, and it was a dream easy to remember, impossble to forget:

He was seated fourth row center in the plaza theater at *Noye-Erdkelle*, watching the Jewish Artists' Production of a new play whose title he could not remember, but it didn't seem to matter.

Shakespeare sat beside him, smelling of ale, cunt, and stale clothing.

The curtain rose, and the play began: it was about a Jew, a Christian and a Moslem. They all had the same name: Aharon. Aaron. Haroun. They were fools who had met during a Crusade, and who, together, had decided to invent a religion in order to save their own lives. It was a strange kind of comedy.

Shakespeare thought the idea was ingenious. He said he was going to appropriate a part of it for his newest piece, in which three suitors vie for the love of a Venetian cock-teasing bitch.

Shakespeare's three characters would be a Moor, called the Prince of Morocco, who, being dark, knew he was merely a second-class citizen; a Christian, called the Prince of Arragon, who would be revealed as "a blinking idiot"; and a third, a Venetian named Bassanio, an enemy of Jews, and a great lover. (After all – said Shakespeare - whoever heard of a Jew who was a great lover? Venetians, on the other hand, were ambidextrous).

"King David, I should think, was a lover," said Dr. Fisch. "Or his son, Solomon. To be factful, sir, the Jewish community in Venice is older than the majority of that city's Christian blood-lines."

"Mmm, you're probably right," said Shakespeare. "But nobody would or wants to believe it. The Jew gets the girl-boy? Never. The Jew gets the money or loses it? *That's* the point. I'll treat the Venetians as I do the Spaniards and the Moors. As a separate race. With both Venetian Christians and Venetian Jews as hypocrites. Still, it *is* a love story. The bitch has to get her man. I can do the bed-trick. That always works. He loves her, but she has to dominate him before marriage, so she tricks him. You should have the sense he's been hammer-holed and sausage-stuffed a thousand ways to Whitsun, and doesn't even know it. This is, after all, Venice, and they are, after all, Italians, and ambidextrous.")

"'*What fools these mortals be*?'" said Dr. Fisch-Hart.

Shakespeare smiled.

"Nice," he said, and wrote that snide observation on his holo-comp.

"Shakespeare is stealing from me," thought Dr. F-H.

No he's not, said Doctor Fisch's nonlocal consciousness. *You're projecting. This is a dream, remember? Shakespeare doesn't* <u>*need*</u> *you to write his dialogue.*

"Then why did he write that into his holo-comp?" asked Fisch.

In fact, said the dfnlc, *Shakespeare wrote: "The quality of mercy is not strained, it droppeth from the heavens as gentle rain." Now he's laughing his head off.*

"Why?"

"Because he loves writing clichés as truths, and watching the audience laugh."

"I still think he gets many of his best lines from me," continued Fisch.

Such as? asked dfnlc.

"From Lear: 'never, never, never, never, never.' From Macbeth: 'Tomorrow and tomorrow and tomorrow.' From Twelfth Night: "With a hey ho."

"You didn't write that," said dfnlc.

"No, but I remembered it."

"It's about the only thing you can remember," said the dfnlc. *"You forgot 'the wind and the rain.'"*

"Can't remember *everything*," whined Dr. Fisch-Hart.

The fifty-second canto

Next, in the dream, the curtain went up as the lights went down.

In the play there was also something about a Jesuit and a bearded rascal. But Shakespeare was too busy, writing in a holo-comp, to notice.

When the play had ended, Dr. Fisch-Hart rose, but the playwright shook his head, waved him away, remaining in the theater and entering more words into his holo-comp.

"I've an entire orchestra of boy flautists and clarinet-players to whom I've promised scads of ice-cream," said the critic to the playwright. "Won't you come and enjoy the fun?"

But Shakespeare merely shook his head, giggling to himself.

"Gentle rain," he muttered, and stifled another laugh. "Don't strain your mercy, doctor," he said and, this time, guffawed.

In a sweat, Dr. Fisch awoke from his medically-induced coma cum ice-cream dream.

In a phrase which would have dreadful thematic implications for the doctor, in a subsequent canto, he screamed:

" WHAT THE FUCK, ALICE!

WHATEVER DOES ONE DO WITH A PREPUBESCENT CLARINET PLAYER?"

The fifty-third canto

And where was the real Shakespeare in all these words?

Not the Shakespeare of the dreams, but the one who had partaken of the interplanetary mussels, and the private muscle-planing with the triple Mollies; the one who wrote "*The Merchant of Venice*?"

He whom many academics believed could never have been himself but, rather, someone else (which statement reflects most gravely on their own careers, and relationships)?

We had learned earlier, in the Natal Nosh, that "to all appearances, Shakespeare had disappeared."

Or something like that.

Wait. The exact line, somewhere...

Here:
"Shakespeare appeared to have disappeared."

The truth was that he could not appear to disappear, if he had appeared at all. Either he disappeared, or he didn't.

Admittedly, to others he was *there* – that is to say, he still appeared as a presence to all; but then he wasn't *there* – that is to say, he was no longer an appeared presence (what the French can an *apparition apercu*) but, rather, a disappearance (what the Argentinians calls a *desparecido*).

The fifty-fourth canto

Where had Shakespeare gone? And how had he done it?

First, he hadn't done anything, except to ask for the restaurant bill.

He had not gone anywhere.

Rather, he had been removed by a crack SW/AT Team, or Saving Writers/Artists Today Team.

Who had given the SW/AT Team the order to remove the playwright?

The FBH, or Folks Back Home.

It is the job of the SW/AT Team from the FBH to accompany all history's great writers and artists from and to the Muse Plane, and to make sure they don't get into trouble when they either incarnate, or soul-swap, or body-surf. When that happens – that is to say, when they get into trouble – history's great writer/artist is poofed, and returned to Piatnik.

That's right: *Poofed.*

You heard me correctly the first time.

The fifty-fifth canto

The Piatniki, as you remember, are saviours of the Children of Israel, created by HaShem as an afterthought. (See the first volume, *Jews On The Moon*).

So Shakespeare became, once again, just another long-legged fuzzy Piatnik - along with Charles Dickens, Marcel Proust, Walt Whitman, Victor Hugo, Jane Austen, Lady Murasaki, James Joyce, James Merrill, Sandro Botticelli, Ditters von Dittersdorf, Casper David Friedrich, Friedrich Handel, Moliere, George Eliot, George Balanchine, Louie Armstrong, Bird and Diz, Lenny Bruce – you get the idea; clearly, the list is much longer, and can be supplied upon request.

Why had the Piatniki been described, in *Jews On The Moon*, as powder-puffs seated atop a daddy long-legs?

Because that's how they look.

And it's the only way to keep autograph hounds away from the silky planes of Piatnik.

Now that I've mentioned how they appear, you'll doubtlessly go looking for trouble by invading Piatnik.

Pay attention to me:

You won't find it.

And even if you did, they'd be long gone.

Merely mentioning their name involves an immediate and general shape-shifting of both plane and persona.

That's how important Muses are.

Adonai's afterthought.

The fifty-sixth canto

The shape-shifting and location-zooming of Muses is done not only to protect plane and persona, but also to protect the public.

Why?

Because Muses can be dangerous.

They can hurt.

The fifty-seventh canto

Meanwhile, back on Piatnik:

Voltaire was the first to stop Shakespeare and inquire, "*Eh bien,* and how was the play? Was I proven to be correct, after all?"

"No, you were not," said the playwright. "It was rather like your *Candide*, but without the charm. Venice was depicted as a world of *merde* from beginning to end. I liked it. Hard to do properly, that play. They made a very respectable effort. More importantly, however, let me tell you about the mussels, and the women."

"You are more Parisian than I," said Voltaire, with a smirk, and took his friend by his seventh leg, and the two of them loped towards the velvety swings.

Waiting for them, hidden within the bark of a Flemish branch, was Hilda Doolittle, also known as H.D., the poet.

She was carrying a message for Shakespeare, from an urgent HaShem and Adonai.

A most dangerous kind of message:

An RPM, 1st Category.

RPM stood for: Rescue People Mission.

If Shakespeare didn't accept their RPM, he'd not be given another chance to body-surf, soul-slam, or dip into a material production of his work, for the next seven procreations.

For HaShem and Adonai, that wasn't even a microsecond.

For all Piatniki, however, it meant billions of wasted time-slots.

"What kind of RPM must I perform?" asked the playwright of the poet.

"Enter the critic's dream and sort him out, I'm afraid," said Hilda Doolittle. "If it makes you feel any better, I did it with Siegmund Freud, and got quite a jolly little book out of it."

"I don't believe in psychoanalysis," said William Shakespeare. And then, *a propos* of nothing he could consciously understand, he exclaimed:

"WHAT THE FUCK, ALICE!

WHATEVER DOES ONE DO WITH A PREPUBSCENT CLARINET PLAYER?"

Then he vanished.

The fifty-eighth canto

H.D. turned to Voltaire:

"*He's in,*" she said, darkly.

"*Mon pauvre Willie,*" frowned the *philosophe*. "*Merde mille fois, comme je deteste les dieux!*"

A eighth riff for Mnemosyne, Before we arrive at fifty-ninth canto

When dad had become the artist and repertoire chief, during the first year of Mercury Records, picking pieces and arrangers for the company's signed musicians, as well as arranging works himself and producing the recordings, he was soon being assaulted by every composer and lyricist in the entertainment industry.

Most of the people he knew, some he met, but practically everyone came to our house or to the office to present their most recent works: Bob Merrill, Sammy Cahn, Frank Loesser, Bob Russell, Jimmy McHugh, even Johnny Mercer, who would soon start his own record company, Capitol, with Clyde Wallach.

I grew up listening to a good part of the Great American Songbook, being played by its authors, in my living-room. It was all about language, and rhythm, and dynamic but above all, that wondrous week-end marriage of words and music.

My favorite moments, however, were spent at the recording sessions, watching dad conduct each section of the orchestra. I wondered how dad would make the melody work with the seemingly disparate ideas of each instrumental section. But when he put it all together, it created a rich and surprising answer to a four-dimensional puzzle.

I loved watching the musicians, their interactions. On the way home, I'd imitate how they played, or spoke with each other. Each section appeared to have its own code of behavior, its separate world:

The horn section was tough, bold, funky, highly individualistic. The string section was generally central European – intellectual, fastidious, technical, highly judgmental. The woodwinds appeared almost uninvited. They were like storks and cranes, gingerly making their way through the string's marshy waters, and unhappy that they'd been invaded by the horns.

The percussion section was definitely the most subversive: in the rear of the studio set-up, the drummers were ready to explode their depth bombs, looking at everybody with sardonic humor.

At that time, in the late 40's, Los Angeles was extraordinary.

Because of the recording and entertainment industries, Dad said it contained the best musicians in the United States, They'd have to be perfect musicians, even though most producers considered them nothing more than a necessary afterthought in the different media. Films were scored musically in ten days, after they were shot, then recorded in three days. It needed genius-musicians to get it right, that first take.

Which they were, and which, most of the time, they did.

And if you think of the composers – Erich Korngold, Leonard Bernstein, Bernard Herrmann, Konstantin Bakaleinakov, Max Steiner, Franz Waxman, Ernest Gold, Dimitri Tiomkin, Miklos Rosza, Charlie Chaplin, David Raksin and, later, Johnny Mandel, Elmer Bernstein, Alex North, Andre Previn, Richard Rodney Bennett – you began to understand the values of the Industry. Although Music was and is at the heart of every heartbeat, by the Money it was given the least attention.

Ditto, television composing.

I must also mention the great European and South American composers and Asian composers of film – Malcolm Arnold, Sergei Prokofiev, Georges Auric, William Walton and Ralph Vaughan-Williams, Antonio Carlos Jobim, Tan Dun and, my favorite, as I write this, Dario Marianelli, whose score for "Atonement" is one of the most moving and elegant pieces of music in film history - - even though I'm speaking of Los Angeles itself, and the Hollywood studios.

Radio also had wonderful pit orchestras, composers, arrangers.

And Television was no different.

Still, composers and musicians were and are treated as afterthoughts.

Think of being a first violinist, and flawlessly recording the full score to "Rebecca" in three days.

Or being a French horn player, in a live orchestra, doing "Lux Presents Holiday" on radio. No flubbing allowed!

Now imagine Stanley Kubrick and Jack Nicholson trying to outdo each other in the number of takes of one scene, while shooting "*The Shining*," and getting away with it: seventy-five takes!

Or Al Pacino methodizing the *dreck* of "*Devil's Advocate.*"

How long did *that* take?

Doubtlessly more time and money was spent shooting those tedious moments than in recording the entire score of Franz Waxman's wonderfully workable accompaniment to "*Rear Window.*"

What mattered, as I learned very early, was the making of things, and the truth of those things.

What surrounded it, or what happened afterwards to it, was by itself unimportant.

What allowed it to happen was, unfortunately, all too important, even though the Man Holding the Key was, more often than not, the King of All Ghouls.

If you were a musician, and you scored a work, and the other musicians dug it, that was enough.

The rest of it was business as usual.

(Think of Miklos Rosza's classic acceptance speech when he received an Oscar for "Ben Hur." Don't forget, he was speaking of a three-day recording session, and a ten-day writing session. In effect, he said: "I would like to thank the Academy for this honor, and especially would I like to thank my colleagues, without whom this score never would have been written: so thank you, Beethoven, Brahms, Schumann, Bartok and, of course, Stravinski."

Dead silence from an uncomprehending Academy.

But the orchestra broke up with laughter, and couldn't play for five minutes, because they understood only too well).

So the real artists in Hollywood lived in two worlds: one that appeared accommodating, but in which they were treated as third-class citizens and behaved as such; the other, in which they served an elegant goddess, and created their work with passionate intelligence, imagination, and novel forms.

That partially explained the peculiarly whacked-out humor and awkward desire to believe the ruling class until it inevitably betrayed him, and which made my father, more often than not, so insanely smart, also so oddly naive.It also explained the constant rebellion against authority, except the authority of music, that shaped his life, and my mother's.

Authorship, to my father and mother, was authority. *Not* external power.

My parents, I had begun to realize, were and remained the divinely rebellious twins, Peck's Bad Boy and Peck's Bad Girl.

As for myself:

During my freshman year at Dartmouth College, my mother met with the College's Dean, Thaddeus Seymour, who assured her: "Don't worry, Mrs. Geller. We'll make a Dartmouth man out of your son yet."

Her response, spoken with an elegant tilt of the head and a captivating smile, was:

"In a pig's ass you will."

The fifty-ninth canto

Moshe, Moses and Moussa were the second, third and fourth travellers to spot the pirate's vessel. The three friends had been dynamically vomiting overboard, by the aft's rail, during the dawn's hours, when the lookout, who was the first to recognize the danger, called out, "Pirates, at starboard!"

The three friends turned, simultaneously, and in different directions, knocking violently into each other, until their eyes settled on a swift-moving ship hosting an English flag and, below it, the dreadful skull-and-crossed bones.

"*Now* what?" whispered Moussa. "It's bad enough having to vomit every five minutes without having to concern ourselves with pirates!"

"Moses, go find your bearded friend," gulped Moshe.

"First," coughed Moses, "He's sleeping. Second, he's not my friend. And, third, I very much would prefer to leave him alone."

"He's right" said Moshe." The man may be now in a dream, and so will be confused enough to think that Moses is the lovely Joslian Herself, and will bugger him."

"The man is like a foul dog with a continuously erect penis," said Moussa. "You're quite right. Let us leave him to his dreams."

Ser Lorenzo appeared quickly, glanced up at the sailor in the crow's nest, then turned to the pirate's vessel.

"They're coming upon us much too fast," he muttered. "We can't out-run them."

"And if they come upon us, Ser Lorenzo, what exactly will they do?" asked Moussa.

"Kill us all, then take our vessel," replied Ser Lorenzo.

"I believe that is not a very good prospect," replied Moshe.

"But Is there no magic you can perform?" asked the captain.

"We're not magicians," said Moses. "We're prophets."

"Get Carliman the Ipnosian," said Moshe, quickly, to the captain. "Dress him in the costliest garments you can find."

"There are no garments," said the Captain. "Only silks."

"Bring us the silks, then," said Moshe. "And Carliman."

After the captain had gone, Moses asked: "So you have a plan, Moshe?"

"Of course not," Moshe answered. "I am simply speaking aloud while praying for inspiration."

"What is the inspiration you seek?" said Moses.

"I have no idea," Moshe replied, "until I see the silks, and Carliman."

"And how will inspiration save our lives?" asked Moses, shivering.

"Inspiration means that one is in spirit," added Moussa, kindly, to Moses. "If one is in spirit, one is not conscious. One is beyond oneself." Then he turned to his friend, Moshe, and said, "You are certain this is no delusion of yours? Being in spirit, I mean?"

"Trust me," said Moshe. "I am absolutely certain of – most precisely - absolutely nothing."

"Excellent," Moussa whispered, quietly. "Such precise uncertainty will either make of us heroes, or dead meat," Moussa.

"I'm still frightened," said Moses.

"And well you should be," replied Moshe. "But understand that being frightened will do nothing to chase away pirates."

"Quite true," said Moussa, and turned to Moses. "I myself prefer to put myself into the inspired state of which Moshe speaks. I am excited to see the silks, and Carliman."

Moses stared at his friends for a moment, considering what they had spoken.

Then he said:

"In fact, this *is* very exciting."

"Inspiration is beyond excitement," Moussa replied. "Feel the breeze of dawn upon your face, and take several deep breaths."

After a moment, Moses said: "Indeed." Then: "I think I will vomit again."

"I think we will join you," Moshe replied.

The sixtieth canto

Ser Lorenzo stood by the ladder, with Carliman shuffling awkwardly beside him.

Two cabin-boys, holding a pile of multi-colored silks, raced towards the Mosaic trio, then stopped, waiting patiently, the captain, cabin boys and the beard, until the three men had wiped their mouths, turned from the railing, and spotted the Ipnosian.

"Fine," said Moshe. "This will be exactly what we want."

"From the looks of that ship," said Ser Lorenzo, "they'll be able to board us in fifteen minutes. May your thoughts be swiftly acted upon---"

"---They are manifest even now, so do as we say," replied Moussa. "First: Lower your sails, then move all the men below deck."

"Lower our sails?" said Ser Lorenzo, stunned.

"You heard him," replied Moshe "The quicker you do this, the easier our task will be."

Ser Lorenzo turned, and began to call orders to the sailors.

Meanwhile, Moshe gestured for the cabin boys to follow him to the foredeck.

"Now then," said Moshe. "Spread out these silks."

Then, turning to Carliman, he said, "Render yourself naked, quickly."

Frowning, darkly, yet doing as he was bid, Carliman soon stood naked upon the deck.

He was truly a hairy man, and this was remarked upon by both Moussa and Moshe. The latter turned to Carliman, and gave him several of the larger silk materials.

"Make a bodice about your waist," he said, "with this red silk. With this yellow, tie it about your neck as a cape. And here, with this deep blue one, cover your head."

While Carliman was following Moshe's orders, the sailors had lowered the sails and, upon Moussa's word, were dropping anchor.

"Have everyone, including yourself, go below, and stay there. Under no conditions, come on deck," Moussa ordered the captain.

"You are sure of this?" said Ser Lorenzo.

"Of course we are sure," said Moshe. "We did this at Agrabad six times, and held off the Sassanid Empire for two days, before we called to the Lovely Joslian for a Compelling and Definitive Act of the Goddess."

Suddenly the Jesuit Tagliacazzo came forward, and stood angrily between the Captain and Moshe.

"How do we know they're not pirates themselves?" he asked. "How do we know this has not been a well-devised plot? Now that you've dropped sail and laid anchor, and now that you're going below, you're giving the pirates the run of your caravel."

Frowning, Ser Lorenzo stared at Moshe.

"We never devise anything until necessity demands it," said Moshe, "and then we let the lovely Joslian work through ourselves."

"*We* have fun," said Moses, then pointed at Tagliacazzo. "*He* doesn't."

"Take the priest with you, below," said Carliman, "or I will be forced to throw him overboard."

"They'll sell us to the English!" yelled the Jesuit. "I know their tricks!"

Moshe, Moussa and Moses pointed to the stairwell, and Tagliacazzo was dragged, crying and howling, down the ladder.

"If he says another word," Carliman called, "I will come down and run him through with this sword!"

All scurried below deck.

When the last sailor had disappeared below, Moses closed the door, and sealed it shut.

"Now lay in the center of these cloths, here, behind me," said Moshe to Carliman the Ipnosian. "And do not move until I say: 'Lovely Joslian, lift him up!' Then do exactly as I say, or Moses, or Moussa. Nobody else can order you about but us. Look at no one but us. When I say 'Lovely Joslian, lift him up!" then you must stand very quickly, and hold out your --- is that a scimitar?"

"No, it is a *yatagan*," said Carliman.

"We call it a *saif*," added Moussa.

"I have heard the Persians refer to it as a *shamshar* myself," said Moshe.

"Good sirs," said the bearded *silkiste*. "The pirates are nearly upon us now. I would suggest----"

"Lie beneath these silks," said Moshe, "and remember my words."

"'Lovely Joslian, lift him up!'" cried the bearded fellow. "Is that correct?"

"Good man," replied Moussa, and took Moses by one elbow, and Moshe by the other, and turned to face the pirates.

"Have either of you seen pirates before?" Moshe whispered.

Both men shook their heads.

"Neither have I," said Moshe, simply. "No matter how old one is, it is always a pleasure to know there's always a first time for everything."

The pirate ship swung swiftly about, as a dozen men threw a dozen grapplers across the rails. All pulled hard, and brought the ship within five feet of the caravel.

"What took you so long?" called Moses to the pirate captain, who stood at the rail, shouting orders.

Below deck, the Jesuit turned red, and started to yell, "I told you---" when three sailors pounced on him, and put several strong hands about his mouth.

The sixty-first canto

The pirate captain was a Welshwoman named Cerridwen ap Gwynnedd.

Moses recognized her at once, and told Moussa and Moshe the following details:

She was as beautiful and as sinful as the priests had said.

She was known to come in the night and take you aboard her ship and you'd never return home.

She spoke Irish and Welsh and Gaelic and English and Latin and Greek and Hebrew, which was proof that she was a typical Welsh enchantress.

"Do I know you?" Cerridwen ap Gwynnedd called to Moses, in English.

"He speaks in metaphors," replied Moshe. "He meant that your beauty was so overpowering to us that we must offer you everything we have - except for the Enchanted Hairy Warrior, - who has protected us from Crusader and Buccaneer and Pope - and who has brought us great wealth - which, as you see, is spread before you."

Cerridwen smiled coldly.

"Let me see this Warrior. If he is as powerful as you say, then perhaps we might become friends."

Moussa replied: "You must send your men below your own deck. As you see, nobody but ourselves is on the deck of this vessel. All the sailors have been sent below for their own safety. If you are to see the Enchanted Hairy Warrior, then you must do the same with your sailors. I cannot be responsible for what will happen, if he spots them."

"There are three of you, and only one of me," said Cerridwen ap Gwynnedd.

"Very well. We're none of us the overpowering personage, but if you think otherwise, then pick three of your greatest warriors to stand by you, and make the rest go below the deck of your own vessel," said Moshe.

"I like you," said Cerridwen ap Gwynnedd to Moshe. "Either you are a skilled magician, or else the stupidest man in the world."

"We have been made dumb by your beauty," said Moses. "Which is, of course, no proof that we're *not* stupid..."

"We are not magicians," said Moshe. "Though we worship a Goddess far greater than you could ever be: the Lovely Joslian."

Cerridwen frowned.

"The name is familiar," she nodded. "Joslian, you say?"

"We are her prophets," said Moses, "and the Enchanted Hairy Warrior her Immortal Protector."

"Which is why he is so powerful," added Moussa.

"Very well," she said and, turning to her crew, called: "Llewys, Crowther, and Profit! Stand by me."

Then she said to the others:

"*Cer goris addurna a gwrandaw bydew. Ai Alwa 'ch, ladd 'u pawb!*"

With a wink at Moses, she added: "I told them to go below."

"You also said that '*if you call for them, they're to come up and kill us,*'" replied Moses, shaking.

Immediately the Pirate Queen frowned, and cocked her head, questioningly.

"The Lovely Joslian speaks all languages," said Moshe, "and our brother hears her voice, and translates for us."

"Have her translate this," said Cerridwen ap Gwynnedd: "*Ai Gwnawn cara atat, 'ch d darfod. Gwna 'ch angen at darfod?*"

Moses blushed.

"You said: '*If I made love to you, you'd die. Did you want to die?*'"

Immediately Moussa replied, "The three of us have died many times in the Lovely Joslian's arms. We do not need your own impoverished arms in which to perish, when we have Hers."

With a cold smile, Cerridwen ap Gwynnedd leaped over the railing and onto the Venetian caravel, followed by the three solidly built warriors: Llewys, Crowther, and Profit.

Immediately they took arms, threateningly, behind Cerridwen.

"Do not stand on the silk," said Moshe, "for it has been blessed by the lovely Joslian in the sacred mysteries of the night."

"And sometimes of the late afternoon as well," added Moussa.

"And sometimes of the noon too," said Moses, "if we are able to rise early enough."

Cerridwen sniffed the air mightily, and shook her head.

"I smell no smells of love on those costly sheets."

"This is not about the mixture of men's and women's bodily odors," said Moussa. "It is about higher purpose. Lovely Joslian, lift him up!"

Immediately Carliman rose, and his chest seemed larger and hairier than it was, and his head seemed fuzzier and darker, and his legs appeared like ship's planks. His muscles bulged so greatly they were obscene. He made hissing sounds from his nose and mouth, and his eyes had turned red.

To all, he appeared most strange.

"How quickly can he cut off the heads of my warriors?" asked Cerridwen, surprised.

"Is that a rhetorical question?" asked Moshe. "Or are you making a joke at your warriors' expense?"

"I am not joking," relied the Pirate Queen. "If he can defeat my warriors, all four of you can have me. Then I will leave."

"But we don't *want* you," said Moussa.

"*I* might," replied Moses. "To see if I die."

"You may have Moses," said Moshe. "In any event, if he dies, that's *his* problem, and no longer *ours*."

"Very well," said Cerridwen, and pointed towards Carliman. "Llewys, Profit, and Crowther: Cut him up."

None of the men moved.

"He has that effect," said Moussa.

"*Ladd 'r 'n flewog bastard*!" yelled Cerridwen, but the men still did not move.

("She said, '*Dammit, kill the hairy bastard*,'" translated Moses, quietly, to his friends).

"Wrong thing to say," replied Moshe.

"Dreadful," added Moussa, then turned to Carliman. "Show them what you can do."

Carliman stared hard at the men, dropped his sword, and kneeled down, licking his lips with mighty lust, before Moussa's fundament.

Profit, Llewys and Crowther shifted, sighed, then swooned.

Instinctively, Moussa took a step backwards.

"And that was done *without* his sword," said Moshe, by way of explanation.

Cerridwen shook her head, and said, "That was indeed passing strange. I fear what he would do to my crew, with one shake of his right hand and one of his left, and with that horrifying sucking movement of his mammoth lips."

"Is that a rhetorical question, or are you asking for a free hand-out?" asked Moshe.

"If I promise you whatever you wish," she said, "will you come aboard my craft?"

"We wish to go to Wales," said Moses.

"Wales?" replied Cerridwen, surprised.

"The Lovely Joslian insists we go there now," said Moussa. "To sing her praises."

"*Ai ddim amgen, 'r Cymraeg adnabod fel at byncio,*" whispered Cerridwen to herself.

("She says: *if nothing else, the Welsh certainly know how to sing,*" Moses translated.)

"You must speak to me of this Joslian, who knows all languages," said Cerridwen. "I can sail to London, but not to Wales. There's a price on my head in Wales. But the Queen and I have a certain understanding. She would adore those silks..."

"We will go with you," said Moshe, "if you release your hooks and take nothing but our gift, which are these very silks. Carliman, lift the silks from the ship and give them to..."

"Cerridwen ap Gwynnedd," said Moses.

Immediately Cerridwen held up a hand and pointed at Moses.

"How does he know my name?" she asked. "I never gave it to you."

"No," replied Moses. "But the Lovely Joslian did. The silks, madam. And your promise to make me die?"

The sixty-second canto

Moshe and Moussa stood at the bow of the pirate's vessel, watching Ser Lorenzo's caravel seeming to recede upon the horizon. Between their by-now familiar retches, burps and pukings (what the Welsh call *yn llindagu, yn codi gwynt, yn chwydu*), they felt strange and discomfited.

Thus far, the Lovely Joslian had enchanted everyone but them.

And yet, Moshe and Moussa had begun to sense Her presence. Or, rather, the presence of Something or Someone who was moving them imaginatively and intelligently towards their destination.

Think of it this way:

First: A murderous Spaniard had purchased tickets for them aboard a caravel bound for Venice.

Then: The ship had been besieged by a Welshwoman's privateer.

And now: they were on their way to Wales, and the only thing they'd paid with was their sea-sickness.

Moses himself was in the pirate captain's cabin, practicing his death in the arms of the mythical Cerridwen ap Gwynnedd, whose door was guarded ferociously by Carliman the Ipnosian.

The entire crew was terrified of the three Moses, for they had learned how the threat of being noisily and lustily fellated by the Enchanted Hairy Giant had made Profit, Llewys, and Crowther so terror-stricken they had fainted – something they had never done before.

"All of this," said Moshe, "is beginning to frighten me, for I wonder---"

"---how long will our good fortune last?" completed Moussa.

"No. But tell me if I do not sound strange, Moussa..." Here Moshe dropped his voice, looked furtively about him, and leaned into his friend, whispering: "I too have begun to wonder...if the Lovely Joslian...is real."

"Of course she is," said Moussa, whispering in return. "We thought of her, and she has protected us, and----"

"Stop being so fatalistic, Moussa," hissed Moshe. "We *invented* her, remember?"

"Did we truly?" said Moussa. "Then who invented us? Whose story is this? We are the heroes of our own invention, are we not, and we worship Joslian, so why shouldn't She exist?"

"It's the endlessness of it frightens me," said Moshe.

"Of what?" asked Moussa.

"Of our imaginations, and of our intelligence. Perhaps we need some rules."

"No rules," said Moussa. "It's what keeps us going. As soon as we have rules, we spoil the game."

"But every game has rules," said Moshe.

"To be broken, or expanded," replied Moussa. "Adam and Eve sinned, and were thrown out of the Garden. Jesus' mother Mary didn't sin, for she was a virgin, and as such gave birth to the son of God. She broke the rules of Adam and Eve's sin---"

"If you're a Christian," said Moshe.

"But I'm not," said Moussa, "and that's the point. Rules may spoil the game, so they're broken and expanded and then new rules appear. It *is* not Progress. It is that Endlessness you've said you fear. It is the very infinity of imagination and intelligence."

Moshe frowned, and shook his head:

"To Senor Gesualdo and his family," he began, "to Carliman and to Ser Lorenzo and the crew; to Cerridwen ap Gwynnedd and her pirates, we're as gods. We're *magic.* I'm beginning not to like it, Moussa."

"Why don't you like it?" smiled Moussa.

"Because I'm *not* a god."

"However, my friend, like God we invent realities. Come, Moshe," said Moussa, and felt himself once again about to retch. "This is the life of every story-teller. And it *is* endless. Once it isn't, one ceases to be a teller of tales. Besides, why do you look for authority, when you have the lovely Joslian staring you in the face?"

For a few moments, Moshe said nothing.

He sighed, took a deep breath, and turned from the railing to his friend.

"What do you think of *Welsh* as a language?" he asked, a propos of nothing.

Then the both of them heard the response, coming across the water like a dove of peace, and flittering before their consciousness:

"Cara'i,'eb Joslian."

They stared at each other.

"'*I love it---*'" began Moshe.

"'*---said Joslian,*'" finished Moussa.

"Now what?" asked Moshe, feeling his blood plummet to his feet. He clutched the rail for support.

"I believe you're correct, after all," whispered Moussa, equally terrified. "It's better to write tales than to participate in them."

"And safer as well," stammered Moshe, trying to focus upon the sea in order to transcend his fright.

"As you said, so meaningfully and succinctly," chattered Moussa: "*now what?*"

The sixty-third canto

In Cerridwyn ap Gwynnedd's cabin, Moses died three times, to Cerridwyn's six.

In between deaths, the pirate queen stretched luxuriously, tousled Moses' hair, and whispered: "*Ai ond baech Cymraeg...*" which meant, "If only you were Welsh...!"

Before he could reply, however, Moses heard a woman's voice come to him from across the water, and hover before his consciousness.

The voice said:
"*Gwisga t ateb 'i. 'ch ll andwya 'm cellwair.*"

Don't answer her. You'll spoil my fun.

Moses' eyes grew wide.
At once, to alleviate his fear, he thought:
Moussa and Moshe will certainly have an answer for this!.

And then, once again, he heard the voice from across the water, calling:

"*Gwisga t chyfrif arni, anwylyd. Fi m yn d atat, acha 'm ffordd!*"

Don't count on it, darling. I'm coming to you – on my way!

Aloud, Moses exclaimed: "*'n gysegr-lân cacha*!"
Which meant: "Holy shit!"

"You bastard Welshman!" roared Cerridwen. "*Adnabyddais 'i o'r cychwyn***!**
I knew it all along!"

With extraordinary rage, she put her hands upon his throat and began to squeeze.

In other circumstances, this would have been quite a treat, but Moses was shaking his head, choking and pointing and staring at an apparition which had appeared at the foot of her bed:

A woman in a Florentine gown, filled with flowers.

A woman with luscious rose-gold hair and green eyes.

A woman who was tall, and lean, and was standing and gazing at the both of them, a soft smile on her face.

"*Ciao, amore,*" she said. "*Sono io, la bella Joslian. Posso giocare, anch'io?*"

"In Welsh, please," chattered Moses.

The apparition smiled, and whispered:

"Hello, anwyliannau. Fi m 'r Lovely Joslian. Alla chwarae, hefyd?"

Which meant:

Hello, darlings. I'm the Lovely Joslian. May I play, too?

Immediately, Cerridwen and Moses fainted.

And the Lovely Joslian, as we will soon discover, quickly, intelligently, and wonderfully indecently, had her way with the both of them.

The ninth riff to Mnemosyne,
Before we proceed to the sixty-fourth canto

Forgive my oxymoron, I know it's showing, but in its own odd way, what I am about to tell you *is* a Hollywood love story:

Frank Sinatra gave a birthday party for my mother, at Jimmy McHugh's house, in the Hollywood Hills. I was nine years old, had never met the extraordinary voice, so my parents had promised to take me to the festivities.

McHugh's mansion might have been designed by Wallace Neff: it was surrounded by eucalyptus trees, elephant ear and banana plants, in Neff's Mediterranean-Meets-the Pacific, Spanish-Style, so beloved in the 'Twenties, and still elegant, in that canyon-high tropical setting.

What was the motive for The Voice to give a party for mom?

I've no idea.

Dad was very friendly with McHugh and Cahn, and Ada and Jackie Gayle, two friends of Sinatra's. Ada and Jackie often lived at McHugh's place. Jackie's brother, Juggy, was a Las Vegas comic. Jack himself was very funny, and so was Ada. Evidently Jackie and Ada had lots of lady friends, which both the singer and songwriter appreciated deeply.

In the early evening, at the party, I spent the first hour staring out of the floor-to-ceiling windows at the city below. Jimmy was playing the piano with his song-writing partner, Sammy Cahn. (Maybe that was it. Dad was still at Mercury Records, and they were plugging their tunes?)

After an hour had passed, Sinatra had not yet appeared.

"I think we ought to put Stevie to sleep," said mom, "until Frank shows up."

"Go upstairs," McHugh replied. "My bedroom's at the top of the landing, to the left."

I didn't like the idea of missing the songs and the views and the chatter, but dutifully I went upstairs with my mom, and was tucked into an enormous bed which faced a gigantic floor-to-ceiling double-window that was slightly ajar, and had an even more impressive view of the city.

The sheets were white satin.

I was very happy to be in that bed. I leaned on an elbow, watching the lights, listening to the distant music, smelling the fragrance of the evening jasmine wafting through the open window. The softness of the satin, the coolness of the evening, the faraway piano and the laughter put me to sleep, gently, as if I were a Cupid figure from "Fantasia," drifting on a satin-white cloud.

I was awakened, I don't know when, by sounds of screaming, running, a door slamming, then, suddenly the bedroom door opening and a woman rushing in, slamming the door, locking it, then leaning against it, breathing hard.

I shot up in bed, not knowing, for the moment, where I was.

The woman patted her robe, searching for cigarettes.

"Are you okay?" I asked, frightened yet curious.

She was startled, and moved quickly to the window, as if she were going to jump out. Then she turned, found her cigarettes, and held them before her as if she didn't know what to do with them.

"I'm fine," she said, shakily, and lit her cigarette, then crossed toward the bed. "I'm sorry, sweetie, I didn't mean to scare you. Are you all right?"

In the thirsty moonlight, I could see her features: her straight blonde hair, wide-set and dewy blue eyes, and busty figure. She had a wide mouth, expressive lips, and a gaze that was as curious as it was unsettling.

She sat on the bed, and gave me a hug.

"Really," she said, "everything's okay, I don't want you to be scared. 'Kay?"

I nodded.

I could feel her heart beating quickly, heavily. Her perfume was delicate, and as fresh as the jasmine beyond the window, clinging to the eucalyptus.

"You have beautiful hair," I said.

She smiled, took my hand, and unconsciously put it in her hair, but her eyes were elsewhere.

There was more shouting downstairs, the slam of a door, then silence, then the sound of footsteps coming up the stairwell. The woman held me tightly against her, frightened, but oddly, protecting me. I didn't know why.

Someone tried the door, and the woman put a hand to her lips, then held me hard, behind my neck, with her right hand, and tightened her left hand on my back, pulling me into her chest. It hurt, but it also felt good.

"Steve?" I heard. "Are you okay? Are you awake?"

"It's just my mother," I whispered, because I did not want the woman to break her hold.

"Steve?"

This time mom's call was worried, and angry.

"Everything's fine," I called, and the blonde lady let go of me, smiled at my attempted manliness, took a deep drag of her cigarette and left the side of the bed, where she had been seated.

"Open up," mom said.

The woman went to the door and whispered, "Is everything safe?"

There was a pause – clearly one of curiousity on my mother's part– what was going on? What was the woman doing, in a locked room, with her son? Then I heard mom reply, "It's okay. He's gone. Just open the door, please."

The woman did as she was told, and my mother came in.

"You have a very nice boy," said the blonde woman with the jasmine perfume, almost guiltily. Lowering her head, she quickly left the room.

Mom was staring oddly at me, and said nothing, until dad appeared.

"Come on, up on my shoulders," he ordered, coolly, as if nothing had happened.

Swiftly he picked me up, put me atop his shoulders, and carried me down the long, wide polished mahagony stairs.

Everyone was quiet: Jimmy, Ada, Jackie, and another woman crying in the corner, with the blonde lady beside her, stroking her back and her hair. The atmosphere was distinctly solemn. Neither the woman who had run into the bedroom nor the crying lady turned to us.

"You'll get to meet Frankie another time," said Ada to me, quietly, and we said goodnight, and went to our car, and mom sat me on her lap, and dad drove down Outpost Drive, and onto Cahuenga Pass, then onto Barham Boulevard, and once again I fell asleep.

Continuation of the ninth riff to Mnemosyne, Before we proceed to the sixty-fourth canto

The next day neither dad nor mom would tell me what had happened.

Eventually I forgot, although the image of the blonde lady standing by the window, the moonlight illuminating her long blonde hair, the quick nervous moments of her hands as they searched for a cigarette, the smell of jasmine and of her perfume would occasionally creep into my consciousness.

When I reminded my parents of the evening, however, they would say nothing.

A quickie riff, legato'd to the above, before we swing into sixty-fourth canto

Nine years later, during the winter of my freshman year at Dartmouth College, I returned to Los Angeles for the Christmas holidays.

On the day I arrived, Dad asked, "Are you too tired to go to the Crescendo this evening? Lenny Bruce's alternating with Count Basie."

"You're joking, right?"

Had I been in bed with pneumonia, after a twenty-four hour no-sleep flight from Australia, I would have dragged myself that same evening to that same nightclub!

The surreality of Dartmouth's "Hanover plain," from an illustration by Currier and Ives, contrasting with the zap of the Sunset Strip and Basie and Lenny Bruce, was not lost on me.

I'd gone to the Renaissance Club, mid-Strip, in Hollywood, every weekend during my junior and senior years in high school, to hear Lenny Bruce, who alternated with Harold Land, Cannonball Adderley, or Miles. That was a major part of my education, which I had carried with me to Dartmouth.

At the staid and moribund Sanborn House, where the English Department held its late afternoon teas, with the poet Jack Hirshman, who was an assistant professor, and a classmate-musician, Chris Swanson, I put together a poetry-and-jazz session of Kenneth Patchen's work. I don't recall any of the English Department faculty attending, but lots of students did.

It was the kind of thing that had begun to take over the Strip.

Chris told the audience of English students at our presentation, "Tomorrow the Hanover police are going to close down Sanborn House, because they don't have a cabaret license."

It made him few friends among the English professors.

The Unicorn, an L.A. coffee house in the European model, was blind-siding the elegant Crescendo in popularity.

The Renaissance Club itself, all burlap seats and plate-glass windows overlooking a flickering Hollywood, was attracting great musicians.

I was caught in the middle, because I was raised with jazz, and what we now call The Great American Songbook, but I also loved the Renaissance Club and the Unicorn, and hung out there, and put on a jazz-play there as well.

I'd begun to have my poetry and prose published in "Coastlines," an L.A. literary journal, whose editors also found the Unicorn a good place to be.

But I also wanted to hear the big bands, the great singers, the acts that wouldn't be happening at the Unicorn or the Renaissance Club: Chris Connors, Stan Kenton, Shorty Rogers, the Sauter-Finegan orchestra, Basie, and the most extraordinary performer in the world, Sammy Davis, Jr. Going back to Hanover, New Hampshire, after that environment, was passing strange.

How had I ended up at Dartmouth College in the first place?

Dad had had heard that an old Party acquaintance, Budd Shulberg, had gone there, and had written that the experience was immensely formative.

Dad had made me apply, even though I was going through enough formative experiences in LA, and had already been accepted to the

Drama Department at Carnegie Tech, which was, at that time, the best school in the United States for theater.

I wrote the application to Dartmouth in pencil.

I could care less.

Besides, it was thirty days after the application date.

When the form asked for my religion, I wrote: Anabapist, and Lonely.

I was accepted within a week.

I had never even read the brochure.

After heavy urging from my parents, and polite phone calls from Dartmouth faculty and staff, I agreed to go. When I arrived, I was horrified to discover it was an all-male school.

When I called dad from the lobby of the Hanover Inn, and told him I was now surrounded by young men, and not by any women, he couldn't stop laughing. Even he hadn't read the brochure.

"What am I going to do?" I said. "I don't know any women up here, in the Northeast, in the mountains!"

"If they're to be found out," said mom, "I'm sure you'll find them."

"Meanwhile," said Dad, hardly speaking for the laughter. "I bet--- you'll have ---great--- *classes*!" and broke up.

To revise Jerome Kern:

As an Anabaptist, indeed: I was never lonelier.

A triplet riff, still legato'd to the above, Before we get down to the sixty-fourth canto

At the Crescendo, during the break between Basie and Bruce, I asked Dad, "Remember that party at Jimmy McHugh's, nine years ago? When I was supposed to meet Frank Sinatra, and instead went upstairs to bed?"

Dad hadn't remembered, so I refreshed his memory.

"You never would tell me what happened," I continued. "You even said: "I'll tell you when you're older," which is something you rarely said to me about anything."

Dad smiled.

Shrugged.

Then waved at his old friend, Marshall Royal, Basie's tenor sax man.

Marshall came over to the table, and he and dad began to reminisce. I loved their rap, but still wanted an answer to the event.

Lenny Bruce came on-stage, and began to count "the number of spades, kikes, slant-eyes, spics" in the audience. Several people immediately walked out. "Whoops," he exclaimed. "There they go, folks. A couple of angry Gentiles just hit the road, but it doesn't really matter 'cause I got two potato-eating Feds taking notes in the front row, all set and ready to do my act for the judge. Hey, Paddy, how's Queen Kong?" he called. "I know your X is for Xavier, 'cause you were named after Cugat, right? but your boss, Mister Hoover, the Chief, right? --- Hey, what does the "J" stand for? It can't be Jewboy 'cause he's got the nostrils of a nig-nog, so maybe it stands for...*Jackson*! Yay-bo! Jackson Edgar Hoover! 'Lissen here, Jackson: we got the dago cornered with the *curveh.* You want to let the poor bastard *come* first, or should we just say fuck it and shoot him in the ass?"

It was so fast, his delivery, the voices so perfect, and the haiku-like imagery so precise you sighed, shaking your head in awe, before you began to laugh. He was that good.

Marshall was shaking his head.

'The man is crazy," he said.

'Yeah,' grinned dad.

'Last night he came out with this guitar-player," Marshall continued. "Eric Miller, you know the cat? and he's chained to him, and the both of 'em come running onto the stage, Eric's yelling, "We gotta go this way!" and Lenny's yelling, "No, nigger, we goin' that way!" and they're doing "The Defiant Ones," and they lose half the audience in five seconds until Lenny rushes to the exit and blocks it with his body and Eric's, and he's yelling: "Listen, you cocksuckers: you gotta understand what we're doin', we're bringin' harmony to the world. Harmony, you sonsabitches! You know how to bring harmony to this joint? Listen to me: It takes both the white keys...." And he holds up his chains, and Eric's hand shoots up: "And the dark keys!" Immediately he loses another twenty people."

"Brilliant," laughed dad, his head between his legs, his feet going up and down in a tap.

"Yeah, but, diggit: everybody loves "*The Defiant Ones*" in this town," said Marshall. "Big Hollywood statement about segregation. Stanley Kramer's a god here. And there's Lenny, showin' it up to be the piece of phoney baloney feel-good shit that it is, shoving it to 'em, right, here, in the Crescendo, man, in the heart of Hollywood!The cat is definitely heading for a fall."

"You don't think he's brilliant?" said dad, laughing still.

"I don't doubt that," said Marshall Royal. "but he's also crazy, and he's gonna fall hard."

Now Lenny was explaining why words were more dangerous than the atom bomb, but that they could be defanged once we faced them and took away their potency by constant repetition. Thus "nigger, kike, spic, potato-eater," etc.

I never really accepted that argument, because I didn't want words ever to be defanged.

I still get upset when I hear the word "nigger," and especially from African-Americans. Young kids, black *and* white, who don't give a damn about history.

"Okay," said Lenny, and pointed to the two F.B.I. agents, who were busily taking notes. "Let's talk about blow jobs. Do we like them, guys? Or are the chicks who give them nothing but a coupla *shikse* cocksuckers, 'cause Jewish chicks are too...'Mmm, I'm not so sure, Marty, I'll touch it, but do I have to eat it?' Where sex is concerned, man, there are no barriers. Or, rather" – sounding like a March of Times newsreel - "let me put it to you this way, men: if you had the choice of being done by Lena Horne or Marjorie Main, who would you choose? And here's one for the ladies, God bless 'em: if you had the choice of being schwantzed by Harry Belafonte...or Adolph Menjou..."

By now the entire Basie band, standing against the wall of the Crescendo, was howling with laughter, while four more couples left the nightclub.

"You're not funny!" yelled an exiteer. "Miscegenation is a serious business!"

"That's why I'm in Hollywood, shmuck!" Lenny answered. "It's the only place that stands behind what it preaches. C'mere, Eric..." And Lenny stood behind his black partner and began to make pumping motions. "You seem like a nice black boy," he said, in a snaky Southern accent. "New to the yard. Now I'm gonna make you an offer you can't refuse, so stand still, gawdammit and bend over...Brought to you by Abe Lastfogel and the Willliam Morris Agency."

No one can ever begin to demonstrate the swiftness of his improvisation, his ability to turn the nightclub into a war zone, using the major themes of American history, popular culture, and the social tensions of the 50's, exposing all the cultural and sexual hypocrisies, the moral cant.

I don't care how many drugs he took, or what his private life was like – "it ain't my business, Jim" - he was brilliant, outrageous, spot-on, a great jazz voice, and so dreadfully needed during the greyness and dread of the Cold War, the Eisenhower era.

I hated Death for taking him away.

I would have loved to have heard him on Reagan, the Great Communicator who broke the unions and lied about Iran-Contra and who was gaga half the time in office; or on William Jefferson Clinton, the self-appointed grand old man of the Democratic Party and former president who helped Reagan destroy American labor and then did in American manufacturing with the passage of NAFTA, and who gave happy hunting notices to the pirate banks and Wall Street privateers with the recall of the Glass-Steagall Act; or on the Bushes, father and son (and who knows who else is presently hiding in the bushes?) and who were proof that Reagan was not the worst president in our history; (of the two, Bush Junior gets my ultimate vote, and what an original vote it is, thanks to the most reactionary Supreme Court we've had in over one hundred years, and which has proved once again that you don't *need to be smart* to not have any justice.)

As for Barry Santoro aka Barack Obama, just ask Larry Summers...why, you ask?

The Basie band and jazz was the only reason I missed America, when I lived abroad, or when I seemed to be living in exile, in Hanover, New Hampshire.

A riff back to the head,
Then off we go to sixty-fourth canto!

Dad and I drove back home that evening, after the Crescendo, going the long way, on Mulholland Drive. Watching the Valley lights, the city lights, the insane landscape of an equally insane town, dad said, “Okay. Now it can be told. Here’s what happened at Jimmy McHugh’s, that evening.”

He paused, and pulled the car into a small parking place, beside a woodland fire station which overlooked the Valley.

Then he turned to me:

“Remember when we put you to bed, because Frank hadn’t arrived yet? Well, next door to that bedroom, which was Jimmy’s, was another bedroom. About a half hour after you went to sleep, Ava Gardner arrived. She was going with Frank at the time. I’m sure you know that. And she’d come to the party with Lana Turner.”

“That was the blonde lady?” I asked, surprised.

Dad nodded.

“You’ve got to be kidding,” I whispered, and remembered that *film noir* image of the blonde lady with the jasmine perfume, standing by the window, lit by the moon and fumbling with her cigarettes.

Dad nodded.

“Shit, and I was nine years old,” I whistled. “How very sad.”

“Anyway,” he said, with a slight edge to his voice; he was on a roll and would not be interrupted. “Frank came in about forty minutes later, and asked where Ava was, and nobody knew, so he went upstairs, and evidently he caught her in bed with Lana, and that’s when there was all the shouting. He threw Ava out of the bed, and Lana went running into Jimmy’s bedroom and locked the door, and then Frank started bawling, and ran out of the house, and that was the end of the party.”

"So that was Lana Turner," I continued. "Wow. And the lady who was crying, in the corner, after we came downstairs, that was Ava Gardner?"

"Indeed, she was, and still is."

"Hmm," I said.

And thought: Women are definitely not like most men.

I was thinking beyond their sexuality, however, and into an arena or psychological state more profound, which I knew was there, but which, at the time, I could not understand: the many ways women comforted each other, so foreign to men they could not deal with it and became so frustrated and impotent that all they could do was hit out, or cry, or run away. Yet another rationalization for rape, war, and the existence of the spiritual Virgin...

We continued to stare at the Valley, but this time in silence.

After a few minutes I asked: "How come you never did any arrangements for Sinatra?"

"You kidding?" Dad snorted, then laughed. "I'd be too afraid! Nelson says he has to medicate himself before every recording session! He's exaggerating, obviously, but the point is Sinatra's brilliant and not afraid to put you down in front of everybody if he doesn't like what you do - whether he's right or wrong. It doesn't matter if it's Riddle or the producer or any one of the musicians. He does *one take*, that's it, and everything's got to be right on target. If somebody other than he flubs, he won't let 'em off the hook. I have tremendous respect for the man's talent, but life's too short. I've been with guys like that before, but who had none of his talent: Tony Martin's the worst. Unlike Sinatra, he's *always* wrong. He's just a bully. Crosby was an absolute prick. He used to pick on Manny Klein all the time, and Manny's one of the best trumpet-players in the business. 'Hey, Jew-boy," Crosby'd yell at him, and nobody'd say anything, they'd just have to sit in the pit and take it. Dinah Shore was that way, too. An absolute bitch on wheels to work with. I feel: *just shut up and make the music. We all know what we're doing.* Anyway, there you are. That's what happened. End of story."

But not quite.

Twenty years later, while living in Rome, I received a phone-call from Artie Shaw's former business manager, and our family friend, Benton Cole.

"Do you mind taking a client of mine around that beautiful city of yours?" asked Benton. "She's doing a guest appearance on a tv show there, and all of her all friends are dead, and she says she's bored."

"Sure," I said. "Just give her our number."

Several weeks later, I got a call from a woman with a deep, husky voice.

"Is this Steve Geller? Benton Cole gave me your number."

The voice was familiar: rich, throaty, and filled with a life well-lived.

"Indeed. And who is this?"

"Ava Gardner. I'm having dinner at Piperno's."

"Inside or outside?" I asked, smiling to myself.

There was a pause, and she said: "Outside. Why?"

I went to the window of our apartment, which was an *attico-super attico* in the historical center of Rome. The top two floors. It looked onto a tiny square, where *Ristorante Piperno* had indoor and outdoor tables.

"Because I'm looking at you right now. Third floor window."

And I waved.

"Come right down," she yelled.

Which I did.

Her eyes were startling, their shape and color.

Wrap-around purple eyes.

Rich, sculpted lips.

Extraordinarily feminine features, and with a gaze that was both comic and tough. She laughed easily, and you had to laugh as well, because her laughter was full and infectious. She was the easiest woman to fall in love with, and I was immediately in love.

"Sit down, Steve, and order for me. I'd eat the whole menu if I could, it just sounds so good."

"The San Pietro fish," I said. "And the *carciofi alla Judea.*"

"S'ior Jay-lor," said the maitre-d'. "*Certo. Anche tu?*"

"*Si, senz'altro. Per me lo stesso,*" I replied, ordering the same thing for myself.

She poured me a glass of wine, from a good bottle of Bertolo, and then poured one for herself.

"We've met before," I said.

"Cheers to our meeting before," she replied, and clinked glasses. "Where was that? I don't remember."

"At Jimmy McHugh's," I replied.

The Bertolo was cold, dry, perfect.

"Really?"

"Twenty-seven or twenty-eight years ago," I said.

"Can't say I recall," she replied, staring hard at me, trying to remember.

"Frank was giving a birthday party for my mother?"

"Who's your mother?"

"Harriet Geller."

"Wait a minute," she frowned, and nodded. "Your dad's a composer, right? Yeah, Benton told me, he was in the Shaw band?"

"Yes."

"Yeah, Benton told me. My friend Lana was married to Artie, for two minutes. Yeah, I remember the party. But I don't remember *you*. Christ, you must have been a fetus."

I had another sip, smacked my lips, looked at the rim of the cup:

"Nope. I was sleeping in Jimmy's bed. Evidently you were in the next room with Artie's ex."

Her eyes widened.

Then narrowed.

Then she started to laugh, and raucously.

"So *you* were the kid in the bed!" she said. "Of course!"

She laughed again, then suddenly cocked her head, and gazed at me as if she were watching me through the cannon of a Sherman tank:

"You just set me up," she said. "You lit-tul prick."

"*Precisely*," I replied. "And that was the problem. I was such a lit-tul prick I couldn't get into the act. Miss Gardner, I count that, as one of the bleakest, if not the most tragic moment of my life. So near, and yet so far. And I never forgot Ms. Turner's perfume. Still, even though it's a nearly two decades later, you *must* let me kiss your hand."

She grabbed my head, and pulled me to her and gave me a big wet kiss on the mouth, then pushed me back into my seat and said: "Now go fuck *yourself*, doll-face, 'cause you sure as hell ain't gonna fuck *me*."

And the both of us laughed, and had a wonderful meal, and if anyone says anything against the memory of Ava Gardner, prepare – as Kurt Vonnegut, Jr. has written elsewhere – "for a knock on the door."

End of my Hollywood love story.

The sixty-fourth canto

RPM 1st Category, or Rescue People Mission, was a holo-disc read by a BBC female announcer, dictated by HaShem and/or Adonai to one of several recording angels. It came with the following instructions:

....

INSTRUCTIONS for RPM 1st Category:

It is crucial for the Rescuer to understand the tortured souls' ORIGINAL INTENTION TO INCARNATE, as well as his or her background, in order to affect an appropriate rescue.

If THE INTENTION TO INCARNATE is not understood, the rescuer will spend eternities trying to decipher the codes hidden within a jumbled life and distorted psyche.

....

Having the holo-disc was an enormous responsibility, and certainly came with risks, which is why HaShem and Adonai had chosen the Piatniki, or "trance-substantiated Muses," to do the job:

The Muses-turned-Piatniki understood ***INTENTION*** better than any other creation of Adonai's and HaShem's.

That's why they were Muses.

They understood what could happen when that Intention, as it were, went off the rails.

That's also why they were great Artists.

And also why they had become Immortals.

Sometimes, however, a few Piatniki were themselves paradoxical tortured souls:

For example, Ezra Pound and T.S. Eliot had desired Intentions, which had gone magnificently off the rails, albeit, occasionally, magnificently expressed.

Ezra Pound (and his *Cantos)* was one of the Great of the Fucked-Up Piatniks.

And for one and a half days, T.S. Eliot (and his *Waste Land)* came in (a distant) second, before Adonai and HaShem let to him go. Eliot himself had been given an entire day to prove himself a Piatnik, but had failed. Instead, he had become another poor soul, and was returned to the mass of humanity.

(This might be explored in a future Sequel to *Jews Beyond Jupiter*, and which will star William Boyd as T.S. Eliot, and Gabby Hayes as Eliot's sidekick, Ezra Pound).

On the other hand, unlike Eliot, Pound had proven himself a comical and flamboyant exception to the other Piatniks: his mind held a variety of skewed Intentions, drawn from a variety of sources. His inner chaos gave birth to many diverse ideas. And it was Adonai Herself who said:

"We'll have to keep that red-bearded anti-semitic Idaho shit among the Piatniki: he was, after all, the one who discovered the works of Joyce and his wife the compositions of Vivaldi. For that alone, we have to applaud that slimebag. And you do have to admit, he does have an odd, shrill sense of humor, unlike his friend, Eliot, who may be accused of many things, but never of possessing a sense of humor – unless you think his American attempts at Anglican dryness and despair a laugh a minute."

So down went Eliot, among the rest of humankind, while Adonai and HaShem kept Pound upstairs, among the Piatniki.

They knew, however, never to give him any Rescue missions. Although now a Piatnik, Ezra was not allowed to be part of the RPM because of the violence of his anti-semitism, which was simply a violence against his own nature and against the children of Israel, which was the nature of much of mankind.

Pound himself was a Jew, from the tribe of Judah, but didn't know it yet.

Adonai and HaShem were simply waiting for the fun moment, when they'd let him have it.

Eliot's anti-semitism had not been as violent as Pound's; it had been drearier, more conventional, mean-spirited and exclusivist. It had none of the wretched, and lunatical literary braggadocio of Pound.

That was understandable,of course, since Eliot himself was part of the *erev rav*, the Mixed Multitude that had followed Moses out of Egypt. He had been a sorcerer, an expert in spells. He worked in the dark, like a pair of claws, on the sea-floor.

The only time HaShem and Adonai had thought of using Pound as a Rescue missionary was for Hitler and Mussolini, not that they saw any future for those two Axis luminaries as potential Piatniki!

They also thought it might be a treat for Eliot, that first and only day he appeared among the Piatniki, but Eliot had immediately bored everybody. The other missionaries themselves had voted to dump him.

Why had HaShem and Adonai thought of bringing Eliot back, if only for a moment? The answer was obvious: so he could bore the hell out of Hitler and Mussolini, adding to the *delices* of their eternal torments!

HaShem and Adonai had a good laugh with that thought, but of course decided to do nothing.

To HaShem and Adonai, however, Pound was outrageous, dazzling, phenomenally fat-headed, and rarely boring. When he arrived on Piatnik, as a Piatnik, he tried to give the Fascist salute.

But with eight new legs instead of two arms, he merely entangled himself and fell all over the place.

It was great fun to watch.

To entrust another psyche to Pound was unthinkable.

The sixty-fifth canto

RPM 5th, 4th and 3rd Categories were simple to treat: generally, they referred to mistaken ideas, and could easily be corrected.

RPM 2nd Category was more difficult to deal with, because emotional cues and life histories were involved. The rescuer had to dig deep into past lives.

Hardest of all, however, was the *RPM 1st Category*, which is where Shakespeare was about to find himself: mistaken ideas, emotional cues and life histories, as well as dreams, fantasies and future world-views were all mixed together, like a *frutta di mare pasta*, in the tortured soul.

The sixty-sixth canto

What was the job of the Rescue People Mission 1st Category missionary?

The missionary had to enter the fantasies, dreams and convictions of the tortured soul, to see the logic and emotional through-lines, and to straighten them out.

What were the specific tasks of the Rescue People Mission 1st Category missionary?

1) From the psychic materials of the Demented One, the missionary had to:

a. construct a biography.

b. define the landscape of that biography.

c. construct a picture of the demented's present moral, intellectual, emotional and psychic scapes.

e. distinguish the influences, both positive, negatively positive, positive-negative, and wholly negative in life, dream, desire, self-projection, and in life themes.

f) demonstrate how the Demented One made external and internal mechanisms of choice;

2) Once this was done, the missionary had to create dramatic or comic situations to test the Demented One's tortured soul, analyzing his or her response to these new situational elements, and then:

3) The Missionary had to fine-tune the gestalt.

4) Finally, hardest of all, the soul-picture that emerged had to be adjusted to that person's original Intention, as presented to HaShem and/or Adonai, expressed by the proto-Demented One, in the holo-disc.

For that original Intention was HaShem's and/or Adonai's contract with the soul of the tortured figure.

That was Their agreement with the pre-demented soul.

Did this agreement deny free will and improvisation and self-contradiction? Not at all.

However, let us not be confused:

Everything is much clearer in the World of Ideas than in the World of Nature.

Things get fucked up much faster around here.

An example:

For this particular incarnation, I have agreed to concentrate on My Desire to become a Composer.

If Comic-Book Art and Cross-country skiing come up, I must not pay much attention to them, but must remain fully involved in My Desire to become a Composer.

After all, if I don't concentrate on Composing Music, why had I bothered to incarnate at all?

In otherwords: *all that matters in this life is the fulfillment of my original Intention.* And if I forget it, or refuse to do it, or am side-tracked, I become screwed-up.

The screws-up - for there were billions - had led to the creation of the Muses and the RPM.

The sixty-seventh canto

The 1st category missionaries were those who understood human nature and saw all its artistic possibilities.

They were those who lived completely by intelligence and imagination:

Shakespeare and Dickens, Goethe, Austen and Proust, Hugo and Merrill, Dante and Rabelais, Swift and the Powells (Anthony and Dawn), Li Po, Rumi, Walt Whitman and Louis Armstrong - top of the line First Categorists, along with Tolstoi, Chekhov, Dostoievsky, Musil, Wilde, Joyce, Chaplin, S.J. Perelman and Luis Bunuel.

These names should give you an idea of how screwed-up were all Category Ones.

If it took a Dickens, Dostoievsky or a Whitman to straighten out the psyche of a human being, rest assured, that being was far from being normal!

The sixty-eighth canto

Why had Shakespeare been given the soul of Dr. Herschel Fisch to repair?

The reason was simple: Shakespeare's problem with Dr. Herschel Fisch was a personal one, and yet the kind which each Piatnik Rescue Member had encountered at one time or another: *a critic or viewer or reader who had so desperately identified with the artist that he or she had lost his or her own identity.*

In the case of Dr. Herschel Fisch, of course, it was much worse.

In spite of his anarchic persona as critic, he was still an academic, and therefore by circumstance, if not by nature, *already institutionalized.*

Though on the surface a supreme maverick, his highly regarded opinion had been created, in word-blocks, as a shadow of the academic institution itself.

Worst of all, he had begun to think *critically* as if he were a poet, and poetically as if he were an unknown critic!

He had begun using the metaphor, God Forbid!, to make categorical comparisons or judgments.

One of the few poets, of course, who had done the same thing was the one poet whom Fisch heartily despised, and that was probably because, although very different, he was also so much like him: the aforementioned Ezra Pound, of Hailey, Idaho.

That being the case, then why hadn't HaShem or Adonai sent Ezra, for the first time in his transformation as a piatnik, into Fisch's psyche?

For the simple reason that They knew that Ezra and Herschel would, the both of them, *fuck each other up,* and even more than they were fucked up already.

Besides, William Shakespeare, and not Ezra Pound, was Herschel Fisch's artistic model, his Muse.

All of Shakespeare's work was inside Fisch, and all of Fisch's metaphors reflected his own and Shakespeare's artistic and creative gluttony.

So, in an act of poetic license, HaShem and Adonai made sure that Shakespeare himself entered the belly of the Fisch, in whose stomach he would have the time, if not the *locus spiritualis,* to figure it all out for the demented critic.

In the Belly of the Fisch,
Part the Firft:

"Now this ill-wresting world is grown so bad,
Mad slanderers by mad ears believed be."

How is it possible to live underwater without any breathing apparatus? How is it possible to see dozens of octopi climbing up and down ladders in an endless library whose books stretch to infinity and who never seem to get wet? How is it possible to hear an orca whale reciting Shakespeare's fortieth sonnet and comparing it with Augustine's description of his pagan youth, followed by Keats' "La Belle Dame Sans Merci," with a chorus of castrated barracudas singing:

"I saw pale kings and princes too,
Pale warriors, death-pale were they all;
They cried—"La Belle Dame sans Merci
Hath thee in thrall!"

Then, suddenly, from Goethe's "Faust, Part II:"

Faust: Lilith? Who is that?

Mephistopheles: Adam's wife, his first. Beware of her. Her beauty's one boast is her dangerous hair. When Lilith winds it tight around young men, She doesn't soon let go of them again.

An octopus, his arms entwined about a volume of the *Zohar*, called to the Orca:

"Further, go back further: She's the Qlipoth in Malkuth. The shells of materialism and self-aggrandisement. She's without thought. Hurry! Go back! Augustine, Shakespeare, Goethe, Keats are too modern. Go back further!"

Several magnificent koi came swimming up to the orca in the library, at the enormous table filled with books, and around which the octopi were depositing further volumes:

"Adam wanted to be on top," they said. "But Lilith wanted to be on top. Lilith was right. Adam was wrong. If he'd had the wisdom to let the Female express her power, there'd be no missionaries in the missionary position, and therefore no nuclear weapons or global warming."

A swarm of crabs clawed their way atop the desk and said:

"God gave Adam dominion over everything. He could fuck any way he wanted! It's Adam's call! What does that have to do with global warming?"

Pythagoras, in the form of a Portuguese man-of-war, appeared ("for the colors alone," he said – "I never sting.") and sang: "The one and the two produces the three. Idea and Imagination produces Form, which realizes the Idea Imaginatively. Nothing ever need be dysfunctional."

And, as he swam away, he was pummeled then torn apart by seven hammerhead sharks.

"If you're not part of the solution," they growled, "you're part of the problem."

Yet Pythagoras returned, this time in the form of a Crab Nebula mussel:

"One plus two still equals three.

Even in the deepest reaches of the galaxy," he chanted.

The Orca retched, the library disappeared, and the sound was so pitiful that even Shakespeare was moved.

In the Belly of the Fisch,
Part the Fecond:

"For I have sworn thee fair, an thought thee bright,
Who art as black as hell, as dark as night."

From Wm. Shakespeare to HaShem and Adonai:

One) Dr. Fisch lives in constant terror, in the most primal depths of self. He uses the world's knowledge and wisdom - Augustine, me, Goethe, etc. - to try to understand why he is so attracted to and terrified by the female. He doesn't know whether to top her or be topped by her. As a result, he castrates himself daily, then grows a new prick with each new book he writes.

Two a) He creates the same dynamic as the Church:
extra ecclesiam, nullus omnio Salvatur."
'Outside of the church, there is positively no Salvation.'

Two b) Fisch's thesis, however is:
"Ultra universitas litterae illic est haud salus" –
'Beyond world literature, there is no salvation.'

Three) He uses world literature as a rationalization to buttress his terror:
(i.e., Lilith wanted to be on top.
God gave man dominion.
Either/Or.)

Four a) Fisch is anxious, confused, unable to move. Images of grasping fears, of terrifying warriors, of the most attractive woman in man's mind - octopi, barracudas, crabs, hammerhead sharks - dominate his inner life. ***And yet he casts***

himself as an orca, and all the other creatures serve him in his internalized underwater library, though they do terrify him.

*Four b) Present, however, is Pythagoras, perhaps the most beautiful of all the sea-creatures, saying the world is "**neither/nor, but yes and no and otherwise, and it is the tension between yes and no which produces a solution: which is otherwise.**"*

Four c) And no matter how many times or how horribly Pythagoras is destroyed, he keeps reappearing and saying the same thing:

1) Father and Mother produce the Child.

2) Intelligence and Imagination create a Work, and although the Work reflects the Intelligence and Imagination of its authors, it is novel, and therefore soon possesses a life and influence of its own.

Five) Numbers act. They do not remain static. In his world, stasis is the only way to play it safe so that he needn't deal with Woman or HaShem or Adonai or planetary forces. But they keep bubbling up, and threatening to drown him, and he keeps reading harder and faster from more sources ("universitas litterae") to stay alive or afloat; to rationalize indecision, which is his fear. Paradoxically, he becomes smarter, appears more cosmopolitan, probably is the greatest reader who ever lived, but he can't put it all together.

*Six) Fisch keeps quoting my sonnets: thus far, he believes I think that the world is so dreadful that lies live as truths (Sonnet 140); that appearances exist to deceive (Sonnet 147). He trusts my work, but uses it as a rationalization to keep from acting. (Personal note: I'm waiting to read "**Those parts of thee that the world's eye doth view/Want nothing that the thought of hearts can mind,**" knowing that he'll use that idea as a rationalization - or an order from me? - **not to act upon anything.** It's Sonnet 69, incidentally, an auspicious sign from which, most certainly, he will dash!)*

I think, though I cannot say definitively that I believe or know, that his meeting me drove him crazy.

Why?

Because I do the very things he is incapable of doing: I eat well, and adore Nature enough to learn from Her, and I fuck madly, and I like listening to people tell stories, even if they're nothing but lies about themselves.

Seven) Fisch closes his eyes when he eats. He shoves food in his mouth and never tastes it. He is probably a virgin. He is even timid around teen-age boys.

Eight) He listens only to dead people, whose words of course are eternal, but who never talk back, which means that he spends his life, in effect, talking to himself.

Conclusion: why does he do this?

Answer: I'm not yet sure.

Action to take: Dive, dive, down again, down I descend in the ocean's depths.

My love to You Both.

William Shakespeare

Post-scriptum: Lo, and he is terrified of suicide ("To be or not to be") because Pythagoras keeps returning to him, no matter how violently he is martyred. So what, to Poor Fisch, constitutes suicide? That is the question.

And that's probably why he loves Hamlet more than any other work of mine, and also why he misreads it so brilliantly.

Post-post scriptum: Have you ever considered the notion that I'm looking at a man from the vantage point of eternity, which point of view may likely be wrong? As Fisch regarded me and my work from the vantage point of the 24th Century?

On the other hand, if stories are eternal, and their themes immortal, then it probably doesn't matter. The particular elements fade (the specific Elizabethan language), but the characters, situations, themes and, paradoxically, a great deal of the poetry, remain.

In the Belly of the Fisch,
Part the Third:

"Say that thou didst forsake me for some fault,
And I will comment upon that offense;"

Shakespeare wanted to know why Fisch feared women.

Shakespeare wanted to know why Fisch lived in a world of stasis, generated by fear.

Shakespeare wanted to know why Fisch used the wisdom of the world to rationalize his own immobility.

Shakespeare knew there was a tale here.

Once told, Shakespeare's job would be to separate Herschel's dreams and fantasies from the poor man's external life.

Shakespeare knew that once he had the answers to these questions, he would have to pry his own work away from Fisch so that the Doctor would no longer rely upon old reading habits – even if it meant that Shakespeare lost his greatest reader.

He'd never thought about that.

He'd never really cared.

The play was the thing. The immediacy of the event.

The truth was: if Will had the chance to act Adam or King Hamlet or the Prologue to Henry V, he was happier than if he had seen all of his plays published in one large Folio!

He'd always adored performance, and liked to lurk upstage to feel the audience responding to the drama's events. He loved the laughter, the awe, the wonder, the recognition of the different levels of his words.

And he liked acting and actors. The Magic of Transformation.

Of course he was Catholic. Rome knew how to put on a show.

The Tudors were still writing their own arrogant first act.

The Puritans, on the other hand, were pure Malvolio, or Ill Will. Good riddance to that lot!

But the Jews, thought Shakespeare, there's the rub. They seemed to see through it all. Or, as Dr. Fisch said: the Children of Israel knew how to read only too well:

While HaShem made up the rules for life, Adonai taught her children how to read into them.

That must be the door that needs prying, thought Shakespeare.

What kind of Jew, or Child of Israel, was Dr. Herschel Fisch?

In the Belly of the Fisch,
Part the Fourth:

"For thee, against myself I'll vow debate,"

Shakespeare began to see Fisch's thoughts and feelings:

A contrarian.

Whatever you're against, I'll consider being for, or will find a different avenue altogether.

The world isn't what you make it. Not at all.
The world isn't what anyone makes it.
The world might even be isn't!

Or the nonworld might even be is, in which case, "we are such stuff as dreams are made of; our little life is rounded with a sleep." Stop-------No Shakespeare allowed.

Mommy says.
Daddy says consider.
Baby Herschel says something else.
And said something else stops mommy and daddy completely.

Mommy is the home, sets the rules.

Daddy works, comes home, goes away to a lady sometimes and mommy cries and takes it out on Baby Herschel and tells him how he should behave with women and what she would do to him if she ever found out he was unfaithful, whatever that means.

Daddy says people behave in many different ways to make them get through the day because life is very hard.

Fuck the both of them, mommy and daddy.

Read.

The more you read, the more you realize that even everybody in literature is behaving like mommy and daddy.

But what makes it different is the language, their perfect colors and rhythms, which means, their ideal poetry.

And what makes the poetry magic is how things that don't seem to go together suddenly go together. How "a morning flatters the mountain tops, kisses the green meadows, gilds pale streams with alchemy." Morning becomes a person, kissing and flattering and making magic.

Words show how everything has breath, spirit, life, consciousness.

It's all connected, words, rhythms, Nature, man, God, Goddess.

And then there's the tension of the ideas in the poetry, in the language, in the stories.

He got all that, Fisch did.
It took time, of course, but it wasn't all that difficult.
He didn't play stickball or get involved with girls. That way he'd get it all.

But there was something else, the thing that produced it, the creativity, which was intelligence and imagination in a particular form, or creating a particular form in which to express itself.

That was something he just couldn't get.

It was a mystery he couldn't solve.

So he spoke of writers as esoteric priests. And sometimes he turned them into saints and prayed to them. And sometimes he turned them into healers and asked for their help.

But none of them answered.

The only consolation he had was when he turned the pages of a book and entered the world of imagination and intelligence and forms.

But that mystery, that sacred trust between the magician and his god, or the poet and his muse, or the Artist and the Supernal, why couldn't he, Herschel Fisch, enter into that contract as well?

Others who had been trained to read didn't care as much as he. They learned Old English. They read into the Oxford English Dictionary. They immersed themselves in ancientness. Or Russian. Or Slavonic texs. Or the Augustan Age. Or the Eddas.

But they didn't care, the way he did. They saw themselves as careerists.

They saw themselves as monks in institutions.

They jailed themselves within their texts, within their walls.

They created a club, and put the club within the institution. They sealed themselves up.

Dr. Herschel Fisch may have been a sealed-up careerist monk in an instution, but at least he had a Confessor: Shakespeare.

The others, instead, they had a Department Chair, who had a Dean, who had a President, who had a Chancellor, who had either Trustees or a State legislature.

Dr. Herschel Fisch needed to possess the idea of the Muse or the God or the Dark Lady or the Young Man or whoever or whatever motivated Shakespeare. That way he could inherit passion.

The others needed to possess tenure, or a MacArthur grant. They needed to publish.

Herschel Fisch published anyway.

He needed an audience. His classroom.

The others could care less about the classroom. That was the least of the institution.

Dr. Fisch's passionhad terrified them, so they shipped him off to Mercury, but he returned, and appeared ready to go crazy.

Whicht was when he met Shakespeare, and had begun the relationship by pissing on his own han-----

Swiftly, suddenly Shakespeare had an insight, a flash, a cartoon bubble with a lightbulb.

*He whispered, "Take that, Ben Jonson: "**δεν βρέθηκαν αποτελέσματα! Παρακαλώ δοκιμάστε πάλι!!"***

*Then: "**Adversus solem ne loquitor.**"*

So much for small Latin and less Greek!

In the Belly of the Fisch,
Part the Fifth:

"Me for my dumb thoughts, speaking in effect"

William Shakespeare to HaShem and Adonai:

Either:

*"**I have the answer! I have seen the sun and it moves.**"*

Or:

*"**Don't argue against the sun!**"*

I asked myself: what kind of Jew, or child of Israel, is Dr. Fisch? I discovered that he is a highly neurotic intellectual who had jumped from the natural world to the world of poetry and literature without any intervening life experience. He collected authors and ideas the way children collect rocks and seashells: but being neither scientist nor artist, until he discovered my plays and poems, he'd been living in a grab-bag of analogies and eccentric, albeit tantalizing, metaphors.

*He understood one thing: that nothing is as it appears, and that anything can be a metaphor for anything else, and that language is natural **and** magical **and** spiritual **and** yet **is a metaphysical truth in and of itself.***

In that respect, he resembles a kabbalist in search of God: all the mechanisms are in place, but the leap of faith that is necessary to prove Your existence is a kind of madness he does not possess, or which he fears.

He saw a dreary parental marriage, and thus had been much too afraid to commit himself to a living being.

What kind of a Jew, or child of Israel, is he? Can he find God, and swing his pendulum in the process? (translation: leap, eat and fuck?)

This may sound not only harsh but also mad, but do bear with me, Lords:

I believe the following idea is essential: You **must** introduce him to Ezra Pound, **for *obviously Pound's bizarre temperament and erudition is equal to Fisch's own.***

Put Ezra inside him, and watch what happens to the both of them.

Render me invisible but active, and I will referee the event to ensure neither hurts the other.

I also suggest You both be present.

Why?

Because this may prove livelier than the book of Job!

I very much look forward to your reply.

Yrs, Wm Shakespeare

Adonai/Hashem to WS:

You are a swine.

We love you.

Tomorrow, at six am, bell tolls times six: Fisch v. Pound

See you then.

A/H, dictated to Metatron

The sixty-ninth canto

Behind closed doors, the guard Carliman had been ordered to bring Moussa and Moshe to the bedroom of the pirate queen.

Moshe thought, with quiet interest: perhaps Cerridwen has a bedroom specialty that involves the three of us?

"Was it Moses, or the pirate queen who called you?" asked Moussa, thinking exactly as Moshe.

"Both," said Carliman.

"And do you know why?" asked Moshe.

"No, sire," replied Carliman. "I merely guarded the door when I heard the three voices."

"Three voices?"

"Two womans, and Onur Bay Moses," said Carliman.

"Two womans?"

"*Iki kadin*, yes. Two womans."

"And Onur Bay Moses?" asked Moshe. "Who is he?"

"The Honored Mister Moses," said Moussa, quietly. "So our Carliman *is* an Ottoman. I'd wondered..."

They arrived at the door, and Carliman said:

"*Ben onları getirdim. Onlar şimdi burada olmayacaktık.*"

The voice of a woman replied from within the room:

"*Benim sakallı savaşçı teşekkür ederiz. Seni tarafindan: kimse girelim.*"

"A Turkish woman in the bedroom of the pirate queen?" whispered Moussa.

"What were they saying?" whispered Moses to Moussa.

The latter shrugged.

"Who speaks Turkish?" he said. "Only Turks."

"But how do you know it's Turkish?" asked Moshe.

"He called Moses Onur Bay. Honored Mister. It's a Turkish phrase. People who look like that and speak like that can only be Turkish, unless they're not."

"I must quote you one day," said Moses, "unless I don't."

The door opened.

And this is what they saw:

The pirate queen was seated at a dressing-table, and the tall woman with the rose-gold hair and flowers in her long flowing dress was combing the woman's tresses.

Moses himself was seated on the bed, half-naked, looking drugged and staring vaguely before him.

"To all of you, I will speak English," said the woman with the rose-gold hair, "although I prefer Italian and Hathorian."

"Hathorian?" asked Moses. "The language of the Goddess Hathor of Egypt?"

The woman turned to Moshe and smiled.

Immediately Moshe felt the blood rush from his face and to his groin, his erection as swift as it was prominent and hopeful.

"You speak English very well," said the woman to Moussa. "Or would you rather I send you my thoughts in your own languages? Which do you prefer?"

"Let us all hear you," said Moshe. "I am Moshe—"

"I know who you are," the woman replied. "I am the one you call The Lovely Joslian."

"*Ahhhh*," smiled Moussa. "Then you *are* our creation."

"If I am," said the Lovely Joslian, "then admit you've done a lovely job."

The pirate queen moved her head back, into the lap of the woman, closing her eyes like a cat while the Lovely Joslian stroked her hair.

"We are sharing a portrait of you, all of us," said Moshe. "That includes Carliman and the Pirate Queen. If we don't think of you, then you must realize you will no longer exist."

"If you do not think of me, I do not exist for *you*," said Joslian. "That is all. But I do exist for others, and in other forms equally pleasing."

"She is magic," whispered Cerridwyn ap Gwynnedd. "And Welsh."

"And Turkish," said Moussa.

"She looks very Italian to me," replied Moshe.

"How do you know that?" asked Moussa.

"Using your own logic," smiled Moshe. "Because she does not look Turkish, unless she is. In which case, she must be Italian, unless she *is* Turkish, which she does not appear to be. But I am most interested in how this happened, and where we are to go from here."

The Lovely Joslian shrugged.

"Where do you want to go?" she asked.

"To Wales," replied Moses. "I want to go home. I miss my mother and my sisters."

Cerridwen grinned, and held up a finger at Moshe:

"He knew Welsh all along," she said.

"So did she," replied Moshe, nodding in Joslian's direction.

"The both of them are coming with *me*," Joslian said.

Cerridwen smiled, and nodded.

Moses nodded as well.

"And where exactly are you going?" asked Moshe.

"Kiss me and I'll tell you," replied Joslian.

"Don't do it," said Moussa. "She may be a *Ghoola.* She will sleep with you and make a baby, which she will eat! I have seen them, many times, in the desert."

"She is not a *Ghoola,*" said Moses. "Perhaps she is of the tribe of Lilith, and uses our power for her own ends."

"She is certainly not of the tribe of Lilith," said Cerridwen.

"Do you have a Welsh female spirit?" asked Moshe of Moses. "Who traps travelers?"

"Kiss me and I will tell you," smiled Joslian once again, and Moshe found himself in her arms, and then Moussa, and she put her left hand around Moshe's waist, and her right around Moussa's, and her breath was sweet, though slightly salty, and her hair appeared even more rose-golden than before, and she smiled as she kissed them both, and locked her lips with each of them, one Moses at a time, and she said, "I am the Queen of the *Gwragedd Annwn,* and we live below the earth's own waters, and now you are all of you mine, for seven years, and you will do as I say, and must never speak of this to anyone else."

"So much for a kiss!" whispered Moshe.

Moussa began to cry, silently, to himself.

Moshe sighed, and nodded.

"Stupid ass," he muttered.

"I should have known," added Moses. "After sleeping with Cerridwen, I had become too greedy."

"As was I, man," said Cerridwen.

"In Wales you will call me '*N arddim 'n aflafar cariadferch Joslian,*'" said the Queen of the Underworld Women. "*The Beautiful Harsh Mistress Joslian.*"

All turned to Moses, but it was Cerridwen who said:

"Harsh but beautiful *Joslian*, Queen of the Underworld Women."

"When I was a babe, my mother warned me about you," said Moses miserably, looking at Joslian, and then at Cerridwen. "About the *both of you.*"

"You're no longer a babe," said Cerridwen, "and here we are, *the both of us.*"

"And proof of my Grandmother's saying, "Be careful what you wish for; God will provide no less," replied Moussa.

"And *you* are a *Gwraig Annwn* as well?" asked Moses of Cerridwen.

"Of course," said Cerridwen. "You think a woman can become a pirate without any aid from her sisters?"

"And the British Queen?" Moses continued.

"She's a Tudor, God help her," laughed Cerridwen. "She'd choose to be an Underworld Woman, '*n gwraig annwn,* if we gave her the choice."

Moshe smiled:

"Really? But we ourselves know her well enough to ask."

Joslian looked up, surprised.

Then she smiled, a bit too sweetly:

"Do you now?" she cooed.

"Of course," replied Moshe. "Don't we, Moussa?"

"That is why we are going to England and Wales," Moussa nodded.

"And will you ask her if she wishes to be an Underworld Woman, and align her power with ours?" asked Joslian.

"If that is what you wish," said Moshe. "We can do that, can't we, Moussa?"

Moussa frowned, nodded.

"We always can, and do."

"The both of you are lying," said the Queen of the Underworld Women. "But I will accept your lie as truth, because that is what we do in the Underworld. If the Queen of the English says no, however, then I will keep you as my slaves for eternity. After I have cut out your tongue."

"An excellent bargain," said Moussa. "My friend Moshe accepts, for all of us."

Moshe smiled. There are times, he thought, when life becomes so pointless it is actually comic.

"Excellent, indeed" replied the Queen of the Underworld Women,*'n arddun 'n aflafar cariardferch* Joslian. "Continue the course for England," she told Cerridwen, "then let us take pleasure with these three *choegddynion*."

"*Choeg*—what?" asked Moussa.

"*—ddynion*," replied Moses. "Fools."

"Such beautiful women sleeping with such fools?" said Moshe. "Preposterous."

"No," replied Moussa, sweetly. "How generous and..." whispering to his friend, "potentially promising."

The seventieth canto

It was insulting!

The poet and lunatic Ezra Pound found himself surrounded by Jews!!

They were all there:

Hannah Arendt, Saul Bellow, the Marx Brothers, S.J. Perelman, Stanley Kunitz, Kenneth Koch, George Steiner, Gershon Scholem, Susan Sontag, Sylvia Plath and, weirdly, George Eliot (who was actually the Invisible Shakespeare, but who, as George, had been handed the coded excuse that, given the success of *Daniel Deronda*, she was writing "yet another novel" about the Jews); Lorenz Hart, Frank Loesser, Irving Berlin, E.Y. Harburg, Alan Jay Lerner, Joseph Brodsky, Allen Ginsberg, Emma Lazarus, Gertrude Stein, Pound's old friend and acolyte, Louis Zukovsky, Moses Ibn Ezra, Yehuda Halevi; and those were just some of the *writers.*

There were also the painters: Jules Pascin, Marc Chagall, Camille Pisarro, Mark Rothko, Sonia Delaunay, Leon Bakst, Amadeo Modigliani, and, of course, Maya Deren.

Pound, that poor *shmuck*, was, as he often said, "being walled-off by pansy-kikes."

His red beard was turning grey.

"Sgoin' on, Gawd?" he cried. "My situation's the only one in the world where firmness and patience are useless!'

Six periwigged octopi appeared before him, and suddenly Pound found himself in the dock, presided over by an enormous orca.

"The Eightieth Canto of Ezra Pound, my lord," said the first octopus. "*Amo ergo sum*," he writes. "I love therefore I am."

The orca replied, "Are you kidding, Pound, or what?"

Pound blinked:

"Am I kidding? You mean, am I kidding about the Eightieth Canto?" he asked.

"Kidding about love."

"I kid about everything but love and money. You don't kid about love and money," said Ezra Pound, sullenly.

"Odd," replied the orca. "I don't care about money at all. I'm sure love has more value."

"Sure does, if you're a whore," said Pound, and laughed.

"Or a pimp," the orca replied.

The second periwigged octopus stepped to the judge's bench and said: "Canto Sixty-nine of the defendant, my lord: "*The capitalists those who have money at interest or those on fixed salaries lose.*"

"What about it?" asked Pound. "Seems obvious to me."

"Are you kidding or what?" asked the orca.

"I never kid about money," said Pound. "That's the point of the Cantos. People kidded about money and blood and love and life. I knew better than to kid about such things."

"I've read your Cantos seven times, Mr. Pound," said the orca. "Between ourselves, your work is deeply-felt and extremely well-researched and wondrously cogent."

"Thank you, your honor."

"My only problem," continued the orca, "is that when it was well-researched it was not wondrously cogent; when it was wondrously cogent, it was not well-researched; when it was deeply-felt, it was neither well-researched nor wondrously cogent."

"Sam Johnson said the same thing to a young poet," snapped Pound. "'Your work is striking and original. Unfortunately, when it was original, it was not striking; and when it was striking, it was not original.' Two can play at this game, blubber-mouth."

The orca was saved, however, by the address of the third periwigged octopus:

"M'lord, let me present the Fiftieth Canto of the poet Pound: "*Wellington was a jew's pimp and lacked mind to know what he effected. 'Leave the Duke, Go for gold!" In their souls was usura and in their hearts cowardice In their minds was stink and corruption Two sores ran together, and hell pissed up Metternich Filth stank as in our day.*"

The orca sat up: "Wellington was a *what*?" he asked.

"A jew's pimp," said the octopus.

Pound strained forward, crying:

"I also wrote: '*Not' said Napoleon 'because of that league of lice but for opposing the Zeitgeist! That was my ruin, That I ran against my own time, turning backward*'"

Pound smiled about him, well aware that he'd made his point to an eternity of well-wishers who, though not invisible, unfortunately were also not there.

"Napoleon opposed the *Zeitgeist*?" said the whale. "You must be kidding! *Napoleon opposed Wellington*, who was a naval officer and not a jew's pimp! Jews don't have usura in their souls any more than you do. Nor do they have cowardice in their hearts. And Napoleon turned backward twice, and that was in Moscow and at Austerlitz. Next?" cried the whale.

The fourth periwigged octopus appeared. "M'lud: I bring before you Canto Sixty-one of a certain Mr. Pound, forenamed Ezra. *"Ma questo," said the Boss, "e divertente." Catching the point before the aesthetes had got there; Having drained off the muck by Vada From the marshes, by Circeo, where no one else wd. Have drained it. Waited 2000 years, ate grain from the marshes; Water supply for ten million, another one million "vani," that is rooms for people to live in. XI of our era."*

"That's what Mussolini did for the *popolo*," said Pound. "*You* tell me he didn't. I fucking defy you!"

The orca replied: "He also took the silt from beneath Venice to create land for the stinking factories of Marghera, thereby helping to sink the Commune of Venice much more swiftly than the sea ever could. And it didn't take two thousand years. NEXT!"

Ezra Pound held up a hand and said, "Who are these gawd-damned octopi?"

A fifth periwigged octopus stepped forward and said:

"Canto One hundred and one, of the same Pound, M'lud: *"Mme d'Houdetot never perceived evil in anyone. 'Sort of ignorance,' said the old priest to Yeats in a railway train, "is spreading every day from the schools!" Obit 1933, Tsung-Kuan, for Honour. Bears live on acorns and come raiding our fields. Bouffier, Elzeard has made the forest at Vergons under Kuanon's eye there is oak-wood. Senper ga-mu, To him we burn pine with white smoke, morning and evening---"*

"I'm fucked here," said the orca whale. "I'm *thoroughly* fucked here! *What is Madame d'Houdetot doing with Yeats and Bouffier and Kuanon?* And what does the old priest and Yeats have to do *with burning pine*? Why am I puffing like a grampus, listening to this? MR. POUND, FOR GAWD'S SAKE, ARE YOU KIDDING OR WHAT?"

The sixth and last periwigged octopus stepped forward:

"If it please the court, may I present the Second Canto of Mister Ezra Pound, of Hailey, Idaho, the first several lines? "*Hang it all, Robert Browning, there can be but the one "Sordello." But Sordello, and my Sordello? Lo Sordels si fo di Montovana. So-shu churned in the sea. Sealsports in the spray-whited circles of cliff-wash, Sleek head, daughter of Lir, eyes of Picasso under black fur-hood.*"

"That's it!" spat the critic-judge, the orca whale. "This time I'm going to have to throw the book at you!" And he hurled the ninth printed edition of the Cantos - published in one volume by New Directions - at the poet's head, and intoned: "I open the floor to the ton of Jews in this courtroom, beginning with Susan Sontag. They have questions. And, poet, you better have answers."

They had questions for him, all right, oh but did they ever!

And he had answers for them, too.

But his answers had nothing to do with the questions, just as the Cantos had been proven to have nothing to do with Napoleon or Jews or Browning or Confucius or Yeats or ----

In tears now, Ezra Pound held up a hand and turned to the orca:

"I may be licked, but I'm not down - which Hem said to me, *a Paree*, that time I threw a left punch and he was expecting a right! *Ebbene, caro dottore, avanti!* Tell me how I could have *improved* the Cantos?"

The orca said, "Mine is not to reason why. Mine is but to read and sigh."

"Listen to me, you fat fuck," said Pound, now trembling violently. "I spent thirty-nine years writing these cantos! One hundred and seventeen cantos!! What did *you do* in thirty-nine years but comment upon anybody ever worthwhile who actually *did* the writing??? You stood at the side of the road, you lily-livered kike, you watched all manner of accidents, and who did you save? Nobody!!! You 'commented.' You didn't create! You *couldn't* create, you wouldn't know how!, you pudding-stuffed circumcised sheeny, you did nothing but----"

Gertrude Stein stepped forward and, behind her, Louis Zukofsky appeared as well:

"Why is a kike is a kike is a kike is a lily-livered sheeny is a lily-livered sheeny too?" asked Miss Stein, and she leaned in, and grinned, with a ferocity that was frightening. "Tell me, Ezzie: Why *you*?"

"Why me?" asked Ezra Pound, cross-eyed and surprised by the swiftness of her attack. He looked to Zukofsky for support,but the latter smiled as much in sorrow as in anger, staring pointedly at Pound.

"Who else is a Jew is a Jew is a Jew *but you too*?" said Louis Zukofsky.

"Look, all right, listen, maybe you two sheenies are different," Pound began, shrugging his shoulders and waving his arms, "and maybe I shouldn't have made those comments, perhaps, but-----what? What is that? You said I'm a *what?*"

"Repeat after me," said Stein, stentoriously. "Pound--is--a--Jew."

"Wait a minute," said Ezra.

The orca began to laugh.

"If I'm a Jew, then he's Mme. Helvetius!" cried Pound, pointing at the whale.

"'*Mais oui'*," said the orca. "'*Ahh but I have to tell you much conversation about the electric eel!*'"

The octopi stared in surprise.

The orca had turned bright red, and had proved himself capable of developing then sustaining an erection. He winked at the octopi and said, "'For this stone giveth sleep!'"

"Those are *my* words!" yelled Pound. "And I'm no more a Jew----"

"Drop your pants," said Groucho Marx, who had suddenly appeared beside Zukofsky, "and show us how many nights you knocked 'em dead in Boise."

"Eh, boss," said brother Chico, pointing southerly at Pound. "At's-a no Boisy. At's a big-a daisy."

Harpo nodded, grinning, then honking his horn.

"Or Hailey," said Groucho. "Somewhere near the mills. Tell us, Mr. Pound, for fifty dollars: What were you doing in Hailey Mills?" and wiggled his eyebrows. "Not that I wouldn't give fifty smackeroos to be in Hailey Mills myself, so long as Lulu's not back in town."

Saul Bellow, Ted Roethke, Karl Shapiro and Stanley Kunitz appeared as baby swans, in tutus, and began to sing, "Chicago, Chicago, that toddlin' town" while the orca stood up and sang as well, and so did the periwigged octopi, and all were singing except Pound, who was staring at the Cantos and crying, "*WHAT WOULD YOU HAVE DONE?*"

James Michener sidled up to the man from Hailey, Idaho, and charged, "In two lines, Mr. Pound, do explain, to all and sundry, the poem's central themes."

"Shut the fuck up, Michener," cried the orca. "That Idaho Jew has proven he has talent. He just doesn't know what to do with it yet."

"And do *you*?" said Ezra, spitefully.

"With *your* talent?" yawned Groucho, pulling Harpo off Karl Shapiro, the most fetching of the swanlets. "Hell, I wouldn't have gone on Mussolini Radio and sung "Mammy" to the Axis! Or was it "Swanee,"

Adolph's favorite tune? Ahh, yes,it seems like only yesterday, I remember Adolph, during cherry blossom time, he and I in *lederhosen* waiting for the gefilte fish to fry, just little ol' *jugend* being *jugend* --- and did he ever have a *jugend*! The police had to fetch an ambulance and three fire companies, just to get his *jugend* back into his *lederhosen,* "Oh Adolph, Adolph, if you'd only listened to me and gone into vaudeville, or even into Madame Sophie, instead of to the Viennese Army!"

Allen Ginsberg began playing a *tabla*, and reciting: "He apologized to me in Washington D.C. on a Friday evening at the crazy house, said he'd never call a spade a spade again, said he was sorry Lord 'bout all them Jews, we all sorry about them Jews."

"Sorry about himself, you mean," said Zukofsky, sadly.

"All right, that's enough. Now listen," began George Eliot. At once, all turned to the much under-rated novelist, and equally under-rated lover of Herbert Spencer:

"Let's let bygones be bygones," she ordered. "The poet Pound promises to be a good Jew from now on. In point of fact, next Saturday he and Doctor Fisch are going to share bar mitzvahs."

"Who's the rabbi?" asked Herman Wouk, author of "*This is My God.*"

"Strangely enough, a most ancient child of Israel," George Eliot replied.

"Who can that be?" asked the orca.

"Why, the old Emperor of Ice Cream himself," said George Eliot. "Wallace Stevens!"

The seventy-first canto

Later that month, it was bruited about that at the Bar Mitzvah of Ezra Pound and Herschel Fisch, the good Doctor ate more mussels, danced more dances, and fucked more women than Shakespeare himself might have done, in three lifetimes!

Admittedly, however, both Pound and Fisch *did lose something* in the translation.

But, I am told, this always happens, at Bar Mitzvahs.

The seventy-second canto

Oh, and guess whom Adonai and HaShem had impersonated, at Ezra's trial, in order to be there in person? Say the magic word and win fifty dollars!

That's right! – Groucho Marx!!!

The seventy-third canto

And if you still don't believe me, ask yourself this:

If you can *never* understand your own mother and father, how in hell can you *even begin to understand God?*

The seventy-fourth canto

London.

The most immediate sensation was its smell:

Depending upon the wind, it was either a perfumed shithouse, or a slaughterhouse manned by three hundred pound thugs, with exposed armpits.

You had keep your head down to watch your boots, yet at the same time stay alert for an open window from which slops were tossed, plopping and splashing, into the dunghill of its streets.

The rain didn't help.

It washed away nothing.

Instead, it made everything you wanted to forget run together in a thick, glutinous wash.

If the weather fogged - and inevitably, once or twice a day, it did - then you never knew *what* you were going to step into, or *who or what* you were going to run into. London's daily fare was shit, piss, pox and murder.

The plague, thankfully, was seasonal.

Moses was happy to hear English, his second language.

Neither Moshe nor Moussa, however - even with English as their sixth and seventh languages - were delighted. For them, you could leave the *souq* or the village, and there were trees and a desert and a sea, a Nature which swept everything clean.

"Look at the people!" called Moses. "Everybody's so well-fed and happy."

Moussa turned to Moshe, whispering, "Do we know this man? The people look like pigs. Only pigs are happy, wallowing in shit."

"Pigs are not happy, wallowing in shit," said Moshe. "Men put them there. The pigs had no choice."

Before them, in a carriage, rode Cerridwen and the Queen of the Underworld Women.

Beside the driver sat Carliman the Ipnosian, gazing ferociously ahead as if he owned the town.

"And just look at Moses," Moshe continued, shaking his head. "I can't believe he'd want to return to this pest-hole. Even that river before us is nothing but a bowel-bog."

"Moses, where are we headed?" called Moussa.

"I don't know," said Moses, grinning and continuing to gaze about him, smiling and nodding at everyone and everything.

"What a provincial fool," laughed Moussa, quietly, shaking his head. "At least *I* warned you about the *djinni. He's* simply thrilled to be walking into horse-dung – say, Moses!" yelled Moussa, once again. "Find out where we're going, won't you? Run ahead and ask the coachman!"

Moses nodded, and began cutting around horsemen, dogs, carters, rushing up to the coach carrying Cerridwen and the Queen of the Underworld.

"Well, at least he's good for something," sighed Moshe, and moved aside as two men in thick green capes and heavy swords swiped into him. One brushed against his leg, and Moshe could feel the man trying to collar his purse. He was about to laugh, then thought better of it.

"That's the third for you, the second for me," said Moshe.

"Fourth," Moussa replied, then nodded towards two harlots who were trying to catch their eye. "Just by gazing at them, you can feel the ooze dripping out of your poor penis," he sighed.

Moshe smiled, and which smile was taken by the whores as a come-on.

One of the women nodded towards an alley.

"We'll give the both of you a pair of knee-tremblers you'll never forget," she said.

Moussa nodded:

"What else will you give us that we cannot forget?" he asked.

Realizing they were being gulled, at once the whores bit their thumbs at the pair, and turned away.

"We're going to see the Queen!" called Moses to his friends. "The Lovely Underworld Joslian says she knows someone who'll let us in Her Royal Highness' chambers."

Moshe frowned, and looked at Moussa:

"What would happen if we were suddenly to become lost?" he asked. "There certainly seems to be enough space for us to hide in, in this town."

"The Lovely Joslian is testing us," said Moussa, shaking his head. "She wants to see if we'll run."

"But how do we know She's real---?"

"Whoever She is, we certainly *know* She's more powerful than the both of us put together," said Moussa. "Don't even think of it."

"Yes, but so was the *Djinn,* and the Giant, and Ser Lorenzo, and even Carliman and the Pirate Queen. In spite of em our own imaginations and our intelligence proved more useful and resilient than all of their combined strengths."

"And which is all the more reason to breathe with the moment," said Moussa, "and use its spirit for our own preservation."

"Don't misunderstand me," Moshe replied, trembling with frustration. "I'm no more impressed with the Queen of England than I am with the Queen of the Underworld. All they can do is act as if I didn't exist. Or they can use me to their ends - if they so desire - or kill me - if I do not meet their desires. Please, Moussa: I'm no more their friend than they are mine. I never was, and never will be."

"Ahh, but the Queen of the Underworld knew how to kiss very well, did she not?" smiled Moussa, trying to alleviate Moshe's frustration and, worse, his terror.

"Yes, I'll accept that," nodded Moshe. "But the fact that she *kissed us both very well* meant that she preferred *the act of kissing,* to ourselves. We're merely objects. To her, we could just as well be farts as men."

"You're extremely unpleasant and unhappy today," said Moussa. "Here we are, in this vomitpile of a town, far from *djinni,* sea-sickness and Crusaders, and yet, somehow, it is not good enough for you?"

"Forgive me" said Moshe. "I have subtle, albeit well-defined, tastes."

"Because you're a Jew?"

"Why should that make any difference?" said Moshe, hotly, lying to himself, and despising himself for the lie.

"Because you know the world could be a better place?" replied Moussa, raising his eyebrows.

"Out of all the people in the world," spat Moshe, "why must one be a Jew to think such a thought?"

"Because that's your contract with God," replied Moussa, "and you feel as if you're not fulfilling it."

"No," said Moshe. "That's *everyone's* contract with God, even if you've never spoken or cared about God at all: to make the world a better place."

"What is 'a better place'?" asked Moussa.

"Anything that's not London or a Crusade," Moshe replied. "Anything that doesn't claim Death is superior to Life."

Moussa looked about, and in doing so, took his eyes off the dirty road.

"Quite true," he said, as his boot disappeared in a pile of horse manure, and the warm stench, as well as a great clod of turd, flew upwards, and covered one nostril, and all of his lower lip.

The seventy-fifth canto

They were seated in the Queen's sixth antechamber, which, as Moses pointed out, "must somehow be between the fifth and seventh antechambers, unless, of course, it is itself the last antechamber, in which case, there would be no seventh antechamber."

Neither Moshe nor Moussa were listening. Moses had not stopped chattering from the instant he had set foot upon that dock by the Thames. Half of his speech made no sense, and nearly all of his accent, which had become, once again, uncontrollably Welsh.

An old man with a grey beard, and a cape covered with strange seals and stars, stood by a richly mullioned window. He clutched several parchments to his breast, staring before him, through the window's rainbow panels.

Across from him, on a couch, slept a well-dressed man with a well-curled beard. On his stomach lay a book, which followed the rhythms of his rising and falling stomach.

Moshe strained to see its title:

"*The Merry Wives of Windsor,*" he whispered and, then, from the cover of the book, continued to read aloud: "*A Most pleasaunt and excellent conceited Comedie, of Syr John Falstaffe, and the merrie Wives of Windsor. Entermixed with sundrie variable and pleasing humors, of Sir Hugh the Welch Knight, Justice Shallow, and his wise Cousin M. Slender. With the swaggering vaine of Auncient Pistoll, and Corporall Nym. By William Shakespeare. As it hath bene divers times Acted by the right Honorable my Lord Chamberlaines servants. Both before her Majestie, and else-where. London. Printed by T.C. for Arthur Johnson...*"

Moshe looked at the sleeping man, whose one eye had opened, and was staring balefully at the cover's reader.

"Did it put you to sleep, sir?" asked Moshe. "This 'pleasant and excellent comedie'?"

"If poorly acted," said the man, closing his eye once again, "it would put anyone to sleep."

"And have you seen it acted?" asked Moshe.

"I wrote it," yawned the man, "It has had a certain success with the Queen," he yawned once again, and scratched his nose. "that I have been held prisoner, in this chamber, for seven hours."

Moshe nodded, staring, still, at the man laying upon the couch.

"Then you must be William Shakespeare," he said, "of the 'right Honorable my Lord Chamberlaines servants,' as the writing says."

"I am indeed," replied Shakespeare, and this time yawned even more loudly.

"I am sorry to hear that you have been in this room for seven hours," said Moshe. "Since none of us are writers of plays but merely story-tellers, that augurs ill for the rest of us."

Shakespeare closed his eyes, thinking: *Not another man with a story!*

The starry-cloaked man with the noisy parchments turned to Moshe and said, "You, sirrah, have the voice of a Hebrew."

Shakespeare looked up, this time, with quiet interest.

Moshe did not reply.

"And are you of the Hebrew race?" insisted the old man. "I have great respect for their knowledge, for I have studied the Book of Formation, which was said to have been written by Abraham himself."

"Written by Abraham, you say?" smiled Shakespeare, pleasantly. "In what language, and with what materials?"

"In the language of the angels," said the old man, coldly. "It was dictated to his son, Isaac."

Shakespeare nodded to himself:

"And might I ask, revered ancient: who translated the language of the angels, and into which language?"

The old man turned away.

"It would have been a desert tongue," interrupted Moshe. "Aramaic, I would think. But the angels did not speak Aramaic. Therefore, like our own, the work was not written, but in all possibilities, vocal, and passed from generation to generation."

"Yes, but what language did the angels *speak*?" asked Shakespeare.

"Nothing we would know," said Moshe. "Why do you ask?"

"If I ever were to write an angel," said William Shakespeare, "I would want to know how he spoke. In "*Merry Wives*" I have a Frenchman, a Welshman, and all manner of verbal unfortunates. In "*Hamlet*" and "*Richard III*", and "*Macbeth,*" I've written ghosts." In "*Midsummer Night's Dream*", fairies. It would be pleasant, some day, to add an angel or two to the company."

"I have spoken with angels, sirrah," said the old man, "and they answer in a form we *do* understand."

Shakespeare stretched, and gazed at the man:

"Then you are Dr. John Dee," he said, politely, and nodded. "Is it true the Queen has made you warden of Manchester College?"

"I am indeed the warden of Manchester College," said John Dee. "At present I am translating my *Necronomicon* into English for Our Sovereign. These pages are my earnest conversations with divers angels. I am presenting several pages of my transcriptions for Her Majesty."

"May I see your work?" asked William Shakespeare.

"You may not," replied Doctor Dee, haughtily. "I am neither a poet nor a play-maker. I am a man of science and of the spirit. There is a difference."

Moussa stepped forward:

"All great men of scientific thought are poets and playmakers as well," he said. "In my country. The dreams of inspiration do not distinguish between science and the spirit, poem and song."

"That is the difference between your country, wherever it is, and mine," said Dr. John Dee, coughing wetly.

"No," replied Shakespeare. "That is the difference between intelligence and reason. Reason makes the distinction you claim, Doctor Dee. Intelligence does not. I know many poets who are as intelligent as any philosopher, and, equally, many poets who are as dim-witted as any doctor."

Dee turned away, stiffly and angrily.

Shakespeare smiled at Moussa:

"I have not introduced myself," he said. "You are---"

"I am Moussa, and this is my friend, Moshe. That is our other friend, Moses."

Shakespeare smiled.

"Truly?" he said. "Are not all those names the same? That is, aren't they all Moses? In the Arabic and Hebrew tongues?"

"Moses himself was not so simple," said Moshe. "Evidently it has taken three different worlds to deal with a mere portion of his fullness: my own Hebrew, his Arabic, and our friend's Welsh-English."

"There were once three Moses, and they appeared in our world, at one and the same time," said Shakespeare, almost wistfully. "A Jew, a

Moor, and a Christian...And what are you doing here, in the Queen's antechamber?"

Before either Moshe and Moussa could stop him, Moses turned from the window and said:

"We are going to ask Her Royal Majesty if she wishes to join forces with the Pirate Queen and the Queen of the *Gwragedd Annwn*, the Underworld Women, who live below the earth's own waters, in order to align her powers with theirs."

John Dee stared, open-mouthed, as Moshe and Moussa turned away from Moses.

Shakespeare crossed himself.

Noting this, Dr. Dee frowned and said, "You are committing a grave mistake by doing that, poet," he spoke, quietly. "How can you be certain I am not a spy for Our Sovereign?"

"I have done nothing," said the playwright, simply.

"And we saw nothing," said Moshe. "What did he do?"

But Shakespeare was not listening. Instead, he stared at Dee.

"You yourself are committing a grave mistake by asserting that you might well be a spy, Doctor Dee," he said. "Even for our Queen."

A courtier appeared, removed his plumed hat, bowed deeply and proclaimed, "Our Sovereign Queen wishes to speak with Doctor Dee."

John Dee nodded, gazing darkly at Shakespeare:

"I take no sides," said he. "I merely issue a warning," and followed the courtier beyond the door, which closed noiselessly.

The seventy-sixth canto

For a few minutes, nobody said anything.

Then Moses asked, "What warning was he issuing?"

"I am from a town of Catholics," said Shakespeare. "And in case you've not heard, the Queen is not Catholic. Thus, I could quite easily have my head chopped off for making the sign of the Cross."

"But *are* you Catholic?" asked Moshe.

"I am an actor," said Shakespeare. "Everybody, Catholic or not, crosses himself in Stratford. It's an old habit. When the Queen asked me to write a play about Sir John Falstaff, a character I'd created in my last work, when she said she'd like to see him falling in love, I crossed myself, as you have just witnessed, and the Queen laughed. It became the subject of a private joke between ourselves. I will know if John Dee is a spy, if she refers to my gesture when we meet. Yet the Doctor is full of wise saws and strange conceits. I enjoy his company, even though I have met him a dozen times and he still pretends not to know me. I would almost give up my portion of the Globe to see his *Necromicron.* I have known several angel-summoners, but none who actually transcribed their discourse."

"Either what he has written is of small interest," said Moshe, "or he has not taken much of it to heart."

"Why do you say that?" asked Shakespeare, surprised.

"His face is as pinched as his manner is mean-spirited," Moussa replied.

Shakespeare turned to Moshe, with a slight cock of his head, as if to ask if he agreed with his friend.

"Exactly," said Moshe.

"The man has been a pauper many years. He is most gifted in divers *arcana*," said Shakespeare. "The Queen has become his friend and protector."

"All the more reason to smile," said Moussa. "If you speak with Angels and the Queen protects you, shouldn't you be of a more generous disposition?"

Shakespeare laughed, and pointed at the trio.

"The three wise men," he said. "What was this you had mentioned about the Queen of the Underworld? Is this another bit of Welsh magic?"

"Ask him," said Moshe, pointing at Moses.

Shakespeare turned to Moses.

"Not at all," replied the latter, seriously. "She is very real. They've met her, and even have slept with her."

"Yes, but did she sleep with *them*?" asked Shakespeare, and both Moshe and Moussa began to laugh.

"We have met a magical creature who is called '*N arddim 'n aflafar cariadferch Joslian, Queen of the Gwragedd Annwn.*" Moses began.

"The Harsh but Beautiful Mistress Joslian, Queen of the Underworld Women," added Moshe. "It's a long story...."

"I am at your service," said William Shakespeare. "Your greatest listener."

"But we're not supposed to talk about Her at all," said Moses.

"Moses, my dear," replied Moussa. "You were the one to mention Her, in the first place."

"I believe," continued Shakespeare, "the Welsh Moses said you were going to try to create an alliance between the Pirate Queen (and is she not the infamous Cerridwen ap Gwynnedd?) And with her ally, the Harsh but Beautiful Mistress, Joslian, Queen of the Underworld Women? With our own Queen? Thus, a triple alliance?"

The three nodded.

"You have a superb memory," said Moshe.

"And now that I know what you are going to do," continued Shakespeare, "there appears to be no reason *not* to tell me how it is you came to do it."

The men said nothing. All stared at different parts of the chamber.

Shakespeare smiled, lowering his voice:

"Here's a bargain: tell me your tale, and if we leave the Queen alive, I'll be your London *cicerone*. I'll play Virgil to your Dante. I'll promise you fine meals, clean women, and several entertainments at the Globe: This week we're performing three new plays of mine - *Hamlet, Twelfth Night, and Troilus and Cressida*."

Moses looked at the others, frowning.

"Two are comedies? And one's sad yet also funny?" said Shakespeare, enticingly.

"The sad one must be *Troilus and Cressida*," said Moses. "I've heard that tale once."

"Actually it's *Hamlet*," Shakespeare replied. "But I promise you, it's also very funny."

"I do enjoy a comic tale," said Moses.

"And I as well," enjoined Moussa.

"Then let's tell him everything," said Moshe, nodding. "Besides, I overheard Cerridwen explaining to Joslian that English plays are very good."

"Bring the two ladies as well," said Shakespeare, with nonchalance. "The lovely Joslian and the Pirate Queen. For me it would be wonder-filled magic to meet them."

"I'm not so sure," began Moussa, thoughtfully. "I'm not so sure how wonder-filled you'd want it. If *your* Queen doesn't kill us, *they* might."

The seventy-seventh canto

"Where to begin the story?" said Moshe.
"With the taking of the town by the Crusaders," said Moussa.
"A wondrous place to begin, indeed," replied the playwright.

A tenth riff to Mnemosyne, Before we proceed to seventy-eighth canto

Two betrayals - which ultimately weren't betrayals, but which, at the time, seemed like them – occurred during the summer of my junior year at Dartmouth:

The Tennessee Ernie Ford Show, in which my father had been musical director and arranger, had come to an end, after five seasons.

A goodbye party was held at the ranch of Ernie's old friend and manager, the musician, Cliffie Stone. The Stones lived in Newhall, California, in high chaparral country. They were a large, talented, bustling family, with great humor, warmth, talent and hospitality.

The musicians, cast and crew, as well as their families, lined their cars along the road leading to the ranch, or parked inside the ranch property itself, all the way to the back, by the stables.

One hour into the sad/happy event, mom said to me: "Could you go to our car and get my bathing-suit?"

I looked at her, confused, as if to say, "Why not get it yourself?" but she was staring at me in such an odd and angry fashion that I knew there was something more to the request than the fetching of a mere bathing-suit.

I went down the path towards the stables, then turned a corner, where we'd parked our car:

Dad was in the midst of a major embrace with one of the singers in his vocal group.

I was shocked, and immediately ducked into a stable.

In less than a minute, the singer passed, head down, and embarrassed. She must have seen me when I had appeared around the corner.

I waited for a minute, equally embarrassed, then left the stable and moved to dad; took the pocket handkerchief from his elegant jacket;slowly and dramatically removed the singer's lipstick from his mouth, neck, and cheeks.

"So tell me," I asked. "How can you trust a girl who kisses with her eyes open?"

"This is very serious," he fumed. "I want you to come with me at once, and apologize to her."

"Apologize?" I asked, stunned. "For what?"

"For what you saw."

"Fuck you," I said. "*You* apologize to me and mom for what *you did*! How could you be so stupid? I don't give a shit if you're fucking around, that's your business, but how come you couldn't *wait*?"

"I'm very serious about her," said dad, "and I resent your tone," and he *was* serious about her, so serious he didn't care who saw him in the embrace, for he could no longer wait for a more private setting.

I went back with him, to the crowds and the laughter, and he dragged me to the young woman, who was sitting in a lounge chair, and trying to pretend nothing had happened.

He said, quietly but firmly, "Steve has something to tell you," and I nodded:

"Yeah, I'm really sorry I interrupted your kissing. It was totally impudent on my part, and I promise never to follow you guys to motel rooms or apartments or cars or wherever the fuck you go to do it," and I turned, and brought mom her bathing-suit, and she glared at me and said, "Thanks. I see you found it," and that was the end of their marriage.

But before Dad left our house and moved in with the young woman and eventually married her, he was asked by Bud Yorkin, the director of the Ford Show, to make a demo reel of his music.

Buddy and one of the writers of the show, Norman Lear, had formed an independent production company, and were going to create and produce films and television series, and wanted my father to do their music.

When dad told me - in one of the few civil conversations we had before he left the house – it was my turn to be furious: "You've been musical director on Buddy's show for five years. Why the hell do you have to prepare an audition tape for *them*? Buddy knows who you are and what you do."

Dad shrugged, feigning unconcern.

"I guess he needs something to show his money people."

"Can't he just say you did the music for Ford and he trusts you completely?"

"It doesn't work that way."

Even then, I knew that was bullshit. If there were people interested enough to put money in Yorkin and Lear, they would accept their choices without question. In the early stages of the marriage, everybody was in love. And even if Yorkin and Lear put their own money into the company, the networks would see an already realized pilot.

Still, I said, in a conciliatory fashion, "Okay, so just give them your "New York, New York" album, and your "Cat Dancers Only" album! That's enough! Jesus, their backers or the networks wouldn't know good music from bad, anyway!"

"I'll think of something," he muttered, ending the conversation.

Several weeks before, when I'd returned from Dartmouth to Los Angeles, I'd stopped in New York to hear Maynard Ferguson's big band at Birdland. The arrangements and musicianship were strong, solid, hip and original. I had brought Ferguson's latest album, "Message from Newport," back to L.A., and had played it for dad.

He nodded and said "Yeah," which was his stamp of approval.

Dad's studio was a converted garage, and which was next to my bedroom.

I went to sleep most nights hearing the piano, as he composed, or did his arrangements.

That night, after our discussion about the audition reel, as I was preparing for bed, I heard "Fan It, Janet," one of the tunes on the Ferguson album, coming from the garage.

Then it stopped, and I heard dad say: "Okay, guys, this time from the top. *One*-two-three, *one*-two-three, and----" and "Fan it, Janet" began once again, and I couldn't believe it.

Was he passing off the Ferguson number as his own, on tape, for his demo reel?

The number finished, dad replayed it, with his introduction, and I found myself hitting the pillow and saying "No no no no goddammit it no!" over and over and over, and crying with rage, feeling even more betrayed than when I'd seen him at Cliffie Stone's ranch.

He never did get the job with Yorkin and Lear.

They gave it to Henry Mancini instead - until Mancini became too famous and was offered something better. (A chorus, please, of "Hooray for Hollywood!")

I do understand all these betrayals, disloyalties, white lies:

"*Making do* is how most people live."

Politics, as we have heard so often, is "*the art of compromise.*"

Compromise, it continues, "*is the art of the possible.*"

Meanwhile, back in 12-point font:

These are the most compromised rationalizations invented by any institutionalized mini-man. Fuck all that shit.

My father's behavior regarding the demo reel was cynical, self-loathing, and a big "Screw you" to everyone: to Buddy, Norman, the entertainment industry and, most of all, to himself.

Dad's behavior regarding his marriage was simpler: it had ceased to work.

Dad had fallen in love; had tried to keep it secret until both relationships were untenable. Either he had to marry the young woman and dump mom; or dump his lover, and try to make a stale and impossible marriage work.

On the surface, his lover was easier. And dad was too tired to take on Mom.

He'd done it three times before.

But deeper within, he had never stopped loving her.

Yet that is not the same as living within an impossible situation.

For me, two questions arose from these events:

First: Would I myself search out other lady friends if I ever fell out of love with my wife, whoever she would be -- or she with me, and children were involved?

Indeed I would, as I eventually discovered, and I did, and eventually divorced my first wife, because after one emotional compromise after another I found it impossible to remain in a lie.

Secondly: Would I ever pass someone else's work off as my own, no matter if the passing was a "white lie?"

Never.

In fact, I fight like hell when someone tries to steal my own work.

It's happened several times: by my boss at a tv station who tried to pass off my daily editorials as his own; by a famous film producer who tried to steal my writing credit; even by a disturbed graduate student, who had claimed I'd stolen his script to shoot my own feature film, although my script was based upon a novel I'd written, long before the student had even been born!

The professional aspect of dad's betrayals demonstrated that the role of the musician was perceived as the lowest rung on the Industry ladder, even worse than that of the writer. Most musicians felt it, and eventually some began to believe it, and thus began to hate themselves.

The love aspect of dad's betrayals, I'd come to believe, was not simply his fault, or mom's, or his new wife's.

As I had written earlier: men are emotionally less complicated than women. If women can't see that, or care not to, and/or are indifferent to their partner's work, there's going to be trouble.

However, when men are treated with respect, love, consideration, care, and interest, the marriage will always work, - unless the man is a sociopath or, like most adolescents, has just discovered masturbation.

Men who are respected, loved, cared for, and whose partners show an interest in their professional lives will always shine for their families.

In spite of our *bella figura*, we men are *not* adolescents: we will wear short-pants until we die.

Cut us off from respect, love, care and interest, and we'll find someone else who at least *professes* to care.

For everything, after all, is a love story.

Even a divorce.

The seventy-eighth canto

Lots of talk on the Jewish Moon-colony of *Noye-Erdkelle.*

Big buzzing, too, among the Piatniki:

Dr. Herschel Fisch, according to the Moon-people, was back and better than ever!! Laughing, Eating, Flirting, and "Imminently Considering a New Career as an Actor!"

Everyone was delighted, including the management of the JAP, who had produced *The Merchant of Venice.* They immediately offered him the role of Falstaff, in *Henry IV, Part One.* He was ready to accept, when he received a letter from Shakespeare.

Bear with me, please. A bit of background:

The seventy-ninth canto

The buzz on Piatnik, the Plane of the Muses, had been of a twofold nature. First, of course, was Ezra Pound's Bar Mitzvah:

Holo-cards of the event were flashed all over the pluriverse, including the parallel universes, which had their own time-sense; in one universe, the Bar Mitzvah photos appeared in the night sky as Pound gave a Fascist salute to both Mussolini and Hitler.

The latter didn't know who in hell Pound was and, when informed, said, "Poetry is for Jewish sissy-boys!"

Because of the photo in that particular quadrant of the pluriverse, Ezra Pound – as will be written by future serious students of history - "languished for the rest of his life in a totalitarian prison."

The Pound of Piatnik, however, was given the Grand Tour of Jewish Thought, with Maimonides and the Ari as his guides.

And what about Shakespeare, Piatnik's man of the hour, the savior of both Dr. Fisch and the savant of Hailey, Idaho?

H.D. had called Shakespeare a "hero," and Voltaire had said the playwright was "the only fool among fools, with balls of steel."

But the man from Stratford knew very well that Dr. Fisch could not be considered cured until he had consciously and actively faced his demon. So when Shakespeare tuned in and discovered that Fisch was being groomed for the part of Falstaff, he shook his head and immediately wrote HaShem:

"*Casting Herschel Fisch as Falstaff is an obvious choice, and proves nothing. The only way we will learn if he has made a complete psychic recovery is to insist he endeavor to play a more demanding character. I think it should be the personage of whom my character Enobarbus said: 'Age cannot wither her, nor custom stale her infinite variety.' That is to say: Cleopatra.*

If Fisch succeeds in the role, then he is cured.

However, if Fisch fails, then we will know he has been hiding behind a curtain of bonhomie. As a result, I fear I will have to plunge my sword, once again, into his psyche, and start anew the rescue process.

Regards to Adonai.

W.S."

HaShem was shocked. One Sabbath afternoon, He told His soul-mate:

"He wants the former critic to play Cleopatra."

Adonai replied:

"Isn't Fisch a bit too *cosmopolitan* for Antony?"

HaShem shook his head and clucked his tongue:

"No, Shakespeare wants him to play the *role* of Cleopatra. The Queen."

Adonai paused, for a moment, then said:

"Oh dear...Well, he *was* inside the man. *We* weren't. Will you set it in motion, or should I?"

That evening, Ahasuerus received a dream analogue from HaShem.

The Janitor was shocked:

"*Shakespeare is no shape-shifter,*" the dream-urging began. "*You are a fool to think so. Bring him back to N.E., and have him direct "Antony and Cleopatra" for the JAP. Although We do not have to bribe you, We will give you a Pillar of Fire for one week. It will answer all questions that are not of a personal nature, and will perform six miracles for the community, and one act of contrition for yourself.*"

The dream-analogue continued:

"In exchange for this production, Adonai will allow the JAP to produce a three week retrospective of Rodgers and Hammerstein musicals," continued the night-fever, *"and without any incursion of meteor showers channeled specifically to destroy the theater, which as you may well remember, occurred when JAP had decided to present a three-month revival of 'Sound of Music.'"*

"Mr. Shakespeare must be given free rein to cast whomever he pleases, and must be allowed to consume all the mussels he wishes, gratis. He has forgiven Molly the Mollusc, and must be allowed full use of the penthouse suite at the colony's King David Hotel, where he will reside with the Mollusc, Molly Malone, Molly Bloom, and any other Mollies who may inspire him."

"To show Me you have received, digested, and agreed to the contents of this Dream-analogue, please burn frankincense and myrrh for Me at nine pm sharp tomorrow, and some lavender and vetiver for Adonai at midnight tonight. If We receive nothing, you will be set upon for the next millenium by pale but nasty Venusian crabs. Don't forget: Adonai may appear to be sweet and lovely, but I am, as always, a jealous God."

Ahasuerus awoke in a dreadful sweat:

How to find Shakespeare?

He'd insulted the man, had called him a traitor and had planned to send him packing - before Shakespeare had done a scarper himself!

Certainly Lord HaShem could easily find a means to bring Shakespeare back to the Moon. But he, the Wandering Jew, had to show HaShem that he was *also* capable of making the effort.

Perhaps an announcement from the JAP, stating that William Shakespeare is being asked to direct "*Antony and Cleopatra,*" and that Ahasuerus and the Cabinet had erred by assuming that the playwright was a shape-shifter?

That would be the easiest way.

After all, nobody had asked the playwright to come see "*Merchant of Venice.*"

One day he had simply appeared!

"That's it," said Ahasuerus to himself. "A holo-vid of the JAP, so enthusiastic about the new production, and then the three Mollys saying that he was the greatest lover they'd ever had, how they hoped he would return, how they missed him, and that the rooftop suite of the King David was waiting for him, and it came with hot and cold running mussels..."

At that precise moment, because Piatnik runs on thought and not physical event, Shakespeare received the message.

He smiled to himself, pleasurably, at the image of the *Bistro Lunaire*, as well as three bedrooms-worth of Mollies in the penthouse suite at the King David Hotel.

And then, of course, there was the play.

He loved *Antony and Cleopatra*. ('It's for old cocks like myself, who've already had a career.')

He identified with Antony, at that particular time in the man's life. ("Just feed me and fuck me"), and adored how Antony could care less about the politics of Rome ("for young souls only; learn to make love, not war, you silly bastards.")

The fellow who'd played Bassanio in *Merchant of Venice* would make a good Enobarbus.

The company's Antonio, however, was too wispy for Antony.

"In which case," thought Shakespeare. "Maybe *I'll* play it. I'm old enough now, and I certainly know the role better than anyone but

Heminge. Besides, doing the part will enable me to keep Fisch and his performance in my sight."

Immediately he heard:

"*Done deal, Willie-boy. This could be the greatest comic triumph of your life. HaShem and Adonai.*"

"Comic triumph?" said Shakespeare, aloud. "What are you talking about? My play is a very respectable and mature tragedy."

Then he heard:

"*Not with Herschel Fisch as Cleo, it isn't, and you as Antony,*" and then the laughter, which hiccupped its way, merrily, throughout the Universe.

Shakespeare found himself, ten seconds later, in the Moon Theater of *Noye-Erdkelle,* facing a company of actors and actresses.

Downstage right, apart from the others, stood a very chastened Herschel Fisch.

He had fallen so deeply into his own guilt, for what he had thought of and done to the playwright, he appeared almost *fetching.*

"Right," said Shakespeare. "First order of business: Dr. Fisch is ordered to lose one hundred and sixty-three pounds immediately. I myself may gain fifteen pounds, perhaps twenty. You?" he said, pointing at the man who had played Bassanio. "What is your name, sir?"

"Pinky Lee."

"Excellent, Pinky. You will play Antony's lusty Enobarbus, companion to my own Mark Antony."

The company was shocked when they realized Shakespeare had cast himself as the cosmopolite conqueror. Then they began to applaud, with many of the members jumping up and down ecstatically. This was certainly a *first*, and a much bigger first than their lunar-Jewish production of "*Merchant of Venice,*" of months past.

"If that is the case," said Dr. Fisch to the others, when the applause had died down, "I will become anorexic. Or better still, I'll practice the gentle art of bulimia. I have heard it's quite engaging."

"Isn't that dangerous?" asked Shakespeare.

"I piss on danger!" roared Fisch, then simpered: "What kind of Queen am I, if I cannot look perfect for my Antony?" and pursed his lips, moving them in and out like a blowfish, while gazing at the playwright with a lewd and provocative glance.

"Indeed," said William Shakespeare, frowning. "And now, let me give some advice to the rest of you players."

And he did, and which I won't repeat, for you doubtlessly have heard it before.

The eightieth canto

Shakespeare said nothing.

He stroked his beard, nodding to himself, and gazing at the mullions in the window of Queen Elizabeth's anteroom.

After a moment he took a long breath, then turned to Moshe:

"And you would go to the underworld realm, because you'd kissed this Queen?"

"We go because we have no choice," said Moussa. "It's all very cut-and-dried."

"You follow in the path of Thomas the Rhymer," frowned Shakespeare, "who met the Queen of Elfland, scraped her, then was made to serve her for seven years without speech. Afterwards, she gave him the tongue that would not lie. For a writer, that is a dangerous thing. When he returned to our world, he produced nothing at all of note."

"Indeed. For if we did not lie," said Moshe, "we would not be here today."

"In truth," added Moses, "we would be dead."

"And look what lying has done, sir!" smiled Moussa, simply. "Lying has brought us to London. Lying has placed us before this very Queen."

"And yet," added Moshe, "I do not consider the telling of tales to be a lie. There is so much in a tale that has more profundity and wisdom than in most men's lives. How can we consider the lovely Joslian to be a lie, when our very faith in our ability to use our imagination, to conjur a vision that would be shared by our hearers, or to demand of our intelligence the ability to survive the violence of the *djinn*, or piracy, or even death, has brought us so far, and in so short a time, and has produced this extravagant Goddess in our arms?"

"Still," said Shakespeare, "we all die, in time."

"I'm not so sure," said Moshe, "any more than to say: we all are born, in time."

"I call death 'the undiscovered country, from whose bourn no traveler has returned,'" Shakespeare replied.

"That is what *I* say as well," nodded Moshe. "But that does not mean that life ends with death. It could mean that one voyages *from* this life to elsewhere, just as one has voyaged *to* this life from elsewhere."

"'*There is more in heaven and earth, Horatio, than is dreamt of in your philosophy*,'" replied Shakespeare.

"Who is Horatio?" asked Moses.

"Would you yourself come with us to the place of Underworld Women?" asked Moussa.

Shakespeare smiled, as much to himself as to the others:

"I have thought of nought else, as you were telling your tale," answered Shakespeare. "But I have plays to write, roles to perform, a wife at Stratford, a farm and a daughter. Were I younger, perhaps----"

"You would stay in this stinking hole of a town rather than follow a Goddess or two into another world?" asked Moshe. "I find that hard to believe."

"If seven years were to pass, as it had with The Rhymer," frowned the poet, "what could I possibly do when I returned? What would have happened to my wife and daughter? Or to my more familiar Queen?"

Shakespeare gazed longingly at the trio, and then smiled wanly, when a courtier appeared, followed by a fat gentleman and then, behind them, Queen Elizabeth.

The eighty-first canto

Queen Elizabeth resembled a vengeful grasshopper with a copper wig.

Shakespeare bowed.

The trio stared.

"My Sovereign," said the playwright, quickly. "I promised you a play, and now I've delivered its lines. Printed by memory, I fear; still, it's a quarto of some worth, and prompted fully by your own regard."

Elizabeth Tudor took the quarto, kissed it, then handed it to the fat man.

"And are these your friends?" she asked.

"They are the friends of a Goddess of Underworld Women," said Shakespeare. "I wish I had transcribed their story, it is so full of factual fable and fabulous fact."

The Queen nodded coldly.

"And what has She to do with ourselves?" she asked.

"Our Lady would align her underworld power with yours, and thereby increase your own power a millionfold," began Moussa.

The fat man, standing slightly to the right of the Queen, snorted, then shook his head.

"I know *that one* to be an Hebrew," he said, superciliously, pointing at Moussa, "and that *other* to be a Moor," he added, gesturing towards Moshe. "Which must make *this other fellow*...Welsh."

"The gentleman is brilliant," Moses replied. "I am indeed Welsh. And my friends are indeed Moor and Jew. But not in the order in which you'd presented them."

"If they are tellers of tales, My Queen, I would not believe them," said the fat man, bouncing up and down on his heels, left hand behind his back, and frowning darkly at the trio. "Certainly, that man" – pointing at Moshe – "is the infidel Moor, and the other an ancient Hebrew."

"My Lord Burghley," replied the Queen. "It is my pleasure to ask you to withdraw, and to tell the Earl not to admit anyone to this chamber."

Burghley raised his eyebrows, surprised.

Then he appeared about to cry.

Without a word to the others, he left the room.

"Is *Cerridwen ap Gwynnedd* a part of this plot?" asked Queen Elizabeth, quietly.

"But there is no plot," said Moshe and Moussa together.

And both thought: there go our heads!

The eighty-second canto

While Shakespeare was directing Herschel Fisch in "Antony and Cleopatra," the much younger Shakespeare, (eight hundred years younger, in fact), was happy to see that Herschel Fisch, who was then Lord Burghley, and eight hundred years younger as well, had been politely disgraced by Elizabeth Tudor, "By the Grace of God, Queen of England and France, Defender of the Faith, Lord of Ireland and of the Church of England and also of Ireland in Earth, under Jesus Christ, Supreme Head."

Moses, Moshe and Moussa, who might seem as yet to have no role in our tale of the future, but who are protagonists in the earlier years of *Jews Beyond Jupiter*, were frightened by the grasshopper-like Defender of the Faith, Lord of Ireland etc.

She gave away nothing.

She watched, like an insect, and occasionally smiled. Coldly, intelligently.

Shakespeare and she seemed to speak a coded language which none of the others could understand. Moses was himself too much the provincial to read their verbal signals and body language, while Moses and Moussa were strangers to the culture.

What made the situation even odder was the Queen's extravagant dress, her dreadful skin covered by intensely white make-up, and her huge and high copper wig. Her eyes were startling. Were they green? Ferny brown? Or so black and penetrating they seemed to possess no color?

Cerridwen was far more feminine.

As for Joslian, She was *The* Feminine.

In the presence of those women, Queen Elizabeth was a clown's grotesque.

"Poet," she began. "Do you attest to the truth of these men's tale?"

"I don't attest to the veracity *of my own tales*, My Beloved Sovereign," shrugged Shakespeare, apologetically. "How then may I attest *to theirs*?"

"Will you accompany them to the Land of the Otherworld Women, and bring us a report of your voyage?"

"If ordered by Your Majesty, I will accompany them to Hell itself," he replied, and both he and the Queen crossed themselves, and smiled.

"*So be it*," said Elizabeth Tudor (by the Grace of God, Queen of England and France, Defender of the Faith, Lord of Ireland and of the Church of England and also of Ireland in Earth, under Jesus Christ, Supreme Head). "If your expedition is prosperous," she continued, "you will be our Ambassador to the Land of the Underworld Women forever, as well as the only Poet to write of such an expedition. You will also receive a percentage of any 'toys and knick-knacks,' which would be the result of an alliance between ourselves and the Queen."

Shakespeare blushed, nodding:

"And the Lord Chamberlains' Men, my Sovereign? What about my work with them?"

"What about your work?" replied the Queen, with an extravagant throw-away gesture of her right hand. "Burbage and Kemp and that marvelous bitch of a boy won't die, if you're gone for a time. We will send Essex to them. He wants us to see your *Richard the Second*, which one hears is supposedly about ourselves."

Shakespeare blushed once again:

"That is a lie," snapped the playwright, "and the speaker has my gage."

"My poet, That was a jest," replied the Queen, "and the writer has our word."

Then she turned to Moshe and the others and said, "Lord Burghley will draw an agreement between yourselves, the playwright, and ourselves, in which I give you leave to explore the Land of the Underworld Women in order for our playwright to report to us privately, and from which exploration we may then decide whether to form an auspicious alliance with --- what is her name?"

Moshe and Moussa turned to Moses, who said:

"'*N arddim 'n aflafar cariadferch Joslian, Queen of the Gwragedd Annwn.*"

"The Harsh but Beautiful Mistress Joslian," recited Moses and Moussa together. "Queen of the Underworld Women."

"It sounds as if Marlowe had a hand in the title, poor beggar," said the Queen, and turned to the door. "Do not leave this chamber, any of you, until you have our letter and seal."

"May I quit London in seven days, my Lady?" whispered Shakespeare, politely but provocatively. "Tonight I am supposed to play King Hamlet."

"You will leave London as soon as we have presented you with the letter, Master Shakespeare," said the Queen. "Do not make us feel you have been 'hoisted by your own petard.' Is that not what you say in this new play - *Hamlet*?"

Shakespeare nodded.

When she had left, and with a mere nod to the trio, the playwright gnashed at himself:

"How did she know I *wrote* such a line? *Who* gave her the text? Tonight is its *first performance!*"

Then he turned to the trio, eyes wide, out of control, and hissing: "*What have you done to cause such a disaster in my life?*"

Sympathetically, Moshe shrugged and said, "Nothing. We told you a story, that's all."

"Yes," said Shakespeare, "*but was it true*?"

"None of us know yet," shrugged Moussa, quietly. "But it might be."

"I'm sure it is," said Moses, nodding vigorously.

"Even if it's not," said Moshe, "I'm sure it will be a consolation to know, as you yourself said: in time, everyone dies."

"Besides," added Moussa. "I've always believed there's a special providence in the fall of a sparrow. The readiness is all, wouldn't you say?"

Shakespeare stared, open-mouthed:"*What do you mean, wouldn't I say? I said it! That's from Hamlet as well!' Nobody's seen it yet!* ***Why are you all reciting my words?***"

And he heard, as they all did, a female voice, distinct but disembodied, intone:

"*Because I told them, poet.*"

Shakespeare turned to Moshe, who sighed, then smiled and shook his head with a kind of comic fatalism:

"What can I tell you, sir? Sometimes the devil, to win us to his side...'

"Enough!" shouted Shakespeare. "I have the point!"

Then, growling, after a moment, he muttered:

"At least I hope they eat well, in the Otherworld."

"As long as it's not *us*," said Moussa, cheerily, "I'm sure it will be fine."

An eleventh riff to Mnemosyne, before we swing into eighty-third canto

This is strange, because now I'm going to have to acknowledge that I've seen fairies, ghosts, have traveled out-of-body to lots of strange places and to stranger times; that I've meditated with monks, shamans, iyaloshas, babaloshas, babalawos, mambas, and with drummers for the Great Spirit.

I've smoked grass twice, and thrown up the second time, and with enough vigor and paranoia to keep me from smoking it again.

I am not a child of the 'Sixties.

I've never dropped acid, taken speed.

I'm not a child of the 'Seventies or 'Eighties either.

I worked with too many coked-up producers and actors, and so had to endure their paranoia by proxy.

I've worked with schizophrenic children at the Childrens' Unit of Camarillo Mental Institution, and organized athletics and taught theater and creative writing to disturbed adolescent girls at the Las Palmas School for Girls, a polite title for one California prison.

I've taught Dostoievsky to blue collar workers, Shaw to junior high and high school students, and how to write screenplays and plays to undergraduates and graduate students.

You may trust me when I write that I can tell the difference between an hallucination, a spiritual vision, and a schizophrenic world view.

I write every day, and have, for the past fifty-eight years.

For over forty years I've been hired to write what has amounted to at least forty feature films and television series.

I've directed documentaries, plays and a feature film.

I've had my good share of acting as well.

Two of the tv series aired, all the documentaries aired, nine of the forty-some features I wrote were shot. You may see me in the first international filmed American tv series, 'From The Secret Files of the French Surete.' More recently, check out Zoefilms International Film Festival, for 2000. Best comedy of the year. "Cuppa Cabby, Piece o' Pie." My wife and I are the leads.

We also acted together in a limited Boston run of our play, "Opportunities in Zero Gravity." (Kae was brilliant).

The independent film I wrote and directed was sold to RAI Film, Italy, which made me very happy because Italy was my soul's film school: Fellini, De Sica, Petri, Germi, Antonioni and Scola were my teachers. My boys' deans, sadly, were Carlo Ponti and Dino De Laurentiis.

Unlike them, however, I was too naive to court law-suits.

So far I've had five novels published, and a book on screenwriting, although I've written over twenty-five novels. That's one out of six screenplays shot, and one out of six novels published.

The plays, however, are always spot on.

And if I schmooz hard about them, they get performed.

The point of this is that I write what I want to write, or am compelled to write.

Whatever my agent can sell - whenever I have an agent - is what he or she can sell.

The point of this is that I write what I want to write, or am compelled to write. Whatever my agent can sell - whenever I have an agent - is what he or she can sell. My only life-long steady job is to write every day, whether or not I have a contract to sell what I am writing.

An additional addition to the eleventh riff to Mnemosyne, before we swing into the eighty-third canto

I have been one of the lead plaintiffs in a class action suit against the television networks, film studios and talent agencies.

The issue was greylisting, which is the blacklisting by the industry of any writer over forty, regardless of sex, race or religion. Greylisting, unlike Blacklisting, is very democratic, in its own way.

It's called age discrimination.

It's also one of the main reasons this country's been dumbed-down since the original Hollywood Blacklist itself, in which Hollywood had agreed to dump some of its finer talents for political jingoism and the studio's film market. (The blacklist in educational institutions merits a book in itself, and far more vomit than I produced the second and last time I smoked grass).

The entertainment industry, most of it, settled our claim.

Only one talent agency held out, declaring with an arrogance that fully mirrors its history, that it is innocent of all charges.

Thus we won all but one of the suits.

After twelve years.

And we created a Fund for the Future, which exists to help older writers to get their works seen, produced, distributed. If it actually can function, it will bring older audiences back to theaters and to television sets and computer screens and cell-phones, for it will help produce works of narrative excitement and dramatic merit.

We consider The Fund the opposite of dumbing-down.

We believe, rather, it's about brightening up.

An addition to the additional additions of the eleventh riff to Mnemosyne, before we swing into eighty-third canto

Are there themes in my work that keep manifesting with an insistence that demands more invention, polish and art, and each time I write?

Yes indeed, and here they are:

One) The universe is a love story.

The feminine lurks in the background, while the masculine struts in the foreground.

Unfortunately, whether the narrative is a comedy or tragedy, the universe's love story - more often than not - is at heart dysfunctional.

Two) The world is a magical place, but we can't see its wonder.

During those rare moments when we recognize the magic, however, we suffer a shift in our perceptions and blame it on the magician; or we create a new church in his or her honor. Immediately we lock the doors, thinking we've found god, when we should have kept the doors wide open and let in the light, rather than growing cross-eyed by the constant and limited stare of our constantly limited vision.

Three) Making things is exciting: from dances to novels to films to babies. Making stories about making things is a key to the mystery of the Jews. (See *Jews On The Moon*).

Yes, and here's another theme, which I think is grand:

Four) Two people looking into each other's eyes, while making love or being made love to, transcends time and space, creating all sorts of universes, and putting the lovers at the center of a (if not THE) universal mystery.

THE ULTIMATE ADDITION

to the eleventh riff to Mnemosyne, before we swing into eighty-third canto

I've lived and traveled throughout Europe a good part of my life, and feel more at home in Paris and Rome and Amsterdam than I do in most places in the United States, except Savannah, Georgia; or Newport, Rhode Island, at five in the morning, in a dense fog; or in Toluca Lake, California, in the early 'Forties, (when we were fighting a different kind of war than we've been fighting, more on than off, since the late 'Fifties), when you could ride your bike all the way from Sarah Street to Riverside Drive without seeing a freeway or even knowing what it would be.

That kind of Toluca Lake is not in Toluca Lake any more, though it still lives in my mind.

Nor, for that matter, are those United States *in* these United Red States or the United Blue States.

I love words, and learning languages, and seeing, sharply, things like paintings and sculpture and films, and learning everything I can about music and languages, history.

Good stories, all of them.

Which ones are more real?

And who's telling the truth?

I don't think anybody is, and I'll tell you why:

Yesterday, while waiting for my daughter's ballet class to end, my wife overheard one of the ballet mothers say, ever so sweetly: "*The Lord doesn't give you anything you can't handle.*"

Not being from the Wal-mart Department of Spiritual Saws, I told my wife I was happy I hadn't been there to hear it. There was already enough saccharine on sale by America's preachers, I'd have become diabetic.

"*The Lord doesn't give you anything you can't handle.*"

Tell that double-negative to a lovely student of mine who was burned from head-to-toe while rescuing horses from a burning stable, and now looks like the lead from "Phantom of the Opera."

Then tell it to every victim of genocide, racism, murder, and greed.

Another mother said, "My son wants to be a missionary in Haiti because he needs to do good works and show the poor that God is Good. Naturally we won't deal with that voodoo stuff."

I'm glad I wasn't there to say: go rob a bank and give poor people all the money, and let them figure out what to do with it.

Or: work for a bank, rob your clients, and give the money to your friends. It's done many times, every day. When the bank finally folds, ask Congress for a bailout.

After all, as these past two decades of Banking/Wall Street/ Governmental piracy have proven, no bullshit is ever too big to fail.

As for all the voodoo stuff, it's older than Jesus, and has kept Africans and Haitians and most of the African diaspora alive, and against impossible odds.

Don't *ever* knock the voodoo stuff.

I've lived too long to believe anybody has a hold on truth and can't let go.

Still, I live for stories.

And I know that until we learn to love each other and to treat each other as we would wish to be treated, there'll always be more than enough material for historians to pretend they're writing the truth; more than enough religious people to believe they're living it; and a few decent writers savvy enough to record, for the future, all the things God knew people could handle, but who, not so surprisingly, didn't.

Poor God.

The eighty-third canto

"*Age cannot wither her, nor custom stale her infinite variety.*"

Shakespeare stared at Fisch, balefully.

This was their first rehearsal.

"Do you understand the implications of that line, Doctor?"

"*Obviously*," said Fisch, drily, the critic elbowing the actor out of his sight-lines.

"*Really?*" replied the playwright, with a slight raise of his eyebrows. "And do you know what that means, *for you, as an actress?*"

"That I'm eternally lovely, and filled with various emotional turns," drawled Fisch, smiling at the others, and pursing his lips.

"No," said Shakespeare. "Not at all. Enobarbus is saying you are the most delectable whore on the planet. A stale is a whore. The pun is in *stale* as a noun, and *stale* as a verb. But what matters to me, and which Enobarbus' line is cue-ing the audience, is that you play every emotional turn for its full value. Every line spoken and everything unspoken, but seen in gesture, is *always different*. I want you remember that, Doctor. Cleopatra is the consummate player. She even creates her audience by her desired action and attitude towards them – whether it's Dolabella, Antony, Charmian, the Clown, or even Caesar. She makes them respond to her, as she wishes to be perceived. She's Playwright. Queen. You've never known a Queen --- well, that's not true. As Burleigh, of course, you knew our Sovereign..."

Fisch stared at Shakespeare, confused.

"I'm a refined reader, not a critic. Burleigh?" he blustered, confused. "I've never played Burleigh. I've never played anyone. You must be mistaking me with someone else."

"Quite right," said the playwright, blushing. "As *Cleopatra*, ask yourself: *what is my intention?* Choose *one*, before you speak the line or do whatever piece of business you've decided to do. Cleopatra is constantly on stage. And who is she? A legend, yet a human being. A Queen. An actress. A divine whore. As Cleopatra, you've been protecting your country and your child's position. You don't want to lose Egypt. Ptolemy, Caesar, Antony, you've fucked them all to maintain your role. Augustus, however, is a thorough cunt, every bit as great as you, so there's no way you're going to seduce *him*."

"Yes, but do I love Antony?" asked Fisch.

"If you didn't, there wouldn't be much of a play," answered Shakespeare, quietly. "But that's not a bad thought. Perhaps you don't realize how much you love him until it's too late. Hear, wait, don't tell me your motives," Shakespeare said, suddenly, and stood up, clapping his hands.

"Why?" asked Herschel Fisch, surprised.

"Because I don't want to know them," smiled Shakespeare. "I'm playing Antony, remember? In fact, I don't think we'll rehearse the play at all, you and I. Memorize your lines, and be prepared to do the play in two months. And if you've not dropped at least one hundred and fifty pounds, prepare to be destroyed on stage."

"But----"

"I'll have the production manager call you for costume fitting and make-up in six weeks. Go home. Lose weight. Memorize your lines. And remember what I told you: *Intention is all. You are the playwright. We're just the audience. You are the play. Antony is your devoted slave.*"

Shakespeare did not feel decadent or ancient saying this, or doing this.

He *wanted* to be surprised.

He knew Cleopatra's intentions, but had written the role in such a way as to give the actor/actress every possibility to deliver the lines in any number of ways.

The masterpiece still ended in two suicides, with the pair fucking their brains out, and having lots of other kinds of fun along the way: fighting sea-wars, eating like divas, love-hating each other in the process, and reciting some very dazzling poetry.

"Go!" Shakespeare called to Fisch, and surprised himself by saying: "Make us proud, *Herschelle*!"

Then he turned to the actor playing Enobarbus.

"You've some of the best lines in the play," he began. "Remember this: *all* monosyllabic words are to be *spo-ken slow-ly*. You can *rush* all the polysyllabic words you wish. But if you speed the monosyllables, you will sound like an actor who doesn't know what he's saying; and because you've a lovely voice, it will sound ridiculously pretentious. Now let's begin, shall we, from the description of Cleopatra's barge?"

The eighty-fourth canto

The Mollies were waiting for him on the terrace-suite of the King David.

They were moon-bathing, the three of them, and the poet-playwright, horny as hell, and happy, whispered to himself, "'*No, Time, thou shalt not boast that I do change.*'"

He felt his penis rise, and added:

"'*This I do vow, and this shall ever be: I will be true despite thy scythe and thee.*'"

The Mollies smiled, and Ms. Malone and Ms. Bloom removed his clothes, and led him to a chair, as the Mollusc said, aloud: "All listeners, will you please go away for half an hour?" and those moon colony listeners who had been attuned to Shakespeare's thoughts swiftly switched to other channels.

As our playwright fell into the differing powers and intensities of each Molly, he whispered aloud: "This is so familiar."

Then:

"Do thy duty, Muse."

Which they did, upon him, singly, and then together.

And yet, in the recess of his memory, he asked, in wonder: "Why is this so familiar?"

Then he recited:

"'*Fair," "kind," and "true" have often lived alone, Which three till now never kept seat in one.*' "

Suddenly he remembered everything, and he began to shake:

"***You!***" he called, and leaped up, with two of the women hanging upon him still: "***Gwragedd Annwn! The Otherworld Women!***"

The eighty-fifth canto

The harsh but beautiful mistress Joslian, Queen of the Otherworld Women, as well as Cerridwen, the Pirate Queen, led the three Moses before them.

They were blindfolded, and tied together with a piece of Joslian's hair, which they could never break.

Stumbling behind the women, bound and also blindfolded, was the Warwickshire poet.

Shakespeare had not yet seen the women.

When the odd trio and the writer had left Queen Elizabeth Tudor and were standing before her castle, they'd found themselves bound, swiftly, then blindfolded and whisked to a cooler clime.

"It is easy to go astray here," Joslian was saying. "Which is why you're blindfolded. Now we are passing the History of your People, and the choices they have made, and because you have the advantage of hindsight, if you saw them, you would interfere and risk altering the course of events - "*which ne'er did run smooth*,"- she smiled. "And now we are passing the Origin of Life, which none of you can possibly understand, and which you would question, and which question would alter the direction life travels; once through History and its Origins, we will remove your blindfolds, and together we will cross the Bridge to the Otherworld of Underworld Women."

Shakespeare said, "I would not interfere with history nor with the origin of life."

"Oh, but you have, playwright," said Joslian. "You have interfered with history in your works, albeit brilliantly. And if I were to ask you the origin of life, you would quote from the Hebrew Bible, and then from the New Testament, and once again you would interfere with processes you could not begin to understand. Be patient."

"Be patient? I could not be a writer otherwise," whispered Shakespeare, almost bitterly. "I listen, I watch. I would not interfere."

"Patience," replied Joslian, quietly. "As your own Lear once said - although he never really said it at all."

The eighty-sixth canto

An enormous wall of water swept over the edge of a enormously wide and clear glass rock, then splashed into a diamond basin.

Two sycamores, on either side of the falls, covered the river as it moved downstream.

And then a breeze, gentle and fragrant with jasmine, wafted towards them.

Immediately, their blindfolds and binding disappeared.

"Spenserian fields" whispered Shakespeare, in awe.

"The woods outside Athens?" smiled Joslian.

"Yes," nodded the poet, "though there never was a woods outside Athens, but 'tis how I imagined them."

"And the fairies?" asked Cerridwen? "Did you imagine them too?"

Shakespeare shook his head:

"I imagined nothing. I'd seen them," he said. "As a youth. Nothing to imagine, except the song," and he looked up at the women who were seated on a pair of white stallions, with gold bridles, holding silver reins with tiny bells.

Both women were glowing.

"Of course," he whispered.

"Of course what?" asked Joslian.

"Your beauty is unearthly. I expected no less."

Joslian moved from her horse, and stood before Shakespeare, smiling. The perfume from her hair and lips, and her lean, perfectly proportioned body caused him to swoon slightly. All the fragrances of Nature were within her, and all of its sweetness and seduction.

"Do not kiss me," said Shakespeare. "I need to stay awake."

"*They* have kissed me," said Cerridwen, pointing to Moshe, Moussa and Moses. "And *they* are still *awake*."

"If we had your beauty," said Moses, almost yearningly, "I could not imagine what our lives would be."

"But you cannot," said Joslian. "And yet, you can be beautiful, in your own human way..."

"I'm not so sure," said Moshe, "that I would want to be as beautiful as that—"

"Too late," sighed Moussa, and held his hands before him for Moshe to see, for they had become softer, and more shapely, with perfectly shaped nails.

"All right," said Moshe, worriedly, "as long as we become men once again..."

"*Here*?" laughed Cerridwen. "In the Otherworld of the Otherworld Women? That's impossible. But you needn't worry: we'll remove your memories, and you'll live here until you're capable of using your newfound powers as magical women. Then we'll send you back to the land of Wales, the perfect place to balance your Otherworld magic with the magic of my sister, Nature. You'll become Muses – Moshe and Moussa and Moses."

Shakespeare watched the transformation, and was thrilled.

"'*I have had a most rare vision*,'" he said. "'*I have had a dream past the wit of man to say what dream it was. Man is but an ass if he go about t'expound this dream...*'"

Joslian, the Harsh but Beautiful Mistress of Otherworld Women, nodded.

"It is all metamorphosis," she said. "Once you are in love, and have fallen under our spell, the world's written by Ovid. He knew it better than any other. He's here even now. Like yourself, Mister William, (if you so choose), he's one of the few men we allow to come and go, as a man, in our world."

The transformation of Moses, Moussa and Moshe was not yet complete, but Shakespeare had turned away from them, and was staring at the glowing, swaying column of perfume that was Joslian:

"Then you are the world within Nature, its secretest world, its essence," he said.

"We are The Philosopher's Stone of the Goddess," said Joslian.

"Then there *is* such a thing, after all," nodded Shakespeare.

"Indeed there is," said Cerridwen, "as there is the Otherworld, which you see before you."

"But you don't come here by boiling root and leaf, any more than you find the Philosopher's Stone by infusing matter with mercury and other substances," replied Joslian. "A woman putting on rare perfumes, and copper wigs is not any closer to becoming one of us than is an alchemist with his alembics, attempting to gain power over creation or to get to its source."

Shakespeare nodded.

Now he was feeling jealous of Ovid. One of the few poets whom he always had loved, but who also had always disturbed him.

"Of course, transformation is the spirit of theater as well," said Shakespeare. "Even the meanest playwright has to master the elements of change in his creations, if the play is to catch the heart of the crowd."

"How many of your creatures become the essence of passions, and change accordingly?" asked Joslian. "How many of your creations are changed by love, or by its absence? Love is at the heart of our own Philosopher's Stone here. You will write of this, in time, how Love is at the very heart of forgiveness and reconciliation. And there will be fairies, and masques, and transformations that finally will make Ovid himself jealous."

Shakespeare blushed, for Joslian had seen into his soul.

He turned to the other woman.

"You stir things," said Shakespeare, to Cerridwen, "for what end? As a Pirate Queen?"

"Indeed," said Cerridwen ap Gwynnedd. "What better way to disturb man and make him dream than to be at the very seat of his anger, lust and frolic?"

"If we don't make you dream one way," said Joslian, "we'll make you dream another. Look at your friends now."

Shakespeare had forgotten about the three Moses who had now become Three Muses: they were seated together, by the river, making crowns of flowers from musk-roses, eglantine, woodbine, oxlips, violets and wild thyme.

"Gentlemen?" called the playwright, and one of them turned. She was darker than the others, with long eyelashes and a soft but penetrating gaze. "You are Moshe," said Shakespeare. "Or Moussa?"

The young woman blushed, saying nothing. Then she turned back to the others, and continued to help weave garlands.

"And will they awaken?" asked Shakespeare, turning to the Harsh but Beautiful Mistress.

"Yes," she said. "Once they've slept."

"As men – once again?" urged the playwright.

"Never more," said Joslian, shaking her head. "They are happier here. The world of men appears to have defeated them, so they have become story-tellers. Now they will become companions to other story-tellers, and will inspire them."

"The world of men would defeat anyone," laughed Cerridwen, "not strong enough to see through it. Don't fret about them, Will. They are much stronger now."

"I myself wish to remain a man," said Shakespeare, calmly, but fearfully.

"As I said," smiled Joslian, "we prefer you as yourself. We would have you no other way. You've served us for many lives, and will continue to do so."

"Served you *as whom*?" stammered the playwright.

"As yourself," said Joslian, with an ironic smile.

Shakespeare sat by a tree, his back to it, and thought: "*These trees shall be my books...*"

And then he said, "*And I, forsooth, in love--I that have been love's whip, A very beadle to a humorous sigh, A critic, nay, a night-watch constable, A domineering pedant o'er the boy...*"

The boy, of course, being Cupid, and Shakespeare "*a corporal of his field.*"

"You've always written of us," said Joslian.

"And we're more than soft," she said, and her eyes darkened, and her hair.

And suddenly she was dressed in black, and standing high above the writer, and whispering: "'*I have given suck and know How tender 'tis to love the babe that milks me. I would, while it was smiling in my face, Have plucked my nipple from his boneless gums And dashed the brains out, had I so sworn As you have done to this.'"*

Cerridwen leaped from her horse and grabbed the playwright by his hair, looking down upon him, her face altered to chilling cruelty: "'*So white, and such a traitor!*'" She spat in his face, crying, "'*One side will mock another. The other too! Give me thy sword!*'" she called to Joslian. "'*A peasant stand up thus!*'"

Shakespeare covered his face with his hands, and both women began to laugh.

"You wrote it," said Joslian. "We didn't. We can be anything you wish. Like an actor. Only with this difference: *our power is real, as is yours*."

"I have no power like yours," said Shakespeare, and wiped his face.

"You have the power of imagination," Joslian replied. "And you serve us well."

"And I may come and go as does the Roman poet?" he asked.

"You already do," replied Joslian, "although you are not awake. We will let you awaken, on occasion."

"With such power as you possess," wondered the playwright, "why do you hide, down here, from men?"

"We are neither their equal, nor are we their betters, nor are we their worse," said Joslian. "When HaShem created Adam and Lilith, they fought because She wanted to be treated as an equal, and so she left Adam. Then Chava was born. So She is considered the mother of all men. But we are older than she."

"They say Lilith mated with the demon Samael," replied Shakesepeare.

"Lilith mated with all manner of angels," shrugged Joslian. "Chava mated with a snake. Do you see the difference between man and woman?

Can you say what it is, or are you drawn to the Feminine by a passion which you cannot define?"

Shakespeare said nothing.

Then:

"What am I to tell Queen Elizabeth? Now that our trio has become muse-like and, I assume, will not be returning to London with me?"

"Tell her what you've seen," said Cerridwen.

"If she wishes to drawn upon our energy, we can change the face of the world together," added Joslian.

"And if she does not?" asked Shakesepare.

"Then she will be known as Elizabeth Tudor, the Virgin Queen," smiled Joslian, "and she will muddle through conspiracy, invasion, defense, and death, as all who have gone before her have done. But you wrote it yourself. You might recite it to her. It is one of my favorite poems: '*For within the hollow crown That rounds the mortal temples of a king Keeps Death his court; and there the antic sits, Scoffing his state and grinning at his pomp, Allowing him a breath, a little scene, To monarchize, be feared, and kill with looks, Infusing him with self and vain conceit, As if this flesh which walls about our life Were brass impregnable; and humoured thus, Comes at the last, and with a little pin Bores through his castle wall; and farewell, king.*' Tell her that."

"Before we left," said Shakespeare, with ironic memory, "My Sovereign exclaimed that Richard the Second was about herself. Now you're asking me to quote him, or at least to quote a speech I gave him. I'ld prefer not to."

"Well, it's time you come with us for an evening's pleasure," said Joslian, with a sly look at Cerridwen. "Then you'll find yourself back in London."

"And if the Queen says yes, that she wants to join her power with yours?" asked Shakespeare, avoiding Joslian's seduction. "How do I find you?"

"Go to your first best bed, and think of us," said Cerridwen.

"Sleep in the woods and fields?" he asked.

"By a stream. We'll find you," said Joslian, and blew in his ear, and nothing else was seen, though everything was felt.

And then he was back in London, at the Globe, and Condell was helping him into a suit of armor, and Shakespeare was saying,"What's my first line?" and Condell replied, "No line, Master. You walk across the stage and stare."

"And who am I this time?" he asked.

"King Hamlet! Don't frighten me, Master Will."

"Is this my first or second appearance?"

"First. Your cue is Barnardo's "*Where now it burns, Marcellus and myself, The bell then beating one*—Go!"

Shakespeare went.

And scared the hell out of everybody.

The eighty-seventh canto

Elizabeth Tudor, in a dark coach and halted across the river from the Globe, was waiting for Shakespeare.

"Why did everybody have to die?" she asked, when he had appeared, then bowed before her door, then entered the coach, as she had commanded, and sat opposite her.

"To what are you referring, Your Majesty?"

"To *Hamlet*."

"Would you wish Hamlet to have lived?" he asked, quietly, eyebrows raised.

"Who wouldn't?" she replied, staring keenly. "Only a Catholic like you would destroy him. Ophelia, Polonius, Laertes – because of him, the entire family's dead; Gertrude, Claudius – his mother and uncle, dead. Those two court fops. Beheaded. That's seven people. And, because of him, we'll never know how many Danes Fortinbras had killed. Am I to assume the theme of the play, if we are to refer to Hamlet, Laertes and Fortinbras, is: *boys will be boys?*"

"What you will, my Sovereign," said Shakespeare with a soft smile.

"Still, you're the best poet, William. One forgives that silly plot of yours."

"It's hardly all mine, My Gracious Queen."

She smiled, patted him on the knee, and handed him a bag of coins.

"Now then: on to serious matters. Your Joslian. Is she real?"

"Yes, she is."

"And does she really live in an Otherworld?"

"Yes, She does."

"How do I know she's not a demon, like Hamlet's father?"

"You don't."

"And would I be endlessly powerful if I aligned myself with her?"

"You would."

"And if not?"

"As you said, Your Majesty, referring to Hamlet: like everyone else in the drama, eventually you will die."

Queen Elizabeth waved away the remark.

"But can you say you know her well enough to trust her?"

"I cannot."

"Is she beautiful?"

"She is."

"More than I?"

"Do I keep these coins, or do I lose my head?"

Queen Elizabeth laughed:

"I have been known as the Virgin Queen, The Fairie Queen, Gloriana, Good Queen Bess. Now I am to be known as the Otherqueen of the Otherworld? What's that in Welsh?"

"*Arall banon chan 'r Gwranedd Annwn,*" Shakespeare heard, and repeated.

"I didn't know you spoke Welsh," said Queen Elizabeth, surprised.

"I don't," Shakespeare replied. "That was She, speaking through me."

Elizabeth nodded. She didn't appear surprised.

"*Ask her: how do we share the Queendom here?*"

Shakespeare closed his eyes, listened, then said:

"You rule here, she rules there, and each helps the other when needed."

"Tell her to come to me herself, Will. You may go now."

Shakespeare nodded, knelt before the Queen, then left the carriage.

Even after he had died, in that time, he never learned what the Queen had finally decided to do.

The eighty-eighth canto

But before Her Gracious Majesty herself had died– Elizabeth Tudor, Queen of England and France, Defender of the Faith, Lord of Ireland and of the Church of England and also of Ireland in Earth, under Jesus Christ, Supreme Head, aka The Virgin Queen, the Fairie Queen, Glorianna and Good Queen Bess –Shakespeare had learned from the courtier, Lord Cecil:

"Passing strange, but in her final days Our Gracious Sovereign had become fluent in that barbarous tongue of the Welsh lands."

The eighty-ninth canto

"In the first place," said Fisch, "Cleopatra the Seventh was related to Alexander the Great, as Appian writes, in his *Syrian Wars.* Her understanding of territorial gains was a principal motive for her supposed interest in Antonius - if *Holbl* and *Porphyrios* are to be believed. Love, as Plutarch describes, was *the least of it*, historically..."

Shakespeare closed his eyes, then turned to Fisch, who was seated upstage left, babbling, in a litter, held aloft by three swarthy Jews, posed as Nubian slaves.

The world's greatest reader looked fabulously *zoftik* - more like Mae West than Glenda Jackson.

And he was sweating in mortal fear.

"Of course," Fisch continued to chatter, "when Caesar himself arrived in Egypt---"

"Here's our cue," said Shakespeare, cutting him off, and smiling nastily: "Listen to me, darling: Forget all that swill you've just been preaching. We're about to go onstage. Instead, why don't you open your mouth as if you had just decided to blow me?"

Swiftly, Shakespeare moved onto the proscenium.

The litter-bearers followed, carrying the terrified Herschel Fisch.

The applause was more than tumultuous.

It was eternal.

Shakespeare had been recognized.

The production, unbeknownst to Fisch, was being broadcast through 75,624 time and space zones, as well as 142 time-travelling links.

Cutting over the applause, and to a fearful Fisch, Shakespeare whispered an ad lib, "I call it love, indeed, and say 'tis much!"

Fisch blinked, then suddenly recovered. He gazed at Antony, shook his head kittenishly, then turned away, with a languid sigh, to one of his eunuchs.

"If it be love "*indeed*," tell me *how* much."

Shakespeare shook his head, disdainfully:

"There's beggary in the love that can be reckoned."

"I'll set a *bourn*" - Fisch pursed his lips, then sucked in his cheeks, pointing at the his own crotch. With a flick of his finger, he covered his seductive acquarium: "how *far* to be beloved."

Shakespeare/Antony gestured to the audience, and to the heavens:

"Then must thou needs find out new heaven, new earth."

Fisch chuckled pleasantly, shaking his head and pointing the finger at Shakespeare, as if he were a school-mistress.

A Messenger rushed onstage, breathlessly:

"News, my good lord, from Rome."

Turning, now, from Cleopatra, Antony snapped, "Grates me: the sum."

"Nay, hear them, Antony," said Cleopatra, in a deep voice, as if she were Caesar himself. "*Fullllllllll*via perchance...is angry."

The eunuchs clapped their hands and laughed uproariously.

Behind a fist, Cleopatra spoke, this time with a baby-voice: "Or who know if de scarce-bearded Caesar hannut sended his powerful-wowerful mandate to you: "Do dis, or dis, Take in dat kingy-dom and enfwanchise Dat!" Perform't, or else...we gonna damn damn damn thee!"

Cleo pretended to cry, and the eunuchs patted her on the back.

The audience howled.

While Shakespeare wondered, surprised:

Is he going to 'camp' all my dialogue? Have we left Antony and Cleopatra for Pyramus and Thisbe?

From the laughter, the playwright began to realize that Fisch had the audience engaged, and surprised, and were loving him, and that singular fat prick was beginning to enjoy it!

Well, he thought, maybe not so fat. But...dammit!

Since when had Antony been Cleopatra's straight man?

The answer, from HaShem to Shakespeare's psychic, was terrifying, and came with the threat of even more terrifying consequences:

"Ever since you told him every actress had open season on Cleo, Willie. 'Infinite variety,' wasn't that the phrase you used? Then 'If you have tears, prepare to shed them now.' Better do something fast! The man is having a field day with your divine creation."

Cleopatra was saying "Hear the ambassadors" - for the third time - and getting a fabulous laugh.

Shakespeare waited for the laughter to settle, and then replied: "Fie, wrangling queen, whom everything becomes – to chide, to laugh, To weep; how every passion fully strives To make itself, in thee, fair and admired!"

He stood back, and applauded her, and laughed, then stared at the audience, but nobody else applauded.

All were watching.

Something was up.

Obviously, Shakespeare and Fisch had lots of surprises in store.

After all, this *wasn't* a comedy.

Or was it?

Shakespeare crossed upstage, until Fisch was turned fully to him, and the litter-bearers had to turn as well.

Oldest trick in the book, this upstaging.

And the stage was Shakespeare's now.

"No messenger but thine," he whispered. "Tonight...we'll wander through the streets and note The qualities of people."

Then he moved downstage right, as if to exit.

Cleopatra strained forward, trying to stop him.

Suddenly Antony looked back at the litter:

"Come, my queen," he said, and passed the Roman's messenger. With a flick of the wrist, he spat, "Speak not to us," and exited.

Cleopatra started in surprise, then pointed like a spoiled child at Antony.

The litter bearers ran after the Roman, bouncing Cleopatra in the litter until she had fallen backwards and her legs were above her head.

It was no longer Pyramus and Thisbe.

It was Petruchio and Kate.

And the audience loved it.

For they believed that the evening was shaping up to be:

An Evening of Shakespeare's Favorite Hits!!

The ninetieth canto

There were two intermissions: the first was after the third act, when Antony had agreed to marry Lavinia, Caesar's sister, and the *triumvirs* had been reconciled to Pompey.

By that time, because of Fisch's performance, the audience was seeing the play as if Cleopatra were also Falstaff, Portia, Gertrude, Cesario, Cressida, Rosalind, both Edmund *and* Edgar, Beatrice, Lady Macbeth as the Porter, Volumnia, Caliban, and, of course, Iago as Antony's lover.

The ninety-first canto

The second intermission occurred after the fourth act, in the monument, when Antony expires in Cleopatra's arms.

Because of the "infinite variety" of Cleopatra's emotions, (*as played by the Fisch, who was on a roll!*), Shakespeare himself had to act Antony as if he were King Hamlet's Ghost, Benedick, Richard III, Titus Andronicus, Bolingbroke, Shylock, Prince Hal, Troilus, Othello, Orlando, King Lear, The Three Witches, Prospero, Cassius, Octavius from *Julius Caesar* (which was totally bizarre, since he was supposed to be playing Antony in a different play, and thus at times appeared to have become his own enemy), and of course Feste, Touchstone, and Lear's Fool; also, interestingly enough, Barabas, Marlowe's Jew of Malta. ("I mean," he thought to himself, "at this point, why not?") He even threw in Stanley Kowalski, when Cleopatra began to resemble Blanche DuBois. He also flagrantly stole from Tony Kushner's portrayal of Roy Cohn, not to mention Arthur Miller's Willie Loman, as played by Buddy Hackett.

It didn't disturb Fisch at all.

He was too busy, during that moment, playing Cleopatra as if she were Ethel Merman belting out Polonius.

The ninety-second canto

The last act of *Antony and Cleopatra* allowed Shakespeare to retire to his dressing-room and to go on a fabulous drunk, with the first of the three Mollies, the Malone, mixing martini after martini and doing everything but feeding them to him intravenously.

The second Molly, the Mollusc, was stuffing Crab Nebulae mussels down his throat as he gestured for "More, more, dammit! To the top!"

The third Molly, Mrs. Bloom, was kneeling before the playwright, on her knees.

The last act, now in progress, belonged totally to Cleopatra.

It led to her escape from slavery, by putting an asp to her breast, and expiring.

Herschel Fisch played her last speech hysterically – sounding at times like Barbara Fritchie ("Shoot, if you must, this old grey head"), or W.C. Fields, ("I shall see Some squeaking Cleopatra boy—wake up, Iras! – "I shall see some ---isn't there a cue here, for the asp, sirrah, my asp is dragging! Wake it up!-- Some squeaking Cleopatra boy my greatness," and drawling, "in the POSture of a whooooooore...." Hmmm..." muttering to himself. "There he goes again, 'squeaking Cleopatra boy, POSture of a whooooooore...' The man is insatiable. Sex for breakfast, lunch and dinner, that Eye-tie's a veritable trifecta of bodily pleasures. Now, Charmian!") and he turned around, falling over his reclining couch, exposing his arse to the audience, legs flailing in the air, "Show me, my women, like a queen. Go fetch my best attires!"

The audience was applauding Fisch's vaudevillian turn, as Cleopatra rose, skirt still over her head, turned around hastily, trying to pull down the garment; instead, she slammed into a column, knocking over part of the set. Six grips, suddenly exposed, ran away, to public laughter.

"I am again for Cydnus," Cleopatra declaimed, "To meet Mark Antony!"

Another column fell, and bopped her on the head.

Iras appeared, holding Cleopatra's best attire.

"Gimme that," growled Cleopatra, grabbing the clothes, and ripping them. "These are *shmattas, you Borscht-belt camel-driver*! Fetch me my jim-jams, the ones with the pearls!"

The universes were rocking with lunatic laughter.

Even HaShem and Adonai were in tears and, with their mirth, had unwittingly destroyed seven planets.

But Shakespeare didn't mind.

He was bloated, stoned, comed-and-*gone!*

Onstage and strange, Cleopatra was surveying the damage around her, stumbling slowly among the crumpled sets, the costumes, the outrage and mayhem, until the theater's public had become insanely quiet, then still.

Like a Beckett clown, Fisch/Cleopatra sat on the floor, center stage, and stared at the audience.

With a barely audible sigh, she waited until the Guardsman brought in the Clown. She addressed all her remarks to the audience, as if all of her strength were seeping from her body, and the comedy was over.

And when the Clown tried to force a laugh from her, her smile was tight, and wan.

"Will it eat me?" she whispered, staring, still, ahead of her.

"Yes, forsooth," replied the clown. "I wish you joy o'th'worm."

And there was silence, still.

In the dressing-room, there was silence as well.

Shakespeare, pants around his ankles and mussels mixing in his throat and stomach with downed martinis, strained to listen to the stage through the dressing-room's loudspeaker. But he heard nothing.

"You think we've struck gold," he whispered, "and the Fisch is dead?"

"Hnnglll?" replied the third Molly.

"*Fisch*!" hissed the playwright. "Listen. Not not a sound in the theater."

"Hnn hnn hnnngll," she said.

"No such luck," said the other two Mollies.

"Ohh," sighed Shakespeare. "Maybe not for *him*..."

And then he heard, and they all heard:

"Give me my robe," Cleopatra whispered, staring ahead, for the party was certainly over. "Put on my crown. I have immortal longings in me." This was spoken almost wistfully, and with a soft smile, to her maid, Iras.

With kisses to the women, pacific and kind, she applied the asp – a small brown snake, hired for the purpose – to her breast.

"As sweet as balm, as soft as air, as gentle." And then, barely audibly: "O Antony...What should I stay..."

And she released the first snake from her hands, and it slithered away, across the stage. She opened her mouth to speak, but her head slumped forward, and she was dead.

Iras sat beside her, and Charmian took her in her arms.

Both stared ahead.

"---In this vile world?" Charmian began, glowering, with Brechtian gloom, at the audience.

The brown snake, now off-stage, began to crawl up the leg of the lighting director, who tried to kick it off, and hit the controls, and the lights began to dim as Caesar and his train marched on stage, then found themselves playing their dialogue in the darkness, until nobody could be seen, so the stage-hand lowered the curtain.

It didn't matter anymore.

All the important people were dead.

In the dressing-room Shakespeare heard the insane applause.

"*Fuckapissshit!*" he exclaimed. "I'm too bleeding fogged to take a curtain call. Let somebody else do it. Take me home."

"Where?"

"Where else?" said Shakespeare. "I'll be the first blottoed Piatnik in history. Fucking deserve it, I tell you, after tonight's performance!"

The applause was now hysterical, but Shakespeare didn't seem to care.

HaShem and Adonai were applauding as well and crying, "Go take a bow, Will! Take a bow! Fisch is stealing your thunder!"

"That's the point, isn't it?" he muttered, struggling into his pants. "Just get me home! Need to sleep! Ladies? Fly me to Piatnik, somebody---!" he called.

"---Anybody!!---Or I'll vile it up, all over this room, this green-room, or the immortal globe itself..."

Immediately, he was back home, tucked into his web, as all good Piatniks are.

And Herschel Fisch, who never could say what had hit him, had become a star.

A twelfth riff to Mnemosyne, Before we say goodbye for now

Acting, and dancing, and singing, and writing, and directing films and plays, and choreographing, and I wish I hadn't let myself get pulled away from the piano to go to the library or to the bookstores, because otherwise I would be conducting and composing now, but you probably wouldn't be reading this book.

Both my parents were great readers.

My dad's side of the bed was a disaster – he would read six to ten books at a time, and they'd be spilling from his bed-stand and onto the floor.

Mom would stick with one vision, until it was finished.

And because she loved writing and writers and acting, mom knew how to read aloud very well. I think they had both agreed to keep me away from the piano.

I had lousy hands, but a keen memory. I knew the music after hearing it once, and watching the teacher play the piece. For the first two months, I simply figured it out on the piano, and played it back.

After several weeks, the teacher was on to me, and told dad either I take her teaching seriously, or she would dump me.

She dumped me.

I continued to play by ear.

But nearly every time I began, mom would say, "Listen, I'm going to Pickwick Bookshop, or to the library. Where do you want to go?"

Pickwick was the spectacular store on Hollywood Boulevard.

When I was about to turn thirteen, mom said, "You can have a Bar Mitzvah, or a typewriter. Oh, and also a charge at Pickwick. What do you want?"

Guess.

Dancing was also always on my mind.

When I was four, I saw the Step Brothers in a concert in which Dad took part, at the Hollywood Bowl. I was so entranced and, during the run-through, stood by the side of the stage, and suddenly one of the Brothers picked me up and said, "Hey, little man: wanna be in the act? We'll teach you how to tap!"

Oh yeah! What could be better than that?

Then I saw the man who would give me my first writing assignment – Gene Kelly – and I wanted to do what he had done.

By then I was acting, making up plays, and eventually, while living abroad, being the kid whenever a kid was needed in that first international American tv series, "From the Secret Files of the French Surete," starring Akim Tamiroff.

After our European stay - when I was thirteen and we'd returned to Los Angeles - I told mom I wanted to take ballet and modern. She said that the best place in L.A. was at Bert Prival's studio. He taught Lester Horton technique, and every summer, when Balanchine's company played at the Griffith Park Theater (before Saratoga became NYCB's summer residence), Igor Youskevitch was more often than not the guest-teacher.

The problem was my father: the first time I'd mentioned dance, he'd said, "Oh, great, that's just what he needs. He'll be hit on within five minutes. No way."

We knew not to pursue it further with him.

"Listen," I said to mom, "how about I take dancing lessons right after school, when dad's at work? Or after my tennis lessons? I can put my dance stuff in my school bag or tennis bag and dad'll never see it."

The plan was elegant in its simplicity.

We went to Prival's.

"He's got peasant feet," said the maestro to my mother. "He'll probably be the smallest kid in his class. He'll never be able to partner, but those feet are perfect for all the fun stuff: *entrechats, tour jetes*, character roles. If he was a girl, he'd have perfect feet for *pointe*. Does he act?"

"Of course," said mom.

"Why do you want to dance?" said Mister Prival, turning, finally, to me, acknowledging my eyes, and not my feet.

"Because I love music and acting and writing and theater."

"Who's your favorite composer?"

"Stravinsky. Then Debussy and Ravel."

He raised his eyebrows.

"What about Latin music? Contemporary stuff?"

"You mean like Villa Lobos or Manuel Ponce?"

Without missing a beat, he said, "No. Like Xavier Cugat."

"Sure," I shrugged. "When I was eight, my dad used to conduct the Larraine Cugat tv show. I went every week to watch. I know all the music, and used to watch the timbales and conga players. They wore beads. And Bird and Diz, they're my favorite."

"What about classical dancers?" he continued.

"I never saw any. I mean, they were dead: Nijinsky and Pavlova. I would have given anything to see them. But we do see the New York City Ballet every summer. I like Edward Villella and Diane Adams and Maria Tallchief. Jaques D'Amboise is too dramatic for me, but I admire his technique."

'When do you want to start?" asked Prival.

"How about now?" I asked.

"We have a problem with his father," said my mom.

But her plan was even easier than mine.

We simply never mentioned it to him, or to anyone else.

The hard part of the hiding, however, was the presence at Prival's of two students from Birmingham Junior High, where I was going to school: because I acted a lot, and was on the tennis team, I was known by many of the students. Fortunately, the other dancing students were gay, and didn't want anybody to know they were studying dance, or doing anything the slightest bit "swishy."

Without any of us saying a word, it was understood that the Bert Prival Studio would be beyond discussion at Birmingham Junior High.

Isn't that absurd?

Life-wasting, time-wasting?

To hide a passion and a gift?

I had and have too much ego to care, but the skulking-around destroyed one of those two young men, as it did thousands of others.

And now, in this age of Clintonian hypocrisy, political Tea-parties given by Glenn Beck and Sarah Palin, and all those soul-destroying fundamentalisms, it's even worse.

'Don't ask, don't tell.'

Why not? Admittedly perhaps it's easier for me to respond, not being homosexualist in desire or taste. Socially, I had nothing to lose. I was already short and Jewish and an artist-in-residence.

Second riff on the twelfth riff to Mnemosyne, Before we say goodbye for now

The Lester Horton classes were tough, fun, and exciting. The rhythms were fabulous, and the counts crazy and eventful.

Youskevitch, however, was not fun: he was strict, slapped your knees if they weren't straight, and yanked you into turn-out position. He didn't smile.

When he liked something, he said, "That was good. More of that," and you felt stronger than you thought possible.

I thought he was the perfect teacher for classical ballet: his eye was keen, his hands were constantly correcting your positions, and he gave you a strong sense of the history of the dance, and the monastic devotion necessary to honor it in practice.

As a result, you worked absurdly well in his presence.

I got enough dancing to know that I only wanted to be a choreographer when I directed, and only a director when I wrote a play to be produced.

Writing had become central.

Everything else, except music, and which was now unreachable to me, had become secondary. By that time, in my mid-teens, I'd given up on composing.

I was busy at theater in school, and writing lyrics professionally when my father needed "special material" for his recording; and because I had begun studying that total theater: opera. Dad was working at RCA as a producer and composer. Each week he received all the albums the record company produced. The operas, jazz, and classical music were my favorites:

I had already enjoyed going to opera when we had lived in Europe – especially Donizetti and Weill – but now I could study the scores, and spent my free time listening to Verdi, Puccini, Debussy, Gilbert and Sullivan, and especially Tchaikovski, Moussorgski, Prokofiev. Poulenc and Shostakovich.

Khachaturian's ballets especially moved me.

One day I asked my father, "Why are the Russians so beautiful, and the French?"

He smiled, toussled my hair.

"Where do you think you're from?" he asked. "Your spiritual home is Russia. Your aesthetic home is France. You're my son. What else is new?"

A Last Riff to Mnemosyne,
For Now.

It's a pleasure watching my youngest daughter - who is an eleven year-old ballerina in training - listening to Khachaturian, Tchaikovsky and Ravel.

"I love that," she says, when we're reviewing a tape of Khachaturian's ballet, *Masquerade*. "I have to dance that. It's so beautiful, and so important, don't you think?"

I do.

Very much.

It's the most important thing in the world.

And may it remain so, Florrie.

That dance.

Every minute of our lives.

Coming soon:

THE THIRD VOLUME OF THE

"JEWS ON THE MOON" TETRALOGY:

'JEWS IN BLACK HOLES"

starring

Newman Fears

AND

Sookie the Human Torch

Made in the USA
Coppell, TX
04 December 2020